RECIPE FOR MR CHRISTMAS

An uplifting rom-com about a second chance at finding love

ANNI ROSE

Recipes for Love Book 6

Choc Lit

A JOFFE BOOKS COMPANY

Choc Lit
A Joffe Books company
www.choc-lit.com

This edition first published in Great Britain in 2023

Cover art by Sasha Alsberg

ISBN: 978-1-78189-620-4

Cousin Mary (Seager)
1929–2022
Whose spectacular annual letters started all this!

CHAPTER ONE

The small label on the back of the envelope told Susie exactly who'd sent the letter. It had finally arrived.

The rest of the post she dumped on the worktop. Taking a kitchen knife, she carefully slit the top of the envelope open, extracting the charity card and a neatly folded sheet of A4 paper. "The Bailey Bulletin". She laid it carefully on the kitchen table and sat down.

Any other year, the Baileys' annual Christmas epistle arrived before Black Friday. It had never been this late.

You can so do this, girl.

She picked up her mug of tea. Ideally, it would've been something stronger, but it wasn't yet nine in the morning and a working day to boot. Her colleague, Luke, was picking her up in fifteen minutes. They both needed to have their wits about them today, too. Thankfully, the Baileys had fitted this year's exploits onto one sheet of paper — albeit both sides.

Over the years, Cynthia and Alfie had perfected the art of the Christmas letter — hardly surprising considering they'd been doing it for so long. This year they'd stuck to their tried-and-tested formula. First, comment on the speed the year has passed at:

The Baileys say it every year and this year is no exception. Time has simply flown by in a whirlwind for them.

And yes, written in third-person. Second, the entire family should sign the letter, including the pets.

Something she and Terry always used to chuckle about. *God, she missed him.*

The whole Christmas-card fiasco bothered her. To send or not to send. Postage was a shocking cost these days   but what should she say? The Baileys' card was addressed to Mrs S Keane — that was something. She'd told most of their friends and family, she was sure she had. Several had clearly either forgotten or not bothered to update their Christmas-card label program.

Was losing a husband a valid reason not to send any cards this year? If she did, then she couldn't not mention Terry's death, but what would she write?

Dear All, hope you're keeping well and have had a good year.

Good start, nice and positive. Wasn't that the way it was recommended one should deliver bad news? Good news, bad news and finish on a positive. "Think bollock burger," her old boss used to say.

Stick to convention, take a leaf out of the Baileys' book, use a third person point of view.

Susie hates being the bearer of bad news, but hey ho, needs must. Terry's dead.

Don't fanny around, say it like it is. He hasn't passed, crossed the rainbow bridge or been lost — well, not since the police found him wandering round Gravesend anyway. And they found him relatively quickly on that occasion.

Susie has been busy. She got a new job, buried her husband and married her boss — not in the Biblical sense of course — LOL!

Always highlight humour. She sighed happily at the thought of today's wedding. Maddie, her boss, marrying her first love, Josh Diamond. And she, Susie Keane, was the deputy superintendent registrar in charge of making sure it happened. It was going to be a great occasion — a couple more loved up, she didn't think she'd ever seen. If they were half as happy as she and Terry had been, they had nothing to worry about. Because she and Terry had been happy. She had so many lovely memories.

This year she is planning a quiet Christmas.

Okay, not that positive, but she didn't feel bloody positive. Perhaps forget the letter and just sign the cards *love from Susie*. Would that do the trick?

There wasn't a huge list she had to send to. Most of their family, friends and colleagues had dropped off the radar over the last ten years. It had got too depressing to visit, so they didn't. There was not much point them ringing either. Terry hadn't responded well to phone calls. Unless he saw someone in the flesh, he often couldn't recall who they were.

There'd only been a handful of people at his funeral, mostly Susie's colleagues, there to support her. From Terry's family, only his son, Max, had come. There had been no sign of his daughter, Jodie, and Max had come alone. But then his latest wife had never met Terry or Susie. In fact, they'd only discovered the birth of Max's last child through a post on Facebook.

She admired pictures of the Baileys. There they all were — as always — doing startling things: up towers; floating on what looked like a giant inflatable banana; eating fish and chips; and dancing at some party or other. Each picture with a witty caption. In all of them, everyone was grinning at the camera.

Cynthia got an electric scooter this year and a new coffee machine. Alfie's health concerns were a verruca, and the cat died.

A quick look at the end of the letter and sure enough the cat hadn't signed it, but there was some scrawl at the very bottom which looked very much like, "*See you in May. Cx.*"

Shit! Now she'd have to read the whole sodding thing.

There was a quick moan about the state of the economy, but:

It didn't stop our annual trip to the south of France, and vineyard country, so Alfie's cellar is well and truly replenished.

No sooner were the Baileys back from their annual holidays in the south of France, apparently, than it was time to apply for Kelly's university place. Kelly was their youngest.

The Baileys' letters for years had been full of Kelly's shortcomings as a troublesome teenager, not that they ever blamed themselves or Kelly for her "issues". This year, there was no mention of which university she'd applied to, or any further reference to last year's concerns about her involvement with some goths. Maybe Kelly had decided to swap the idea of studying medicine for a degree in witchcraft and herbal medicines.

Then came a line Susie hadn't been expecting.

Next year sees fifty years since Cynthia started secondary school. She's frantically trying to arrange a reunion. If you were at Bridgefield Grammar with her and have contact details for any classmates, please let her know. More details to follow in the New Year.

Susie stood and washed her mug.

Was it really fifty years since they'd started secondary school? She and Cynthia had sat next to each other on that first day and remained friends throughout school. They'd both gone their separate ways since, but always kept in touch through Christmas cards, letters and the occasional email.

A reunion — Susie hadn't thought about most of her class for some time. The school had high aspirations for them. How many of her year, she wondered, had got anywhere close to meeting them. What was the Latin motto they'd had to recite after morning assembly? Something about hard work conquering all.

Well, she had worked hard. Very hard. And it hadn't conquered all, not where Terry was concerned. She couldn't have done more. For ten years she'd become his sole carer and been there for him twenty-four-seven until it finally became too much. It was their doctor who insisted she find a nursing home for him because she wasn't coping. It had been a tough year and not one she'd really want to share in a Christmas bulletin.

On a happier note, she loved her new job in the Register Office. It was always a privilege to help people through the major events in their lives and she couldn't imagine that she'd ever tire of conducting weddings. She smiled at the thought of today's wedding. It was going to be something else.

She, Luke and Charlotte, her other colleague, had talked about little else apart from Maddie's wedding for the last few weeks. They'd planned it like a military operation. Luke had set up a WhatsApp group "The Diamond Plan". At first there'd been the occasional post, but in the last forty-eight hours, as the tension ramped up, her phone pinged with new posts every couple of minutes:

Josh arrived home safely from the States.

Maddie's parents arrived and are staying with her.

Lisa, the wedding coordinator at Grey Towers, reported the library decorated.

Clara, Lisa's wife, has created a remarkable menu for the wedding breakfast and the cake should be spectacular.

The car is ready.

There had been a panic yesterday, until Maddie's neighbour saved the day with the wedding flowers. Bouquets and buttonholes would be at the hotel in plenty of time this morning.

It was just down to Susie and Luke to sort out the preliminaries and get the show on the road.

She glanced at her watch, checked her make-up in the mirror and put on her overcoat. Luke would be here any minute. She went through her usual routine of making sure she'd locked everything and had all the paperwork she needed. *Ceremony — check, schedules — check, reading — check.*

Jane Eyre's "I have, for the first time, found what I can truly love — I have found you." Maddie's favourite.

Looking down at the page, Susie's eyes smarted. Josh would read it. It wasn't normal for the bridegroom to do a reading, but there was nothing normal about this wedding. Susie was primed to take over if he found it too much.

She tidied the Baileys' letter into a drawer and put their card on the pile of Christmas cards still waiting to be arranged around the house or put straight out for recycling.

She would refuse the reunion invitation when it came. Make an excuse — a reason she couldn't attend. Hopefully she'd be working. If she wasn't, then she'd offer to swap so she was. Anything to avoid hearing endless tales about everyone's wonderful lives and all their children's achievements, especially at the moment.

She needed to take up a hobby, do something interesting. Perhaps she'd explore some of the places she and Terry had always talked about visiting. Only wear purple on Thursdays and learn to cook macarons. Next Christmas she would join the annual Christmas-letter brigade, and she would write an upbeat letter about her achievements. A letter that would knock spots off the Baileys'. No one would care what state Alfie's wine cellar was in once they got her letter.

Terry had made sure she would be taken care of financially and she was too young to be written off. There were loads of things she'd always wanted to try. She would make a list and see where it took her.

She looked out of her kitchen window onto her small garden. She'd always wanted a pond. Maybe she could try her hand at garden design or landscaping. She flicked through the college prospectus to see if there was anything garden or landscape related. Nope, so she checked the "P" page for ponds. Philosophy, Photography, and that's when she saw it — the course tucked in between Pilates and Positive Thinking.

Susie smiled as the doorbell sounded. Maybe, next year, this middle-aged widow would really have something to write home about.

CHAPTER TWO

Across the Grey Towers' library, Susie saw her colleague Luke talking animatedly to his wife. They looked like they weren't going anywhere, anytime soon. Not that he had to. Tomorrow was Sunday. Neither Susie nor Luke were working. Their work here was done — Maddie and Josh were married. It felt good — no, it felt brilliant. There had been tears and laughter in all the right places. Susie didn't think she'd ever seen Maddie look so happy. Yes, as weddings went, it hadn't been strictly conventional, but it had worked.

She pushed her chair back.

'You're not going yet?' Josh's father said. Was that disappointment Susie saw flicker across Bob Diamond's face as she stood up? Her heart gave a brief flutter. A nice flutter. Her pulse speeded up and a warm, pleasant sensation rose through her body.

A couple of hours earlier, she'd experienced a similar feeling. At the time, she'd put it down to being nervous about conducting her boss's wedding. But as the bridal party had entered the library at Grey Towers, Susie had caught Bob's eye and smiled. He'd given her a thumbs up and smiled as he started playing the pre-agreed recording of a motorbike starting up on his phone. Susie had found she was reluctant to drag her eyes away from the tall handsome man in the leather jacket as Maddie's two bridesmaids walked solemnly down the aisle, with Maddie's tri-coloured terrier, Miss Phyllis, between them. The motorbike recording gave way to the opening bars of "Born to Be Wild" which Bob sang with Maddie's father. They were good. More than good. Bob had a lovely tone to his voice. There was something about watching and hearing him that made Susie feel as if she'd just drunk a mug of thick, creamy hot chocolate. Not a sensation she'd experienced in a very long time.

She was feeling the same thing now as she turned and looked at Bob.

'You shouldn't go. The bride and groom will be disappointed if you disappear off so soon.' Bob pushed back his chair and stood up. His dark-brown, almost black eyes never leaving her face.

'They won't notice.'

'Of course they will. You're an essential part of their wedding. They couldn't have done any of it without you. They'd want you to stay, kick back, relax and celebrate.'

'I've already stayed far longer than I intended.' Susie had been surprised to find a place had been set for her at the top table next to Bob.

'It was a fabulous meal, wasn't it?' he said.

'It was.' Susie stroked her stomach. 'I don't think I'll be able to eat for another week.' It had been lovely and made even more special by the company. She found Bob easy to talk to and they'd chatted throughout the meal. She'd even found herself telling him about her Christmas letter idea. She'd explained about the Baileys' letter and the car-bumper sticker on a pick-up truck she'd been stuck behind the other day on the motorway: "You have one life, live it."

'Good idea.' He'd laughed and held her gaze. 'I'm thinking of starting early-bird swimming, perhaps after Christmas.'

'Don't put off today, what . . .'

'You can put off tomorrow.' His dark-brown eyes sparkled as he stared deeply into hers. 'Isn't that what they say? Maybe I should look at the college prospectus too.'

'I meant to say earlier—' she swallowed, glancing away — 'you have a lovely voice.'

Bob performed a mock bow. 'Thank you. It's been a long time since I've sung in public, and we didn't have long to practise. Maddie's parents only arrived yesterday.' He nodded towards Maddie's dad, who was looking slightly inebriated but blissfully happy in the middle of the room.

The DJ announced the first dance and invited everyone to join in. Susie should go. It was time. She reached under the table for her handbag.

'Don't you want to dance?' Bob asked.

She froze, unsure whether he was asking her to dance. She searched his face for a clue.

He had six inches on her, broad shoulders and the creases round his eyes suggested he laughed a lot — or squinted. No, Bob Diamond was definitely a laugher not a squinter.

'Sorry. I didn't mean . . .' He looked embarrassed as if reading her confusion.

Susie blushed.

'I'm not your man, I'm afraid. Two left feet. The last time I threw anything close to shapes on a dance floor, probably would have been to "Kung Fu Fighting". More years ago than I care to remember.' He smiled. 'I'm not sure I still know all the moves to that.' He rubbed his forehead. 'There were a lot of "oohs", a few "aahs", even more thrusting, high kicks and, oh God, I've just remembered, we wore our ties as bandanas. I'm guessing a fair amount of alcohol was also a major requirement. Trust me, your feet are safer this way.'

Susie turned away. She didn't want him to see her disappointment. She loved dancing.

They watched Maddie and Josh sway together on the dance floor, lost in each other's eyes. Susie sighed, for a moment imagining it was her on the dance floor with Terry. Their first dance as a married couple had been to "Could I

Have This Dance?" Terry had been a wonderful dancer and loved country-and-western music. They both did. Whenever they were in the car, they often ended up singing along together. As his dementia got worse, he struggled to remember events and people, but rarely forgot a song.

On their wedding day, he'd held her tight into his chest as they whisked and chasséd in time with the music. He'd sung along, and she'd felt like a princess, happy and in the certain knowledge she'd made the right choice. The way Maddie and Josh looked at each other as they danced to an Ed Sheeran number, they looked like they felt that way too. The song was Lisa's idea of a joke, not Maddie's choice at all. But the couple twirling round the dance floor looked oblivious to everything other than each other.

She'd considered playing "Could I Have This Dance?" at Terry's funeral. Because they had danced together for the rest of his life.

Susie's eyes itched with tears. Very soon, she'd start crying. So far, she'd held it together. She needed to get out. 'I couldn't knit a more perfect couple,' she mumbled as she turned to go.

Bob turned, his eyes sparkling too. 'You knit?'

'Only dishcloths.'

'In that case, you're probably right — you couldn't.' He grinned. The music stopped, and the DJ asked everyone to go outside for the bouquet toss.

'Shall we?' Bob said, his hand gently resting on Susie's shoulder. It felt warm there. She liked the sensation. It had been a long day. Luke and Charlotte were busy talking to others. There was no point interrupting their conversations just to say goodbye. She'd see them on Monday.

Bob walked her down to the front of the hotel, where Maddie's yellow Capri stood on the drive, with the engine running. Tied to its rear bumper were several tins. Balloons filled the back seat and a "Just Married" banner was visible through the back windscreen.

'Thank God for that,' Bob said. 'We left the car decoration to Poppy.'

'Josh's sister?'

'Yes, and anything could have happened, although she was under threat of death to use lipstick on the paintwork.'

'You did such a brilliant job with the restoration,' Susie said. 'Her first car. It blew Maddie — and her dad — away. They both had a good cry when they saw it again.'

'It looks good,' Bob said, visibly straightening, his pleasure at her comment, evident. 'If I say so myself. And I enjoyed doing it. Car maintenance is so different these days. They are increasingly governed by complex electronics. Nowadays, the car tells you when it needs a service or what is wrong. Gone are the days when you'd pop open the bonnet, have a look and listen.'

Maddie and Josh were poised to get into the Capri. Someone called something and several flashes went off.

'Are they really going? So soon?' Susie frowned. 'I thought Lisa said they had the bridal suite here tonight. Charlotte and Luke both went up to doctor it earlier. Do you think we should warn Lisa?'

Bob shook his head. 'It's a symbolic driving off. They're just going to park round the back, then Maddie's going to get changed out of her wedding dress so she can dance all night if she wants to.'

'One, two, three.'

Susie felt something graze her ear as Bob reached out and grabbed something.

'I look forward to taking your notice soon.' She laughed, glancing down at the bouquet in his right hand.

* * *

Bob looked down at the bouquet then up at the back of the woman walking across the car park. He wondered what was so important that she had to get home. Her dark-blonde bob moved in time with her paces. He wished he'd been quicker. He'd briefly toyed with giving the bouquet to her, but she'd gone before he had a chance to fully engage his brain. Would she'd appreciate flowers? Or was it too soon after her husband's death? Would it just seek to remind her of wreaths and funeral flowers?

'It's normal to let a woman catch it, Dad,' Poppy joked, coming up behind him.

'There weren't any women nearby,' Bob argued. There had been one woman, but she seemed to be completely oblivious to the large object heading towards her. Certainly, she didn't try to catch it. He'd acted instinctively, and reached up, snatching it, before it took her out.

'Here, you have it,' he muttered. 'Maybe it will encourage you to think about relationships.'

'I don't want or need the bouquet. I've had lots of relationships.' Poppy tucked her arm through her father's as they walked back into the hotel.

Bob bit his tongue. Now was not the right time to have a conversation about his daughter's biological clock. He just wanted to see her as settled and happy as Josh had looked today. All the way through her twenties, he and Elaine had both hoped she'd find someone. There had been one or two promising boyfriends, but the relationships had all died out within months. Now in her early thirties, Poppy seemed to be making less of an effort than ever to find a partner, spending more and more time on the hire-car side of the business at Diamond Cars.

There was music and dancing until midnight. Bob felt sad Susie had gone. He'd have liked to sit and chat some more. He'd enjoyed their conversation over the meal. He'd thought she'd been about to cry as they watched Maddie and Josh take to the floor for their first dance, and for a moment there, he'd wished he could dance. She'd smiled when he'd joked about his last dance routine, except the smile hadn't quite reached her eyes, and he'd have had to be blind not to see the look of disappointment on her face.

For a while there, she'd looked miles away. Was she wishing her husband had been there? He could remember how raw he felt when Elaine died. That was eighteen months

13

ago, and a day still hadn't gone by when he hadn't thought of her. He wasn't sure he could have held it together as a wedding guest so soon after her death, let alone been the celebrant. Elaine would've loved the party. She should have been there. She should have stayed to see her children married. Bob fingered the bouquet and set it gently down in the middle of the table, unsure what to do with it.

He finished his drink, noticing Susie's glass, still on the table, half-full. Clearly, she wasn't a big drinker. Elaine would never have left a glass like that. But then she wouldn't have left any party before the end either. There had been many times when he'd wished she would. He never found parties fun or relaxing — he had to keep a close eye on the amount she was drinking. Although Elaine wasn't a mean drunk, she just seemed to get louder and think everything she said was funny.

Bob sighed. Christmas, in a couple of weeks' time, would be the second one without her. This year would be very different to the last. Last year was difficult for many reasons. Josh was just back from the States and not in a great place.

Poppy, equally upset, had kept herself busy and away from them most of the time. Bob had felt lonely, strange. The first year, every occasion — birthday, anniversary, Christmas — had felt like another hurdle to get over. This year, time had started its healing process. He wasn't worried by Christmas in a fortnight. Josh and Maddie would be honeymooning with her parents in France for the festive season but planned on driving back at New Year. Christmas in the Diamond household would be a quiet affair. They'd never been big on Christmas decorations in the house. They always put a tree up in the showroom, and this year it had been up since the beginning of December. He'd probably spend Boxing Day taking it down, so it was gone by the time the garage reopened the day after. But Christmas Day, he'd cook a meal for Poppy, then maybe they'd flop in front of the telly in the afternoon and argue about whether to watch *The Sound of Music* or *Easy Rider*.

CHAPTER THREE

'Get this down you,' Fiona O'Dwyer, Treetops' new manager, said, handing Susie a gin and tonic. 'I'm sure you need it by now. It was so kind of you to come in and help today.'

'My pleasure,' Susie said.

'New Year's Eve is always tricky. Families turn up en masse for Christmas, but few bother to visit twice in a week.' She kicked off her shoes and settled onto the sofa in her small office. 'Let's put our feet up for a while. We've still got three hours until Big Ben strikes and the residents begin to think about going to bed. We'll join them in the lounge later for the countdown to midnight and a rousing chorus of "Auld Lang Syne".'

'Not me.' Susie laughed. 'I'll be gone long before midnight.'

Fiona raised her glass. 'Well, thank you again. It really is appreciated. Staff need time off too — we'd have been really stretched tonight without you.'

'I enjoyed it,' Susie admitted, half-surprised to find that she had. She hadn't known that the old manager, John Fielding, and his partner had been moved on when she'd first popped in to offer help over Christmas.

Fiona had explained they'd been promoted to look after a new retirement village that the company was building near

Allingham. Maybe she would visit them there one day. John Fielding had been so kind while Terry was at Treetops. At first, Susie had been upset to hear he'd gone, but she'd immediately warmed to Fiona and her husband, George. They were delightful company and the Treetops' residents seemed to have had a blast all day.

Volunteering at the nursing home was beautifully anonymous, and not at all depressing. No one looked at her sympathetically or asked her how she was coping, and all with tilting heads and bland words. Terry hadn't been there long, but he had been happy while he was, so there were no distressing memories. 'Maybe I could help you out in the new year too,' Susie said, as she took a sip of her drink.

'We'd bite your hand off,' Fiona said. 'You enjoyed it. Really?'

'Really.' Susie grinned. 'And not just because, on a purely selfish basis, it meant not spending New Year's Eve on my own.'

'I can't believe you didn't have better offers.'

'None I seriously considered.' Small lie — she'd had none. But if she had been inundated with alternative offers, she'd have probably still ended up at Treetops. Somehow, it was easier doing things for others than spending endless time on her own. Especially tonight of all nights. She and Terry had never made a big deal about New Year's Eve. Most years they'd have been in bed well before midnight and slept through any fireworks.

'I hope you've poured me one of those,' said George, Fiona's husband, as he came into the room.

Fiona nodded in the direction of the coffee table.

'I'm pleased to report all's quiet on the western front, madam,' he said, with a mock salute in Fiona's direction. 'Well, the conservatory anyway. Everything done, dusted, and the tables are laid for breakfast, mainly thanks to this lady here. And most of the residents are in the lounge.'

Susie checked her watch. Fiona was right — it was only nine. Still three hours to go.

'You didn't think of putting the meal back tonight?' she asked Fiona. 'Some pubs I know tend to try to serve the mints and coffee with a glass of champagne at the end of the meal, and time it to ensure everyone just finishes eating by midnight, ready to cheer in the New Year.'

'The medicines at Treetops are always dished out at mealtimes,' Fiona said. 'It could get awkward . . .'

'The trouble is—' George put an arm round Fiona's shoulders and winked at Susie — 'that lot might look like nice, docile old ladies and men, but that's because they're medicated up to their eyeballs. A late-night gala dinner sounds nice, but trust me, put supper back by three hours and we'd need to stock up on tranquilizer darts, and be prepared to use them at the first sign of trouble.'

Fiona raised her eyes. 'Don't listen to him. He's only joking.'

'I know that,' Susie grinned.

'Yep, I love them all really,' George nodded. 'But they can be challenging at times. You do need eyes in the back of your head, and then some.'

He nodded at the gin bottle. 'Another?'

Susie shook her head. She still had half a glass left and had been at Treetops since mid-afternoon. She ought to get going. Maybe another half an hour, she'd finish her drink and leave them to it. That way, she could still be in bed by ten thirty.

She stretched her legs out and sat back in the chair. 'Who was the guy running the celebrity-and-Treetop-resident death sweepstake?' she asked, taking another sip of her drink.

'Don't,' Fiona said, shaking her head. 'One of our new residents — Reginald Stanhope — Reggie. I try to stop him, but the minute my back is turned he gets his little book out and takes more bets.'

Susie grinned. 'You know, Donald Trump is currently the even-money favourite, with the woman in Room 4 coming a close second?'

'Doesn't surprise me.' Fiona rolled her eyes. 'I caught him the other day offering Violet odds on her not making the year. The awful thing was, they were such great odds, I actually considered a flutter.'

'You mean you didn't?' George said. 'I did.' He put down his drink. 'Hang on. I've had an idea.' And with that, he disappeared from the room.

'I'd like to think he was joking.' Fiona looked firm, but Susie sensed there was a smile waiting to happen.

'Who's in Room 4?'

'A lady who came in for respite over Christmas and hasn't left her room since.'

'That explains why one resident, a man in a dressing gown and slippers, asked Reggie to check she wasn't dead already.' Susie remembered the conversation in the lounge that had been going on while she collected empty cups.

'She's not. We'd have seen the private ambulance,' another resident said.

The woman had a point.

'Unless they are keeping it secret. I watched a film about Stalin where they did just that,' the dressing-gown man replied.

'Why did you watch a film about Stalin?' a blue-rinsed lady asked as she shuffled into the centre of the room.

'I saw that one. Jason Isaacs,' a woman, in what could only be described as a handmade cardigan that looked like someone had run out of wool, switching to a different shade halfway down the last sleeve, said. 'I watch everything with him in it.'

'She thinks he's her son.' Blue-rinse woman turned to face Susie and whispered loud enough for the rest of the room to hear.

'He's not my son, he's my toyboy,' the cardigan woman had come back with. She looked perfectly serious.

'I'll give you 200/1 on Prince Harry,' the man with the book told Susie as she gathered up his cup and several sweet wrappers. 'He's this year's rank outsider. Him and Great Uncle Bulgaria.'

'The Womble?' Susie asked. 'You're taking bets on a Womble?'

'I'll take bets on anything.' He grinned. 'So much easier than explaining to this lot he's not real. That would be like telling them Santa's dead.' He shook his head. 'Most of their hearts wouldn't be able to cope with that shock. I couldn't live with that number of deaths on my conscience.'

George came back into Fiona's office, balancing a large plate of cheese on top of a Tupperware box Susie recognized to be the one she'd brought in earlier.

'I thought we could do with some food,' he said. Fiona rose and cleared space on the table so he could put the huge plate down. As soon as he had, she handed him back his glass.

'A hangover, because we've been drinking on an empty stomach, wouldn't be a great way to start the new year. And, Fiona, you really need to try these crackers.'

Cooking was Susie's happy place, and since Terry's death she'd done a lot. The Register Office usually tasted and devoured anything she produced. Today's offering was buttermilk crackers best eaten fresh.

Susie took a lump of cheese and two crackers. They were delicious. She was pleased with how they'd turned out, but watched closely as George ate two and a lump of cheese.

'Truly wonderful,' he managed with his mouth full, then helped himself to another couple.

They spent the next hour chatting, Fiona and George asking her about her plans for New Year and she told them about her Christmas letter idea and the courses she'd already signed up for. 'I was explaining my ideas to a friend at a wedding.' She blushed at the thought of Bob Diamond, and hoped they'd assume her heightened colour was down to the drink and cheese.

'Maybe you should call it the trials of Susie,' Fiona laughed.

'What about labours?' George suggested. 'The labours of Susie.'

'I don't think so,' Fiona giggled. 'Didn't Hercules have to do them to atone for killing his wife and kids, and didn't most of them include slaying or capturing things?'

'Sounds fun. Maybe I should think about "labours" for next year instead of resolutions. I can think of a few people I'd like to slay.'

'George!' Fiona said, her eyebrows mid-forehead.

'I know, I'm joking.' George briefly held up his hands in mock-surrender as Fiona gave him a withering look.

As soon as she turned away, he took another cracker. 'I don't know why she's worried,' he said to Susie. 'I've always forgotten my resolutions by the end of New Year's Day.'

'Especially any that involve losing weight, more exercise or giving up alcohol.' Fiona took another cracker too.

'Is volunteering one of your labours then?' George asked.

'No.' It wasn't. Susie hadn't thought of it like that.

'Definitely should be,' Fiona said. 'We'd love to see you again. You'd be more than welcome any time. Or, if you'd rather, we could give you a regular slot — either to help in the kitchen or just to sit and read to some residents who don't get regular visitors. They'd appreciate that. And there are others who sometimes need a bit of help with admin, letters and things.'

Susie drained her gin and tonic as the door opened and a woman came in holding a bottle of champagne.

'Hello, Edna,' Fiona said.

'Edna Oldroyd,' George whispered to Susie. 'One of our permanent residents. She made our lives here hell when Fiona and I first arrived, not least because she's got the *Redford Chronicle*'s editor on speed dial, but she is a real character.'

'The name rings a bell,' Susie whispered back.

'Made a bit of a name for herself when she got involved with our local Olympic three-day eventer champion and his horses.'

'Of course,' Susie nodded. 'Didn't she sponsor them all?'

'Uh-huh. Edna, how are you?' George smiled at her. 'You look gorgeous this evening.' Susie found herself smiling too. He might have a wicked, inappropriate sense of humour, but he seemed genuinely fond of all the residents.

'Can you uncork this?' Edna ignored Fiona and passed George the bottle. 'Reggie offered to do it with his teeth, but they look false.'

'Is this for us?' George asked. 'Only it's late and we probably can't do it justice. Why don't I put it in the fridge and maybe we can celebrate tomorrow?'

'For you?' Edna looked at him with steely eyes. 'Don't be silly. This is for Reggie. Such a nice man — he's sorted out the problem with our television.'

'What problem with the television?' Fiona paled visibly and put down her glass. 'What have you done to the television? It was fine earlier.'

'No, it wasn't.' Edna nodded at the bottle. 'Are you going to open it or what?'

George deftly unhooked the top and massaged the cork out of the neck of the bottle. 'What was the problem with the television?' he asked.

'We couldn't get Mad Mike the biggest size.'

He held the bottle over his glass so any overspill could run into it as he twisted the cork until it popped.

'It's for Reggie, not you.' Edna eyed him suspiciously.

'She'll be the death of me.' Fiona shook her head as Edna left the room.

'What's Reggie's story?' Susie asked.

'A femoral fracture, after a fall from an electric scooter,' George said. 'Pretty horrific really. He had to have a couple of operations because it got infected and was in hospital for ages. He's been here for nearly three months. Just before Christmas, he suddenly decided he enjoyed being looked after and now appears to have no intention of leaving.'

'Don't be hard on him,' Fiona said, then, turning to Susie, added, 'It's what happened with many of our residents. They come for short-term rehabilitation and the next thing we know they've moved all their belongings in and want to stay. Did you hear our cleaner say that yesterday she'd overheard him talking and he referred to Treetops as his for ever home?'

'You really know how to make my day.' George sighed and rubbed his temples.

'Maybe he's lonely.' Susie paused. 'I was wondering . . . I mean . . . You don't think Edna could've meant *Magic Mike XXL*, do you? You know — that film about male strippers? I saw it was on one of the pay-to-view channels this week.'

'We don't get pay—' Fiona's face metamorphosed through several expressions before she jumped up. 'I'd better get to the lounge,' she said, heading to the door. She stopped with her hand on the handle. 'You didn't give Violet back her credit card, did you?' she asked George.

'Of course not,' he snapped.

'Sorry. No, of course you wouldn't have needed to.' Fiona turned to Susie. 'Violet's good with figures,' she said. 'She can remember any number — her birthday, her first telephone number, the long number on her credit card, the date and the three digits on the back — and will happily recite them to anyone who asks. Although, strangely, her memory when it comes to family and other things can often be vague.'

'It drives her family to distraction,' George said.

'I swear she only needs to hear a number once and she'll remember it for ever.'

'If that lot are watching a film about strippers, maybe I should make sure we have the defibrillator on hand . . .'

'George!' Fiona said, sharply.

'It's all right, Susie's a friend,' George said, and Susie felt a warm blush creeping over her cheeks. 'She knows I'm joking. Can you remember the direct line number for the hospital?' He ducked as Fiona threw a cushion at him.

'Come on,' she said, 'we'd better go and see what's going on.'

They arrived at the residents' lounge to find a young man Susie recognized as the nursing home's gardener, gyrating, naked to the waist, and swinging his shirt above his head in time to the music coming from the large television at the other end of the room — to the obvious delight of most of the residents — while Edna and Reggie, oblivious to the gardener's side show, stared fixedly at the large screen.

It had been a memorable day and Susie had found herself both busy and laughing most of the time, until it hit her that she hadn't thought about Terry. This had been her first Christmas without him.

He'd been such a big part of her life for forty-odd years. It hurt so much that he was no longer here.

Tomorrow she would walk to the woods. She'd scattered him on the hill there overlooking the town. They'd often done the walk together in the past, always pausing at the top to enjoy the view. A bench had been installed there sometime in the last few years. Tomorrow, maybe, she would sit for a while, enjoy being close to him, and wish him "Happy New Year".

She'd planted some tulip bulbs beside the bench before Christmas. Maddie's neighbour had recommended the variety. Susie wasn't the best gardener in the world, but the snowdrops she'd planted last autumn already looked like they were pushing through. She could imagine herself in years to come sitting there among the flowers. Terry would have liked it there too.

In the lounge, George had managed to get the gardener to stop dancing, while Fiona lowered the sound on the television, having wrestled the remote from Edna.

Susie put a hand on Fiona's arm. 'I should get going,' she said.

'Nonsense.' Fiona pulled her towards the television screen. 'Sit down.' She nodded towards the seat next to Reggie. 'You and I have a film to watch. It's been paid for, so we might as well make the most of it. Edna, could you spare a couple of glasses of champagne over here?'

The cardiganed woman from earlier came and stood between them and the television. 'Is Jason Isaacs in this one too?' she asked.

* * *

Bob looked round the table and wondered how soon he could slip away. Miss Phyllis needed a walk, and he needed his bed. He'd never felt the need to stay up and see the New Year in. What was it that Tennessee Ernie Ford had said? "Another year older and with bigger debts," or something like that. He couldn't see any reason to celebrate that, but he was never one to turn down a Chinese meal, and Maddie and Josh had pushed the boat out this year.

At Christmas they were still on their honeymoon, or mini-moon as they were calling their trip to France to stay with Maddie's parents, but they'd made it back earlier today. It was good to see them. Bob smiled and reached for another spare rib.

Their proper honeymoon was a trip to America that, according to Josh, was, the last time Bob had asked, still at the planning stage.

The pair of them hadn't stopped talking since they started the meal. If one took a breath, the other one would finish the sentence, or laugh and say, 'Do you remember . . . ?'

The meal was a surprise. Poppy had been down to cook pasta but had made no attempt to get started. Just when Bob thought he ought to do something for supper, Maddie and Josh had turned up with two overfilled bags and three bottles of expensive-looking French wine.

Poppy was in on the surprise, apparently. And the food, Bob had to admit, was good.

Miss Phyllis, their dog, was beside herself to see her owners again. She kept bringing in odd shoes and spinning round, wagging her tail while they thanked her and made a fuss of her. When she thought they weren't paying her enough attention she'd find another shoe, and the whole rigmarole would start again. On the table there was now a growing collection of odd shoes.

At one point, Poppy squawked, 'OMG, I haven't seen those shoes for ages. Where did you find it?' Miss Phyllis wagged her tail. Despite Poppy telling her what a good dog she was and asking her to find the other one, she didn't. Her next find was a Wellington boot.

Bob would miss her. Miss Phyllis had been his constant companion for the last couple of weeks. He'd taken her for walks twice a day and she'd stayed so close wherever he'd gone, it had been like having a shadow.

Of course, he'd still see her. Josh and Maddie lived close by, and Josh would be bringing her with him when he came to work in the office at the garage. Bob couldn't imagine his workload ever being so onerous that he couldn't take her for at least one walk a day. That should keep his heart consultant happy. He put his hand down, and after a quick sniff, just to make sure he wasn't offering food, Miss Phyllis wagged her tail and pushed her head into his hand for him to stroke. They were fast becoming firm friends.

He'd even started to recognize the regular dog owners on the common, and often walked with them. While Miss Phyllis played happily with the other dogs, he enjoyed chatter about everything from the state of the country to suggestions for that evening's meal. Everyone was known by their dog's name. He was Mr Phyllis, and usually walked with Mr Duke, Mrs Rodney and Miss Bert. Sometimes Rocky and Brian would join them, along with their owners.

It was Miss Bert who'd suggested the deconstructed kebabs they'd had for tea last night. Poppy had declared them a triumph. They must've been good. Poppy said she'd happily eat them again.

What a year. So much had changed. Josh was married and back in the UK, still working part-time for his old company but looking after the bike side of the recently renamed Diamond Cars and Bikes. Poppy had taken over the wedding limousine hire side of things and had expanded it considerably.

'Another year over . . .' Josh looked at Bob and started tapping his fingers.

Bob coughed. On the other side of the table, Poppy raised her eyebrows. 'No. Please. Not that John Lennon Christmas song,' she groaned.

He offered his daughter the plate of spring rolls, and she took one as he laughed and raised his glass. 'Thank you, everyone,' he said. 'Especially my daughter — the heathen. Here's to health, wealth and happiness all round.'

'And "lurve",' Poppy added, lifting her glass too.

'We ought to make resolutions,' Maddie said after everyone had clinked their glasses. 'What do you plan on doing next year? If we all make a resolution, then next New Year's Eve we can look back and see if we have achieved them.'

'I resolve to get through it,' Bob joked.

'Don't ask me,' Poppy said. 'Every resolution I've ever made has been broken on New Year's Day. And before you ask, I'm not planning on a dry or meat-free January.'

'There must be something you want to achieve next year?' Maddie said. She wasn't giving up, Bob would give her that.

'Nothing apart from the usual: marriage to Chris Pine, or an equally acceptable-looking multimillionaire.'

'She's had a thing about him since she went to see *Outlaw King* a few years ago,' Bob said. What he didn't add was that Poppy might also have designs on a certain data engineer working with Josh. Tony had popped into the garage to check on post and make sure all the systems were working while the newlyweds were away.

In all likeliness Poppy's feelings were reciprocated. Josh had said Tony would pop in once a week. They were away for three weeks, but there hadn't been many days when he hadn't just "popped in", "because he was passing" and always stopped for a coffee with Poppy.

Come to think of it, he looked a bit like Chris Pine. Bob had sat through the film at least once when he'd found his daughter watching it. From memory, there was dark hair and designer stubble, so yep, a lot like Tony. But he knew better than to tease Poppy in front of her brother about a budding romance.

'I love what I do. Really, I'm happy.' Poppy shrugged. 'What about you two lovebirds?'

Maddie grinned at Josh. 'We've got our honeymoon proper to look forward to.'

Josh needed no more of a prompt. He was off. 'It's turning into a bigger event than we originally discussed. Latton

Data Inc, my head office, wants us to combine our visit with some presentations they've asked me to do, so we're looking at going to America for at least a month, maybe six weeks now.'

'And we're going to ride the Pacific Coast Highway,' Maddie added, her face split with the widest grin Bob had ever seen.

'Finally.' Bob grinned back. He knew how much that ride meant to Josh. It had been something he'd dreamed of doing since he was a kid. 'Good for you.'

'Maddie's had her leave approved. She's allowed to take a block of her holiday in one go,' Josh said. 'So now I can start to firm up the arrangements.'

'If I need more, then they've agreed I can take unpaid leave, as long as I'm back before the wedding season gets into full swing,' Maddie interrupted.

'I'm going to spend time at head office while we're out there so I can catch up with the American team,' Josh added. 'Which means . . .'

'I'm going to have plenty of time to shop and enjoy Los Angeles,' Maddie giggled.

'I was going to say . . .' Josh laughed at his wife. 'Before I was rudely interrupted.'

Maddie stuck out her tongue.

'That it means I've started looking at places to stay and explore on the way.'

Bob smiled. Last year Josh had finished restoring the ancient Triumph bike, the same model that his hero Steve McQueen rode.

Steve McQueen had died a good few years before Josh was born but had come alive again with all Bob's father's stories. It had been Grandad Steve's dream to ride the Pacific Coast Highway. He never managed it, but perhaps dreams were transferrable.

For various reasons, Josh's plans had been put on hold so often that Bob stopped asking his son about it. Just this last year he'd finished restoring the bike, and now next year it seemed he was finally going for it.

Bob speared the last pork ball. It was too good to leave. With Josh and Maddie making eyes at each other and Poppy checking her phone, he seemed to be the only one eating. He hoped everyone wouldn't suddenly realize where they were and feel hungry, because he was doing a great job in clearing up.

He had dreams too. He'd wanted to join the Ace-to-Ace run from London to Beijing, ever since he'd bought a bike from someone who had done it. The Pacific Coast Highway sounded like a much more civilized option. The Ace run was a lot longer, thirteen weeks in total, and you had to cross some hostile environments to get to Beijing. Not everyone made it. He wasn't sure he'd ever told Poppy or Josh that dream, partly because he didn't want them to laugh at him, or worse, tell him he was just being a daft old man. Poppy certainly wouldn't mince her words.

The trouble was, you had to be capable of handling a bike and riding up to five hundred miles in a day, and he'd barely handled a bike in thirty-odd years. While Josh was away, he'd taken the Ducati out daily, to keep it ticking over. That was his excuse anyway. Boxing Day, when Poppy was at friends, he'd taken it to Blackpool and back. Over four hundred miles. As far as he knew, Josh hadn't checked the bike, so he hadn't needed to make excuses. He was only supposed to be turning it over and keeping it going.

He'd been stiff afterwards, but other than that, felt good. Like his dream was possibly back on track.

He had Maddie's colleague, Susie, to thank for her words of wisdom at the wedding. 'You have one life, live it,' she'd said. He wished Elaine had thought like that. She could have done so many things if she'd wanted to.

Bob's heart attack last year had been a bit of a blip. His doctor seemed pleased with his progress and said there was no reason the stent should stop him from doing what he wanted to do. And he wanted to do the Ace-to-Ace ride. He wondered whether Susie had decided what her trials would be for next year. He wished he could ask her.

He'd certainly be interested in reading her next year's Christmas letter. And if ever he saw her again, he'd tell her.

CHAPTER FOUR

'Next?' A face appeared at the hatch in the shed, otherwise known as the Lorry Park Café.

Bob looked up from the local paper and ordered a sausage sandwich and a mug of tea.

'Brown or white?' the girl asked.

'White bread, brown tea.' Bob handed over the exact money and moved to one side so he could wait for his order. The person behind him moved forward — he was sure it was a woman, but difficult to tell given the quantity of clothing she was wearing. Bob hadn't heard a forecast that morning, but it looked like she had all bases covered weather-wise. There was something familiar about her, but she was angled away from him and he couldn't be certain.

She was probably not dieting seeing as she ordered the same as him. Both orders appeared together. The chef put a tray with the two sandwiches, two steaming cardboard cups and a handful of paper towels on the counter and nodded at Bob.

'Excuse me.'

Bob turned to find the woman smiling at him.

It was her. Bob was suddenly lost for words.

'Bob, isn't it?' she asked. 'Josh's father and Miss Phyllis too. I thought I recognized you both from Maddie's wedding. Hello, little one.'

Without waiting for a response, she bent down and made a fuss of his dog, who seemed to be equally as delighted as he was to be recognized, except in the terrier's case she expressed it better — she had a tail to wag, and did. She didn't just stare back open mouthed.

Bob coughed and tried to recover his composure. 'I'm not sure I can follow that,' he said. 'Hello . . .'

'Not you. I meant Miss Phyllis.' Susie straightened up. Her smile was infectious.

'Susie.' Bob had a lightheaded moment and felt happier than he had in a while. 'Are you eating in, or just collecting a takeaway?' To be fair, if they ate in, they'd have to sit on the patio outside the café. The café had cordoned off a large square and arranged tables haphazardly there.

'In.' She grimaced. 'It's mild for January and dry, so I thought I'd chance it. What about you? Do you want me to carry the food over to a table, seeing as you've got your hands full with the dog and paper?'

'Only if you'll join me.' Bob cringed. *Did he really just say that?*

They sat on opposite sides of one of the wonky wooden benches. 'So . . .' Bob took a bite of his sandwich, then wiped his hands on the thin napkin that came with it. 'What brings you to Redford Industrial Estate on a Saturday morning? I've got an excuse — I was walking the dog to the lake and back.'

Miss Phyllis sat looking at him with the biggest eyes imaginable. Maddie wasn't keen for her to be fed from the table, but Bob wasn't sure how long he could resist that pained expression. He moved the roll out of her eyeline and took a sip of the tea. The good thing about the Lorry Park Café was that the tea was always hot and strong, and the bread always buttered.

'I've started one of my new experiences for this year. You probably don't remember my Christmas letter idea . . .' she tailed off.

'I do,' he said. 'Go on then, tell me, what brings you here on a Saturday morning?'

'A pole-dancing class in the unit across the way.'

His mouthful of tea came out in a spray as he coughed. Thankfully, she wasn't directly opposite him, so escaped being covered. He used the paper towels to mop up. 'Pole dancing?' he said.

'Yep.'

He wrapped his hands round his cup again and eyed Susie suspiciously over the top.

'It's top of the list of things I want to achieve, although I am rethinking the taxidermy course.'

Was she taking the piss? He didn't know her well enough to be sure and dared not risk another mouthful of tea yet. 'And the pole dancing?' he asked cautiously. 'What's that about?'

'Extremely good for your legs, and it was the only dancing class the college offered that started before Easter. I might do burlesque next term if I get this nailed.' Her mouth twitched and there was a twinkle in her eye as she took a bite of her roll. Bob watched as she chewed. He'd have liked to have had something funny to say, but his brain was empty.

'I needed to get started on my list before I lost confidence and did nothing,' she carried on. 'So here I am, week one of a six-week course. Only today, the knee-hook slide was way beyond me. As for the carousel spin, I didn't attempt that one. It just looks like a disaster waiting to happen, especially seeing as I couldn't climb a pole at school. I'm still trying to figure out why I thought it would be any easier fifty years later.'

Bob chuckled. Her eyes sparkled in the weak sun. And despite what she said about January being mild, a small white puff of breath punctuated each of her sentences.

'They say practice makes perfect.'

'They do, don't they?' There was something about the way she tilted her head. Clearly, she hadn't expected that reply.

'Otherwise, how are you going to nail it before Easter?'

'How do I practise? The nearest thing I have to a pole is the post at the bottom of my stairs and that's only about three foot tall. It's way too late to add one to my list for Santa and I'm not sure he'd take me seriously, anyway.'

'Oh, right. When you said Christmas letter, I assumed you were planning on sending a friendly, chatty, newsletter-type thing to your friends. I didn't realize you meant Santa.'

'That's not what I . . .'

'Dear Santa, I have been a good girl this year. Look at the things I've studied at college — pole dancing, flower pressing, soap carving . . .'

'Stop,' she laughed. 'That's not what I meant.'

'But you do still believe in Santa?'

'Of course,' Susie said. She threw him a look, which he suspected was her trying to look indignant, but failing miserably. 'Don't you?' She bit her bottom lip. 'Actually, being serious here for a moment, there was a pole for sale in the *Redford Chronicle* this week. A nearly new one. I guess they didn't find pole dancing easy either, considering the ridiculously low price they want for it.'

She put down her sandwich. 'Do you think I'm being ridiculous to think about buying my own after just one week?'

'Not at all. How else are you going to practise?'

'There is that, but every time I think about buying anything frivolous, I just hear my mother's voice saying, "What were you thinking?" and "You must have more money than sense".'

'Well, I wouldn't dream of saying anything that crass. If you think you're going to use it, then what's the harm in getting it now? It would mean you could practise between lessons. Maybe the knee lock . . .'

'Knee-hook slide.'

'That . . . would be a doddle by the end of the course.'

'I doubt it, but I was tempted until I googled what you'd need to install one — it's way beyond my DIY skills. Which means I'd have to ring our usual handyperson and ask him to install it.'

'And that would be a problem?'

'It's silly, really, but he's always given me the creeps.' She looked for all the world like she was trying to suppress a shudder. 'This would give him the ideal opportunity to come out with just about every innuendo you can imagine and wink unpleasantly.'

Her smile dropped. 'Sorry, I'm being silly. It will be fine. I guess I'm feeling vulnerable. It's still early days since Terry died. Now, what about you? How was your Christmas?'

'Good, thanks, apart from another apron-and-oven-glove set from the in-laws. It says they're for cooking but gives no instructions how long or on what temperature. Or, for that matter, what they should be served with. I shouldn't be unkind. They're both in their eighties, but it is the second set they've sent me since Elaine died.'

Susie giggled. She'd finished her roll and tea but was making no move to get up. He wanted to stand her another drink, but if he reminded her she'd finished, she might suddenly remember something she needed to do. He didn't want her to go. 'Poppy's even less happy. She got the pants back that she sent Elaine's mother last year. I think she's planning on sending them back this year. Was Santa kind to you? Or will you be writing to him to complain?'

She shook her head. 'No point. He never writes back.'

'Come now.' Bob felt in his jacket for a pen and started to write on another napkin. '*Dear disillusioned . . .*'

'What are you doing?' Susie leaned over and looked at the napkin.

'Christmas reply from Santa,' he said. '*I'm sorry to hear Santa did not deliver the Christmas present of your dreams, but this shouldn't mean you give up dreaming. It's never too early to plan for this year. May I suggest in future years, to avoid such disappointment, you are more specific about your choices? Santa is not a mind-reader and really doesn't have the time to shop around. Catalogue numbers and sizes are always useful where appropriate.*'

'Christmas is a time for children,' Susie said.

'*Please also consider all presents should be of such a size that they can fit down your chimney. Santa is a delivery driver, not a professional wrestler.*'

Susie grinned and held up a hand.

'And, while we're on the subject, if your required delivery method is via a chimney, then please make sure said chimney is free from all obstructions.'

Her eyes crinkled and she let out a burst of laughter, deep and unexpected.

'For that matter, do check that you have a chimney,' Bob added. *'Also, please bear in mind there are strict weight limits. The sleigh is pulled by a herd of elderly reindeer, not a fleet of Eddie Stobart trucks. Argos might give a fourteen-day money-back no-questions-asked guarantee, but Santa doesn't.* Anything I've forgotten?'

'No.' Susie laughed. A deep, hearty laugh.

'Maybe I should make a list too.'

Susie's smile dropped.

Bob felt immediately lost.

'I'm sorry. I should've asked. I know you lost your wife. How are you coming to terms with her death?'

Bob sighed. She'd worded it nicely. Most people said "getting over". "Coming to terms" meant acceptance. He still missed Elaine every bloody day, but he was starting to accept she was dead. Although, over Christmas when he'd taken Miss Phyllis out, he found himself saying out aloud things he wanted to tell, or discuss with Elaine. Last week, a couple crossed the road to avoid him. He hardly blamed them — he'd been in the middle of an argument with himself about the practicalities of fixing up an old banger.

Susie seemed to take his silence as a reluctance to answer her question.

'I'm expecting some pretty impressive bruises in the next couple of days,' she said, not looking at him. 'Thank goodness it's January and I can cover up. Otherwise there's every danger I'd be mistaken for a cage fighter.' She swirled the dregs round in her cardboard cup. 'Can I get you another tea?'

She was looking at him. Straight and direct. Her eyes looked grey from where he sat.

'Or do you have somewhere you have got to get to?'

Miss Phyllis lay at his feet, either farting or snoring — he didn't look down to check. He didn't want to break eye contact. There was something happening in the rest of his body, like he'd inadvertently plugged himself into an electric socket. A strange but pleasant sensation.

'Thank you,' he whispered hoarsely. He should've been the gentleman, and offered to pay. He'd intended to, but it was too late. Standing up right now could be embarrassing for them both.

Susie came back not only with teas, but two shiny Chelsea buns. 'I shouldn't really,' she said, 'but figured if I made a meal of breakfast I could call it lunch.'

The other tables around them had changed occupants several times while they'd been sitting there. It wasn't the sort of place you stayed for any length of time. The food may be good and the portions may be sizeable, but its entire *raison d'être* was fast food in a convenient location.

'I received another Christmas letter this morning,' Susie sighed. 'Another happy family. They would have sent it earlier but have been abroad skiing for a month. Kids all geniuses, pets winning various shows, parents both incredibly fabulous cooks, rally drivers, all round good eggs, in line for New Year knighthoods, yadda yadda. That sort of thing.'

'They're knighting rally drivers these days?'

'Okay, I exaggerate, but you know the kind of thing. Four pages of fascinating facts about interesting people.'

She'd already finished her tea, but her bun sat untouched on the plate. She started shredding her cardboard cup. Bob gently removed it from her hands, collected their rubbish together, and moved the bun in front of her.

'Eat,' he whispered.

'Do you think "the labours of Susie" is a silly idea?' she asked. 'After today's pole-dancing class, I think maybe I am just an uninteresting person who should stick to knitting dishcloths. Sorry, I bet you wish you hadn't asked me to join you now, don't you?'

He jerked his head. 'Not at all. And for what it's worth, I don't think you should give up pole dancing. Not after just one lesson anyway.'

She looked up and smiled. Not a huge smile, but there was definitely one there.

'I admire you,' he said. 'I haven't sent Christmas cards for the last two years for the same reason. What are you supposed to write as a widower? "Here's hoping for a better year next year". That just sounds so shallow.'

'Are you? Hoping for a better year?'

'I suppose I am.'

'Then you have to plan it. Look at what you want to achieve and go for it. Try something new.' Her phone buzzed, and she reached for it. 'God, is that the time? Look, sorry I'm working this afternoon. I really ought to think about making a move.'

'Apart from pole dancing what else is on your "to-do" list?' Bob asked.

'It's quite extensive, but if it's going to take this long to master any of them, then a few of the ideas are going to have to go, otherwise it's probably going to take me the rest of my life before I'm ready to write a newsy letter to my friends.' She stopped speaking and wrapped the rest of her bun in some paper napkins. Bob didn't feel the need to break the silence.

'Although, thankfully, not everything requires that much effort. My next idea is to attend a laminated dough or macarons workshop. They're day courses — I just can't decide whether to do croissants or macarons — and they're both running on the same day.'

'The biscuits?'

She nodded.

'Annoying little bleeders with little taste, in my experience. Go for the other one,' Bob said as he got up, then picked up the napkin he'd written "Dear disillusioned" on. He took up his pen and wrote a number on it. 'When you're ready for that pole, or any pole, to be fitted, call me,' he said. 'I'd like to help. No innuendos, I promise.'

CHAPTER FIVE

The following Saturday, Bob paused as his hand found the door handle. The kitchen door was ajar. He could hear Poppy's voice.

'I tell you, Josh, Dad's turned weird since Christmas. He's even started bloody swimming.'

'Dad?' Josh sounded surprised. The cheek of it. Bob had always been an excellent swimmer. Who was it who'd taught them to swim?

'First thing in the morning, twice a week.'

Bob enjoyed his twice-weekly swims, despite never having been keen on unnecessary exercise. He'd never jogged anywhere in his life, but swimming was different somehow. Although getting there sometimes felt a bit of a chore. This morning he'd have rather had another hour in bed, but once there, the early bird regulars seemed to encourage each other.

In the last couple of weeks since he'd started, he'd already worked out he wasn't as fast as Mr Crawl, who always went for the end lane. Bob took the lane next to him and stuck to the breaststroke. He may be a good deal slower, but he didn't make nearly as much of a splash either. On his other side a couple of women usually swam in the same lane, unless the lane next to them was empty, then they'd split up. At the other end were the married couple who swam for fifteen minutes and then got out, giving everyone more space.

Everyone had their preferred lane. Bob tried to avoid Two-Paddle Frank, who was only swimming for therapeutic reasons and insisted on doing it with floats. He preferred to swim in Mr Crawl's lane if he got there before Inflatable Eileen who wore armbands. She didn't come every week, according to the women normally next to him — she was usually a Monday and Wednesday attendee.

Bob aimed for fifty lengths, give or take. Sometimes he wondered whether the others had a name for him, and what it would be. "Breaststroke Bob".

He'd usually lose count of the number of lengths he'd swum somewhere in the teens, about the time he'd stop thinking about anything important and start to relax. He could shower and still be home at a reasonable hour with his head clear and feeling good.

Considering he'd spent his youth racing bikes, he had to accept these days he was not an adrenaline junkie. But he did feel alive when he heard an engine purr, or when a car was restored to factory condition, or when a dark-blonde-headed woman with deep grey eyes sat across a table and laughed with him. Those feelings stayed with him and made him feel good, in a way that a half-marathon run around the town never could.

'Exercising without being prompted. Do you think his consultant gave him bad news, and he hasn't told us?' Josh asked.

Not the consultant, it was the flaming dietician. He'd told Bob to replace butter and cheese with vegetable or olive oil, which, combined with a list of highly saturated foods Bob needed to avoid, too, meant their last appointment had been a real downer.

Miss Phyllis stuck her nose through the gap in the door. Bob couldn't hide any longer. He'd been sussed. He could see her wagging tail through the gap. Poppy and Josh might not have noticed his arrival, but the highly sensitive nose of that mongrel had.

'And he brought a catalogue from the local college home last week.'

'Why would he do that?' Josh asked.

'Apparently, he's considering a blacksmithing course.'

Just a day. And not considering — it's booked. Bob smiled. The course had looked interesting. The local farrier was running it at the Old Forge, which was behind the most gorgeous pair of metalwork gates, made from horseshoes. He liked the idea of making a gate — maybe using some of his car memorabilia collection. Bob figured he'd be unlikely to create something of that size in a day, but who knew? And as Susie had said, "You'll never know unless you try". That hadn't been about metalwork. He couldn't remember exactly what she'd been talking about at the time — another of her mad Christmas letter ideas. He smiled.

'Why would he do that?' Josh asked.

'Because the glass-blowing course was full,' Bob said.

They both stopped talking, clearly trying to backtrack and work out just how much of the conversation he'd heard. He pushed the door open fully and made a fuss over Miss Phyllis. 'Hi, you two — up already?' he said, smiling. 'I hope you've got a brew on.'

Poppy turned her back and busied herself boiling the kettle as Bob threw his damp trunks and towel in the washing machine.

'I wasn't expecting you today,' he said to Josh, who was perched on a stool. 'Nothing wrong, is there? Maddie okay?'

'Maddie's fine. She sends her love. She's working today, so I thought I'd make a start on a couple of reports. Where have you been?'

'That's a trick question, right? I've just come in carrying a towel and a pair of trunks, both clearly wet, like my hair. And, before either of you call it that, it's not some sort of mid-life crisis. I'm just trying a few new things out for size.'

'And one of those is swimming first thing in the morning?'

Bob ignored the sarcasm in Poppy's voice.

'I sometimes find myself at a bit of a loose end. The business is running smoothly, so from time to time I get bored. I'm just looking at other opportunities.'

Two slices of thick toast popped out of the toaster.

'If I'm in danger of being pensioned off early, then I need to consider other options.'

Poppy put the toast on a plate, got some butter out of the fridge and topped the mug of tea on the counter up with milk. Josh passed the mug over to him.

'No one's pensioning you off, Dad,' he said.

'Good.' Bob pinched the slice of toast that Poppy had just finished buttering and took a large bite out of it, as she shouted, 'Oi'.

Pulling the age card had been wicked. Now they'd both feel guilty that they were taking over, even if nothing was further from the truth. He loved having Josh back, even if most of his time was still taken up with his part-time consultancy role for Latton Data Inc.

The wedding limousine hire side of the business was thriving under Poppy's control. Bob had no intention of interfering there. He was still nominally in charge of the sales and maintenance side of the garage, except he'd come back from his appointment with the dietician yesterday to find Josh holding the service meeting that Bob had put in the garage diary, then completely forgotten about. He'd arrived to find Josh allocating tasks to the mechanics. He had also quietly taken on a lot of the business admin. Josh said he didn't mind, so Bob had no intention of interfering. Why would he? He hated that side of the business. As far as he was concerned, it kept him away from his first love: sourcing and servicing classic cars.

They'd decided at Christmas not to push the bike side of the business until Josh had settled in. Although, there had been several bike enquiries over the last month. Josh had already found one bike for a customer. It had meant Josh and Maddie having to make a trip to Cumbria to collect it. They'd driven up last Saturday afternoon and spent a couple of nights in the Lake District with Miss Phyllis before Josh had ridden the bike back on Monday while Maddie brought the car home, calling in at some relatives along the way for lunch.

On Tuesday, Bob and Josh worked on the bike together, servicing then cleaning it. And on Thursday Josh sold it to a man who'd happily paid the asking price, netting the garage a healthy profit.

Bob had wanted to go to Cumbria with Josh and Maddie and ride the bike back for them. If they had asked, he would have jumped at the chance. Sadly, they hadn't, and it hadn't been something he felt he could suggest, seeing as his family and consultant still considered him to be in recovery.

The idea that he must be protected at all costs must surely end soon. Maybe he should stand in the garage and shout, 'I'm okay. I'm fully fit.' Or, perhaps take out a full-page advert in the *Redford Chronicle*, announce to the whole town there was nothing wrong with him anymore. Even the consultant, at their last appointment, had said, with a straight face completely devoid of emotion, that Bob could return to having a "normal sex life".

'Whose?' Bob had asked. Which, apart from a slight splutter, hadn't got a reaction, and certainly not a sensible response.

It had been the dietician who'd been less enthusiastic and waxed on about prevention being better than cure. It was him who suggested Bob look at college courses. Okay, he'd suggested vegan cookery not blacksmithing, but he had handed over a brochure.

He really shouldn't wind the kids up. They were great, but he didn't want them second-guessing his reasons for swimming and keeping fit. He thought back to Susie last Saturday and the way her eyes had glittered when she'd told him about her pole-dancing class, and he'd practically covered her with tea. He was going to tell her about the swimming but figured it would be best to give it a couple of weeks.

Bob wondered what a certain woman with a love of sausage sandwiches would make of him announcing he'd become vegan. He smiled at the thought of her forehead creasing and those grey eyes searching his face for a hint he was joking.

'Dad, this weekend . . .' Poppy had her mother's knack for changing the subject. He wondered where this conversation was heading.

'I've got a problem.'

He smiled. 'Really?'

'I'm double-booked. One of our drivers has called in sick.' When Poppy drew her words out like that, it was because she wanted something. 'Could you do a local one? *Ple-e-ease*?'

'What time?'

'Thanks, Dad, you're a star.' She wound her arms around his neck. He made a grab for her second slice of toast. He was too late. In an almost balletic move, she whipped the plate out of his reach and spun away. When she turned back, she was holding the toast aloft and it already sported a mouth-sized hole.

'Pick up at eleven,' she muttered between chews. 'Church ceremony at noon. Drop off at the Badger and Fir Tree. You'll be home by one.'

Damn. That meant he'd miss Susie leaving her class. He sighed and went to look for a pair of overalls.

CHAPTER SIX

Susie had walked home with a skip in her step last week after her first pole-dancing lesson, but that had been more to do with meeting Bob again than the class. That had been painful, and she'd been ready to give up. But two cups of tea, a sausage sandwich and a Chelsea bun later, he'd persuaded her to have another go. She was glad he had — this week had felt a lot more positive.

She'd hoped to see him at the burger van again today and had been disappointed to find him not there. She'd spent most of the week practising the exercises their tutor Tara had showed them, and this week received congratulations for her bent-leg side plank.

'That's great, Susie,' Tara enthused. 'You've really got the idea. Drive your hips forward, just make sure that you're actively pushing that lower shoulder down as well.'

Susie decided against eating her own body weight in sausage sandwiches and cake on her own and set off home, slightly dejected. Last week she'd stuck Bob's "Dear disillusioned" serviette to the fridge with a magnet. It made her smile every time she walked past.

He'd offered help, and even if she'd misread any other signals, she needed that. It would have just been nice to run it past him again, but by the time she'd got home she'd made up her mind.

She was going to buy the pole. One of the other women had a washing-line pole that she was using to practise. 'I don't think it's strong enough to take my weight,' she'd said. 'But I can spin around it to my heart's content.' Her moves had improved from the practice. Susie hadn't told anyone about the pole this morning. She didn't want one of her classmates jumping in before her. Not until she'd seen it and ruled it out.

'I was wondering,' she said as the phone was answered. 'Whether your pole is still for sale?'

The young woman who answered the phone sounded sulky and strangely familiar, when she said it was. She wondered if she'd been a recent client.

As soon as Susie asked why it was for sale, the person — whoever she was — went into a diatribe about how her ex, who was also her landlord, objected to it being in the sitting room because, "It made the house look like a brothel". That thought alone made Susie determined to own it.

'It's the proper thing,' the girl said defensively when Susie said she'd think about it. 'Really easy to install. Doesn't need any permanent fixings if the height of your room is somewhere between 2.25 and 2.75 metres. It works on secure pressure between the ceiling and the floor. Have you checked the height of your room?'

Susie frowned. No, she hadn't. Her hesitation must have given her away.

'Check it, and if you still want it, come and see it. I'm in all day.' She reeled off an address which Susie noted was only two streets away, one of the smaller new builds that had sprung up recently.

She hadn't figured on making an instant decision.

There had been times over the last week, despite Bob's encouragement, when she'd debated going back to the class at all. At times she wasn't sure she ever wanted to see another pole again. But she was glad she had. They were a nice group.

Bob hadn't said that he'd be there. They hadn't made any arrangements to meet again. Still, she felt like she'd been stood up. Ridiculous. They weren't dating. They weren't even friends, just casual acquaintances. She'd met him twice in her life. It wasn't as if she wanted to spend the rest of her life with him. She *humph*ed with exasperation.

The address she'd written down was in a small cul-de-sac. The terraced house looked like its only non-attached wall was the front one. It had a small window and a door. No bell. Susie rattled the letterbox, and the door was opened almost instantly — by Tara, her dance teacher.

The two women stared at each other.

'Tara!' Susie said.

'Susie!' Tara exclaimed, clearly just as surprised. She frowned. 'Was it you I just spoke to? You rang to buy my pole?'

'I didn't know it was you.'

Tara shook her head but opened the door wider into the sitting room. Behind her, in the middle of the room, in a centrepiece sort of way, was the pole. The house looked beautifully clean and tidy, but in her wildest dreams Susie hadn't planned on making quite such a feature of it.

'I'm sorry,' she said. 'I don't know what I was thinking.' She turned to go, but Tara took hold of her arm.

'No, I'm sorry.' Tara looked upset. 'You've made really great progress this week. Come in and have a look.' She appeared genuine. No hint that she was taking the piss, or surprised by Susie's deathly pale face.

'It looks almost new.' Susie followed Tara in.

'I haven't had it long.' Tara shook her head. 'Only since the end of last year, when I was signed up to teach the class for the college.'

'What about the classroom?'

'The industrial unit is only available on Saturday mornings.' Tara shook her head. 'No, that's not true, they did say I could use it anytime, that was part of the arrangement, but Mondays to Fridays the double-glazing warehouse next door use the room as their storeroom. When I put the pole up, every one of them made some sort of comment, from innuendo to downright obscene. It was so uncomfortable. I am not an exhibitionist, and I certainly don't want to be ogled by a group of middle-aged men. I just need to do daily exercises to strengthen my core muscles, stay fit and practise our new moves. I can hardly teach students something I can't do myself.'

Susie felt sorry for the girl. Normally so confident, Tara looked dejected as she stroked the pole lovingly.

'I've been given until the end of the month,' she said quietly. 'Jason has demanded I get rid of it before then, otherwise he'll evict me.'

'Can he do that?'

'How should I know? I can't afford to take the chance.' She shrugged. 'If he throws me out without references, I'm buggered. It's hard enough to find a place to rent if you have good ones. You want it or not? If you don't, I suppose I could store it at the industrial unit until the end of the course, then if I can't find a buyer, I'll just have to take it to the local tip.'

'What about next term?' Susie asked.

'Two people have already dropped out,' Tara said.

Susie nodded. There had only been eight of them today. They'd waited a few minutes before starting in case the others turned up, but they didn't. The class was mixed ages. Susie thought she was probably the oldest, although Sharon and Paula were not far behind. One young girl's mother sat at the back of the room last week. She insisted on staying to watch, but this week she'd dropped the girl off, seemingly happy they were an all-woman group without any male groupies. Last week, the girl seemed to spend most of the lesson with a fixed pout, but this week she looked a lot more relaxed and on one occasion, laughed.

'The council won't run the course if there are any less than six people.' Tara sniffed. 'It's not cost effective.'

'If I buy it . . .' Susie said.

'Yes.' Tara looked up. She didn't seem to have noticed Susie's stress on "If".

'I only live a couple of streets away. Maybe you could come round and train on it there?'

'What, in your house?'

'It's okay. I don't have a landlord.'

Tara's eyes widened.

'Maybe you could even help me with some of the exercises. Today was only my second lesson. Last week I toyed with the idea of giving up, too, but something someone said persuaded me to give it another go, and I am glad I did.'

Tara took a while to answer. 'You don't know me,' she said, eventually. 'What about stranger danger and all that? How do you know I won't trash your place or steal from you?'

It was Susie's turn to shrug. 'Would you?' she asked.

There was a vigorous shake of the head.

'Of course, if you're planning on moving in, changing all the locks and demanding squatters' rights, I'd rather you said now, while there's still a chance for me to change my mind.' She grinned.

Tara smiled. 'Now there's a thought.'

'Great. I'll take that as "no" then. Do we have a deal?'

There was another moment of silence, punctuated by Tara squinting at her. Susie figured she could practically hear the cogs in the woman's brain turning.

'How about you don't pay?' She was talking fast. 'We can say you're borrowing it. That way, if you don't get on with it, I can still sell it later. I'd probably get more for it if I had more time.'

It was Susie's turn to think. 'Okay,' she said eventually. 'When would be a good time to arrange collection? Someone I know has offered to help with installing it.'

'No need,' Tara said firmly. 'We can take it apart together and I'll carry it back to your place and help you install it. That way I get to see where you live. Is there a problem with that?'

Susie shook her head. She'd been disappointed not to see Bob at the café. She wanted to ring him and ask for his help. Hearing his voice would be good, therapeutic even. In her head she'd planned for him to come round, and help

47

her install the pole. Probably not in the centre of the room, maybe between the lounge and the dining space. She could've offered to cook him a meal to thank him. Then they could've sat and talked, maybe over a good bottle of wine.

Sometimes, of an evening, she was lonely. Which was crazy because Terry had been in Treetops Nursing Home for months before he died. Even before that, most of the time conversation had been very one-sided. But while he was still alive, she always felt that she could talk to him, tell him things. Now she felt empty. Something was missing. Something more than just the crap TV schedules of late.

She wasn't looking for a relationship, but Bob was easy to talk to and made her laugh, and she hadn't done much of that for quite a while. Then there was a certain feeling she got when he was around that made her warm inside. A feeling she enjoyed.

Also, it was nice to talk to people of her own age. She loved working in the Register Office, but she was the oldest by quite a stretch. Tara was easily young enough to be her daughter, probably even her granddaughter.

'And you can test it by sitting on the pole.' Tara's smile was wide now. Susie tried to smile back. Tara had mentioned at length this morning that it was a staple beginner move, but it could be painful. Very painful until her muscles strengthened.

'You have to learn how to grip the pole with your thigh,' she said as she expertly dismantled the pole into sections and slipped on a pair of shoes.

'Yeah, right.' Susie laughed, glad that it was now in pieces, and she wasn't expected to do anything more than hold two sections. The only time she'd be likely to be able to "sit on the pole" was if it were lying on the floor.

'We'll soon have you climbing up it.'

CHAPTER SEVEN

As always seemed to happen in the UK these days, the new year started reasonably and then got colder and wetter. Today, Susie had woken to discover a layer of snow covering the ground. She hated snow. It always put her in a bad mood, but today's mood wasn't helped by listening to an answerphone message from Max, Terry's son, threatening a visit that afternoon. It would be interesting to see his reaction to his stepmother's latest purchase.

No one had left a message to say pole dancing had been cancelled that morning and she was within easy walking distance, so had no excuse not to go. It would be too cold to meet Bob at the lorry park. He probably wouldn't be going, anyway. He didn't make it last week, but it would have been nice to see him. She pulled the paper napkin off the fridge and put it back about half a dozen times before making up her mind to ring.

She couldn't remember the last time she'd felt so nervous as she typed the number into her phone and waited while it rang and rang. She was just about to hang up when the phone was answered by a woman.

'Diamond Cars — how can I help?'

Susie had steadied herself for the call and now didn't know what to say, so she did the mature, grown-up thing and hung up without saying a word.

49

She had wanted to suggest that if he was thinking of going for a walk today, they meet after her class, but perhaps somewhere a little warmer than the lorry park. There was the café at the garden centre which allowed dogs in. If he happened to be out and about, she could buy him a sausage sandwich there to thank him for being kind to her when she was having a meltdown after the first class and persuading her to keep going. Somewhere along the line she figured she could mention buying a pole last week.

He'd given her a landline number. She had assumed it would be a direct line, maybe his home number, but clearly not.

Had she misjudged the situation completely?

He'd looked like he wanted her to ring — hadn't he?

Maybe all he had offered was help fitting a pole? If her middle-aged brain had just accepted that instead of tossing all the possible scenarios around and making two plus two come somewhere near to 376, she'd feel a lot more settled.

Susie berated herself — she wasn't a love-struck teenager anymore. She refocused on her intention to go to the pole-dancing class. Not that the pole dancing was getting any easier, but Susie had paid for the six-week course and intended to finish it. The exercises Tara set her to work on at home may have helped, but the jury was still out on that. The bruises were still very much there, and surely she must've misunderstood what Tara said about doing cobra lifts. She'd tried on a couple of occasions, and fast concluded that the woman must be mad — they were physically impossible, and she'd ached for ages afterwards.

In fact, so far, at home, all she'd really managed was walking around the pole elegantly, pointing her toes, leaning outwards and turning as gracefully as she could. That bit she found easy. Her dance training had helped. She had a good posture. Then with her hands in the right position, she'd sometimes slide down to a crouching position — less graceful — and getting up was sometimes a bit of a challenge.

New year, new challenge — pole dancing. Met some lovely people.

No need to explain she'd met one of them outside the unit. Or that the class was held in the ground-floor office of a double-glazing warehouse next to a granite merchants and tyre centre on an industrial estate. On a need-to-know basis, and no one she planned on sending her Christmas letter to did.

The snow was starting to melt. She remembered Tara stressing the importance of a proper warmup before a class. Going to be hard with today's freezing temperatures. Susie went back upstairs to rethink her wardrobe. Thermal underwear, thick socks, heavy trousers and Wellington boots were given. She dug out a heavy coat, a hat and a pair of gloves and took a last look in the mirror. It would need to be seriously warm in the unit for her to be persuaded to remove any layers, but the trouble with wearing so many was that it was difficult to bend. Oh dear, she might have to give the cobra lift a miss today as well.

On impulse, she rang Bob's number again. She'd leave a message with the garage, asking him to call her. She could be anyone — a potential client.

'Hello,' she said, when a woman answered this time and announced it was Diamond Cars. Susie must have hesitated so long that the woman asked if she could help, in the sort of voice that suggested she wanted nothing more than to be of assistance.

'Sorry,' Susie said. 'I think I got cut off last time. I am trying to get hold of a Mr Bob Diamond. If you could just tell me when he'll be in the office next?'

'Sorry,' the woman said. 'He's at a wedding today until lunchtime. I don't know what his plans are after that. Is it urgent? I can give you his mobile.'

Max's impending visit couldn't be classified as urgent. Hardly life-threatening. Susie had just been about to thank the woman and say she'd try again another day, when she started reciting a phone number.

* * *

51

For the second week in a row, Bob checked the car over for unsightly marks, straightened the white-ribboned bow on the grill so it was as ready as it could be for the next set of photos, and got back in the car. The snow overnight had started to thaw into a less-than-attractive mush.

The woman in the church office had looked surprised to see him back and suggested he sat inside with her for the duration of the wedding because of the outside temperature. He thanked her and explained that with a car that age, it was better to turn the engine over every now and again, even take it for a run round the block if it looked like there was any danger of the windows starting to freeze. By keeping the inside temperature warm there was less likelihood of the bride and groom making all the windows steam up the minute they got in, less chance of them feeling the need to wipe the windows over with their hands to clear them, or worse still, write slogans on the misted glass — always a pain to get rid of.

Bob glanced down at his phone. No calls since he'd last checked. He had watched it like a hawk over the last fortnight — he'd felt sure Susie would ring. Maybe not about the pole, but he'd felt a connection. He was an old man and had had several strange feelings over the last year, what with his heart attack and all that, but the sensation in his chest when he saw Susie at the Lorry Park Café had been different. A flutter, but warm and pleasant. He'd even rung his mobile from the office phone just to make sure he could hear the distinctive ringtone and it was working properly.

Thinking about her now made him smile. Had she taken his absence from the industrial estate last week as evidence he wasn't interested? He hoped not. Did she care that he hadn't been there? Probably not, but he wished he'd taken her number. At least then he could have rung her and explained.

He still wasn't sure how he'd got roped in by his daughter to help again today. Yes, the driver was still proper poorly, but Poppy had had a week to sort out additional help.

Had Susie gone back for more pole-dancing lessons? This must be week three. How many classes were there? He'd forgotten to ask. She'd clearly found the class hard but didn't look like the sort of person who would give up at the first hurdle and hopefully not the second or third. He would definitely be at the lorry park next week. He had a whole week to come up with a plausible excuse why he shouldn't be roped in to drive, if needed.

Tony Longworth had offered to do the wedding that morning, only apparently, he wasn't on the insurance. Bob wasn't going to be caught out again — he'd make damn sure next week he was.

Bob checked the clock in the car and tried to remember what Josh had told him about Susie Keane. Both Josh and Maddie had gone to Susie's husband's funeral late last year. He thought Josh mentioned her husband had been quite a lot older than her and been ill for some time. Alzheimer's, wasn't it? He'd spent the last few months of his life in Treetops nursing home with twenty-four-hour care, often not recognizing Susie. When the end came, it sounded like it was a relief, although nobody would have wished him dead.

If it was anything like Elaine, there were times when they'd go weeks without communicating properly, but when she was actually gone, he missed her. He might not have appreciated at the time how comforting it had been to know she was there, and he could have had a conversation if he'd wanted to, and she'd been sober. Eighteen months on, it was getting easier. That first Christmas had been difficult. Every bloody thing he did reminded him that Elaine wasn't there. Last month, with Josh and Maddie's wedding just before Christmas, he hadn't had time to think about himself, and some days about Elaine either. There had been a lot of people around and it had been very different. But different in a good way, and the main thing he remembered was laughing. Like last week, sat at a wooden table in a lorry park in the weak January sun with Susie. She'd laughed a lot.

He looked at his watch again. How long did photos take? He wished he'd put his foot down and refused this gig. No, he didn't. It wouldn't have been worth the hassle.

'What reason would he have given for not helping?' Saying he wanted to go for a walk to the industrial estate with the dog sounded like a flimsy excuse even to him. He could imagine Poppy's face if he'd suggested that. She'd throw him her best disgusted look, teeth bared, nose wrinkled as she squinted at him. it was the look she'd perfected from an early age, designed to reduce grown men, him in particular, into a quivering heap. He appreciated quicker these days when he was on to a loser. Added to which, Miss Phyllis wasn't keen on water. He wasn't even sure she would be happy to be out in snow.

Today's reception was being held in a local community centre. Maybe he could swing through the industrial estate on the way to the centre, just to see if Susie was there. A minor diversion. The bride and groom probably wouldn't even notice, except he was likely to be followed by a raft of guest cars on their way to the same place, because it was easier to follow the limousine than reprogramming their satnavs.

As soon as he could get them back in the car, deliver them to the reception, then he'd be finished and free to spend the afternoon in his workshop with the old Sunbeam Alpine they'd collected during the week. Once he'd got into a pair of overalls and resembled a grease monkey, he'd be less likely to get browbeaten into another favour for his beloved daughter, today at least.

He reached across and took the brochure from the local college out of the glove compartment, found again the two pages he'd folded back and turned on his phone. The woman in the church office had given him a Wi-Fi code and assured him it would work while he was parked in their car park. She was right. Bob entered the password when prompted and waited for the symbol to indicate he was connected before he scanned the QR code on the first of the two pages. It asked him to confirm the course he was interested in. He made sure it was selected and pressed return. The next screen asked him for personal details and the phone asked him if he wanted it to fill them in for him automatically. He entered his age when prompted and the course fee automatically came down. Life was getting cheaper now he'd reached his sixties.

He entered his card details before it rethought its calculations.

He was going back to college — that would be an interesting conversation over the dinner table tonight. He watched through the car windows as the photographer arranged various groupings on the grass outside under the rose arch. Time to retrieve his uniform cap, a bottle of prosecco and two glasses from the boot. He checked his reflection in the wing mirror and undid the cork, ready to pour the drinks and congratulate the happy couple as soon as they made their way across the tarmac.

* * *

Bob came out of the workshop, rubbing some cleanser on his hands to try and get rid of the last traces of grease.

'How's the car going?' Poppy said.

'Looks like all the pieces are there but no nuts or bolts, which could be a bit of an issue. I'll have to give the guy a call and see what he's done with them.'

'Did you speak to Freddie Brompton about the vintage Vauxhall he's interested in?' Poppy handed him a wad of tissues from a holder on her desk and watched Bob dry his hands.

He raised his eyes. 'The auction doesn't finish until this evening, but I am really hoping the silly old bugger doesn't start bidding on it.'

'I thought he wanted you to do that.'

'I told him not to be so bloody ridiculous. How the hell are we supposed to get it home from South Africa?'

'He was talking about driving it back, wasn't he?'

'He's bonkers. There's no way I'm going with him. We'd need to drive up through Africa, take a ferry across the Mediterranean then up through Europe. That's the shortest way, or we could take an out-of-the-way diversion through Iran and Saudi Arabia.'

'Is there no other way?'

'Yes, but last time I looked, the route through the Middle East had been blocked by civil war.'

'Freddie said it would only take eight days.'

'It might, but you'd have to be driving twenty-four hours a day and be in a four-by-four. I'd figure at least two weeks on the road, assuming we didn't have to wait for spares and we could find fuel. Freddie doesn't seem to appreciate there won't be services every thirty miles or so, or that Premier Inns might be few and far between. And you know Freddie — there's always the chance he'll get bored and want us to take off somewhere else. You know what he's like. I think he saw us doing a *Thelma & Louise*-style road trip.'

Poppy frowned. 'I hope not. That didn't end well.'

Bob reached for his phone and looked at the call history. There was one call and his heart skipped.

'You don't think Freddie will do anything stupid? Dad?'

Bob looked at the phone and then his daughter.

'What is it? Has something happened?' She sounded concerned.

'I've had a call.' Not someone already in his contacts. There was no name attached.

'There was some woman this morning who came through on your office line and I gave her your mobile.'

'What did she sound like?'

'I don't know, some demented harpy who doesn't know how to use a phone. How was she supposed to sound?' Poppy tucked some papers into a file and stood up. She'd pulled open a drawer when she twirled round. 'Why? Who were you expecting to call? You've been acting strange recently. What aren't you telling me?'

Bob shook his head. 'I don't know what you're talking about.' He turned away and set off towards the house. 'Dinner will be on the table at seven.' He didn't wait for a reply or look round to see Poppy's face. She'd be watching him. He knew that, but he didn't want her to see the colour he could feel racing up his neck. He showered before he checked the phone again and then he hit the number that was staring at him.

* * *

'Are you on your own?' Max said. There was no smile. His eyes were narrow and his stare hard. Susie knew he was coming, but now, stood on her doorstep, she wished she'd put him off. He made it sound like a sinister question and she had to fight the urge to shake.

Her mobile rang. She looked at the screen. No caller name, but the number was familiar. Her pulse sped up.

Max was watching. 'Are you going to get that?' he growled.

She lifted the phone to her ear but didn't wait for the caller to speak. 'Ten minutes would be great,' she said. '37 Whitemead Road. Great. Great. I'll see you then. Sorry, Max, do come in. What were you saying?' She rang off.

Max stalked past her into the sitting room and looked around. His eyes settled on the pole. His face went red. 'My God, you don't waste any time, do you? Who was that on the phone. A client?'

'Absolutely none of your business,' Susie said. 'Now what can I do for you? Only, as I'm sure you'll have heard, I am busy.'

'I wanted to talk to you about Dad's will. My solicitor said he couldn't have been in his right mind when he made it and he probably only did it under extreme provocation from you. He told me Jodie and I are within our own rights to challenge the terms in court, but I know you'll probably want to avoid this, so if you've got any sense you will make us both a reasonable offer. Jodie and I aren't greedy. We don't want to see you homeless, but we are his only children.'

'Right,' said Susie. 'Anything else?' Max was big, he'd filled out a lot as a middle-aged man. His colour and beer belly suggested he wasn't living the healthiest lifestyle.

At five foot six inches tall, Susie wasn't small, but she was acutely aware of him looming over her. She didn't want to get into an argument. In all the time she and Terry had been together, Max had never missed the chance to have a go at her. It used to start with a snide comment designed to provoke a reaction. She'd always figured that if she didn't rise to the bait then he'd get fed up and leave her alone. How wrong can you be? She'd been married for thirty-eight years but a forty-nine-year-old Max still had the power to make her feel awkward and an interloper. As a teenager his temper often resulted in something being damaged. Three wives and seven children later, they hadn't had a lot to do with him over the years, but Susie wasn't sure it had got any better.

There was a ring at the door, followed by a hard, urgent knock.

Opening the door, Susie was incredibly relieved to find Bob standing there.

He came.

It couldn't have been more than five minutes since she'd put the phone down — he must have driven like crazy to get there.

'Are you okay?' he asked. 'What on earth has happened?'

'You came,' she whispered to his chest, as suddenly she was pulled into a warm and comforting embrace.

She was shaking.

'I'll get going, then,' Max said, from somewhere behind her.

* * *

Bob looked up and saw a large red-faced man standing behind Susie. 'Jeez. Who the f—?'

'Max,' a tearful Susie whispered.

Bob felt in his jacket pocket for a tissue and handed it to her.

'Just remember what I said.' The statement was accompanied by a hell of a lot of finger-pointing from the man mountain who now stalked past them without a second glance and marched down the drive.

58

Bob kicked the door shut after him and let Susie go.

'Thank you,' she said, leading the way through to the lounge. 'I'm so sorry.'

'No problem.'

They stood side by side, watching through the window as Max levered himself into a small red car and started the engine.

Bob winced at the noise and the plume of smoke that came out of his exhaust as the car lurched forward. 'If he's a friend of yours, maybe you should tell him to book that in for a service.'

'No friend of mine,' Susie said. 'He's my stepson.'

Bob watched as the car roared up the road until it was out of sight.

'There was nineteen years between Terry and me, so Max is coming up to fifty now. Age hasn't mellowed him, and he thinks I've cheated him and his sister out of their inheritance.'

There were so many questions bubbling around his head, Bob did the sensible thing and stayed quiet. Susie still looked upset. He put an arm round her shoulder. 'Come on,' he said, turning back towards the room. 'The pole — you bought one, then.' How had he missed that?

She looked up, then her face cleared. 'What that thing? No that's holding the roof up,' she said. 'The whole place is in danger of falling down.'

He may have not spotted the pole, but he would have had to be blind not to see the spark in her eyes and the way her mouth twitched upwards. He grinned back. 'Bob Diamond,' he said. 'Specialist subject — the bleeding obvious.'

CHAPTER EIGHT

February: Did a bakery course with a master baker and conquered laminated dough. Croissants, pain aux raisins and any other viennoiseries on me next time we meet!

Susie looked at the croissant. Not as elegant as the ones she'd been shown how to make on the course. She needed to stretch the dough, both before and during the rolling process. That way, she'd been told, she would get more layers. The result wasn't as laminated as she hoped. Okay, if she was being honest, it wasn't laminated at all.

What was it the chef had said? Except he wasn't a chef, he was a master baker. "Rest dough overnight, prove for longer, two hours rather than one. Use harder butter than normal supermarket butter." She liked the bit where she beat the butter with a rolling pin.

"Don't roll it. Beat it into submission, until it has the same flexibility as your dough," the master baker had told them. "Imagine it is your worst enemy."

That was particularly satisfying. Today's butter, "Max", hadn't stood a chance.

"Never work dough hard." She didn't think she had.

She thought she'd mastered all the elements but had clearly missed something essential. She buttered and ate one of the warm offerings. It may not be laminated, didn't look much like a croissant, but its texture was light and it was tasty. She could happily imagine warming the other lumps up and serving them with ham or cheese. On the other hand, her doughnuts and cinnamon twists were a triumph. And deep-frying the ends of the dough then covering them with cinnamon sugar as well — genius idea.

It had been fun. She had enjoyed the course. Twelve people from many walks of life. All eager to learn. Some professed to have a lot of experience with baking. They'd all come from some distance to be there. No danger of running into someone she knew. Some had been on courses at the same place before and sycophantically extolled the virtues of the baker. "Life-changing experience" she'd heard on more than one occasion. Clearly, she was in the right place. That was exactly what she was there for.

Susie knew which flavours worked well together. She was great at combining them for outstanding results, providing you could overlook the slightly bodged decorations at the end. If you wanted taste, Susie was your girl, but a *Great British Bake-Off* contestant, she was not.

She kicked off her shoes and put the Tupperware box full of tasty offerings in her cupboard. She'd been treated all day to tastes of cooking, and she really wasn't hungry. She planned on curling up on the sofa with a small glass of wine. She was glad tomorrow was Saturday and her last pole-dancing class. She'd take a bag full of goodies in for her classmates. There was no way she could seriously eat that amount of dough any time soon.

It would be good to catch up properly with Tara. She'd come home from work a few times over the last month to find a note saying she'd been in. Often the post was on the kitchen worktop and on one occasion she'd found the bins had been put away after the dustmen had left them at the end of the drive. Other than that, there was never any sign of her. Jason must've wound his neck in once the pole had been removed. Although, last week she thought she heard

Tara telling one of her other classmates that she was going to have to look for somewhere else to live.

A green light was blinking on the telephone docking station in the hall to suggest someone had left a message. Susie pressed play. Most people used her mobile, but family still tended to use the landline, as did double-glazing salesmen, although they rarely left a message or a return phone number. There was a pause before a male voice said, 'This is Max . . .' Susie shut the machine off. She was too tired to listen to another of his rants tonight. But by the time she curled up on the sofa, her small glass of wine had turned into a large one.

* * *

'Today is our final lesson,' Tara announced, once all eight women had changed into their classroom attire. She had joked when they'd started six weeks ago that their clothing would decrease as their pole-dancing ability increased. She only wore a black one-piece costume with a zip-up front, in shiny material that could well have been PVC, but Susie and most of the others had not accepted her assertion that skin-on-pole contact would help them grip the pole better and improve performance.

Susie may have swapped her oversized tracksuit bottoms for slightly tighter leggings, but that was as far as her clothing transition had gone. She certainly wasn't ready for "booty" shorts or, heaven forbid, a bloody thong. As soon as the class finished she'd slip back into tracksuit bottoms, while Tara would just throw a coat over whatever she was wearing, pull on a pair of leather boots and be off. Susie didn't remember having that sort of confidence in her body shape in her twenties, and she certainly didn't have it in her sixties. While she was sure her core was undoubtedly being strengthened by her classes and home exercises, she really wasn't ready to inflict acres of flesh on the public or the rest of the class.

Today, Tara looked tired and pale. What had happened to make her smile look so thin and forced? 'I hope you're all starting to feel more confident with the basic moves,' she said, as they stood in a line ready for the warm-up exercises. 'You all seem to have developed greater co-ordination and understanding. I'm seriously impressed. So today we're going to try a full dance routine, using some of the moves we've learned, to celebrate just how far we've come.'

'Are you planning on doing another course soon?' Sharon asked. 'I don't want to lose my fitness.' She made a show of flexing an arm, which to Susie's untrained eye didn't look entirely toned.

'No.' Tara shrugged. 'I'm afraid the college say there isn't enough interest. And the double-glazing company are getting busier, so they want this room back.'

Susie felt sad. Saturday morning classes and her chats afterwards with Bob had become part of a regular routine. He'd been there for the last two weeks, and she'd got a text from him this morning saying he hoped he'd see her later.

'And,' Tara continued, 'I'm not sure where I'm going to be living either. I've got to find somewhere. It's quite expensive in Redford. I think I'll move further away. So, ladies, I'm afraid this is goodbye.'

There were certain times in her life when Susie had acted before she'd really considered the repercussions.

Not properly thought everything through.

Usually, she was a rational person who covered all bases.

Today, she raised a hand, before her brain had clicked into gear. She guessed she knew she'd always planned on making the offer. Max's phone call last night had upset her. She'd woken in the middle of a nightmare where they were both in court and he was listing all her shortcomings as a stepmother to a judge who was nodding sympathetically to everything Max said.

'Ladies, I've brought some buns and pastries that I made yesterday for you to try. Could we have a five-minute bun break? I just need a quick word with Tara.'

Tara looked concerned. 'Is something wrong? Did I leave a door unlocked?'

Susie put a hand on her arm. 'Nothing like that. I was wondering—'

There was a chorus of oohs and aahs from the other side of the room to suggest the buns were a success.

'—whether you'd like to have a room at my place. Because if you did, well, there's no reason why you couldn't continue the Saturday morning class from there. We could put this pole up as well for classes. There's enough room.'

For a second Susie thought Tara was about to refuse, but suddenly she found herself wrapped in a hug. 'Are you one hundred percent serious?' Tara asked.

'Yes, I've got a huge amount of space,' Susie said. 'It makes sense. I think we'd probably get on okay and I feel a bit lost and vulnerable just now. I'm having issues with my husband's son, so in many ways you'd be doing me a favour.'

'Your husband?'

'Dead husband. Max is my stepson and giving me a hard time about his father's will.'

It was difficult to see from Tara's expression what she thought about that.

'I'm not asking you to move in to protect me. He's not dangerous. Nothing like that. He's just unpleasant.' He hadn't threatened her physically and he'd disappeared as soon as he'd seen Bob. He was more of a finger-pointer and shouter. The message on the phone last night hadn't suggested he was thinking of turning up, just that he didn't like her very much and that his solicitor was going to be in touch.

A bully and a menace rather than a boxer. 'I'm asking because . . . well, I like you and it would be nice to have the company.' Susie shrugged. 'I probably won't be able to attend classes every week. The wedding season starts to get busier after Easter, but hopefully, as it's my house, if I was there, you'd let me at least drop in and see everyone.'

Tara smiled for possibly the first time that morning. 'Done,' she said and stuck out a hand. She looked at the women on the opposite side of the room. 'Do you mean what you said . . . you know, about liking me?'

Susie nodded.

'Nobody's ever told me that before. I could move in tomorrow. Can I tell them our news?'

Tara didn't wait for a response. She clapped her hands and called everyone to attention.

* * *

Bob kissed his daughter on the top of her head as he walked past her in the showroom. He was mid-stride and almost past her when he caught sight of the naked torso of a tattooed man on her phone screen. 'Jeez. Who's Gerry from Cheltenham and why is he naked?' he asked.

'No one,' Poppy said sharply, clearly embarrassed that he'd seen. She laid her phone face down on her desk.

'So why were you looking at him?'

'Poppy's signed up to a dating app,' Mike, his young apprentice said as he walked across the office. 'Looks like she's real popular. Her phone keeps pinging with new likes.'

'Really?' Bob raised an eyebrow and tilted his head as he watched her. Very little made his daughter blush. 'And does Gerry from Cheltenham like you? More to the point, do you like him?'

Poppy shook her head vigorously. 'God! No! He says he's thirty-six, but I'd say he's at least ten years older than that, if not nearer fifty. He's ancient.'

'She's only got eyes for one man,' Mike said.

'Shut up,' Poppy hissed. 'That's not true.'

Bob looked at the young lad, grinning from ear to ear. 'Go on.'

'She heard he's on this dating site, but it sounds like someone was winding her up, unless he's lying about his age or gender, or both. She must have spent all afternoon checking them all to find him.'

'Have not,' Poppy argued.

'Do I know the man in question?' Bob tried not to let his surprise show. Poppy had had a few dates in the past, but

65

she'd never seemed keen on getting involved with anyone. He assumed she was happy single. He'd thought there might be something going on with Josh's colleague but hadn't seen much of him lately and hadn't liked to ask.'

'Yep. The guy who works with Josh,' the apprentice said, matter-of-factly.

She was *keen on him then.* 'Really?'

'Shut up,' Poppy growled at the young lad. Her pink blush had now turned into a far deeper shade of red. 'Look what you've done. Dad will probably do something stupid and tell him I like him.'

'Cross my heart,' Bob said.

'Uncross your bloody fingers when you say it.'

'What about you, Mr D,' Mike asked. 'You ready to step into the dating world again.'

'That's not a bad idea.' Poppy spun round. 'You should. We could set you up with a profile. Who knows, there might be the perfect woman for you out there.'

'There'd be no point,' Bob said. 'I'm not looking for anybody.'

'Okay, we know you thought Mum was perfect, but it's been eighteen months now, going on two years. There's probably another woman out there who would be perfect. After all, you're not that old.'

'Thanks.'

'You could live for another thirty-plus years. You don't want to do that on your own,' Poppy said. 'You should have a bit of fun. Why don't we upload your details, take a picture and write you a profile. You won't need to do anything. We can sort it out and filter your responses.'

CHAPTER NINE

Now time allows, Susie has signed up for a second pole-dancing course. Maybe this time she will be able to leave the ground.

Best not mention she was hosting it yet, or that she had a lodger. It seemed to be going well. Tara was quiet, tidy and happy to share meals in the evening. For the first couple of weeks, whenever Susie had been held up at work, she'd arrive home to find Tara and a meal ready waiting. She couldn't remember the last time that had happened. After that, they'd always arranged to eat together. Plan menus around their schedules. One or other would cook, and as often as not they'd share their day's events over a meal and a glass of wine.

Tara was gradually starting to open up and talk about her ex. Sounded like Jason was a complete wanker, but Susie had so far avoided saying that was what she thought. Tara still seemed to think he would one day open his eyes and realize what he was missing and come looking for her. Or more likely his current squeeze would throw him out and he'd come round wanting somewhere to stay.

Tara's old home now sported a sold notice which went up within a week of her moving in with Susie.

She plans on doing Introduction to Taxidermy and Mediumship courses at the local college soon — not at the same time. That way lies madness — ha ha!

Susie hadn't really planned on signing up for the mediumship thing, but the course had caught her eye and it would certainly give Max something else to moan about. Once that idea had taken root, she'd signed up. Maybe there was something in it. Perhaps Terry would make contact — there were a couple of share certificates she still had to find for Norman Fairchild, her solicitor, before he could finalize the probate application. And if Terry was feeling chatty, she could ask him what he thought about Bob Diamond and her pole.

She stood up and walked over to the pole, kicking off her shoes. She'd promised Tara that by the start of next term's class, she would practise staying off the ground for at least ten seconds before she slid into a heap at the bottom. Tara said she was doing well, but Susie sometimes wondered whether she could see disappointment in the girl's eyes as she watched Susie struggle. Did she think she should have made more progress? She remembered the arm positions and lifted herself off the ground as her phone pinged to announce someone at her front door. Saved by the bell. Susie landed and went to answer it.

Max stood on the doorstep. 'Is this your idea of a joke?' he asked. He was sort of a mottled red shade and waving a letter with such force he could have been using it as a fan. 'I can't believe you've stooped this low.'

He jerked it at her. Susie took a step back in surprise.

'You want me to take a DNA test to prove I'm his son.'

Okay, that was news to Susie. She had mentioned to Norman Fairchild that Max was threatening to challenge the will. He'd said something about Terry expecting that and there was something in place to protect her if he did.

But a DNA test? What was that about?

'Take it back. Tell your bloody solicitor you're only joking, that you were just being malicious — I don't know. Tell him to take back the request or you'll be sorry — really sorry.' Then came the finger-pointing. 'You should be worried, because the way you're going, something unpleasant might happen to you real soon.' He lunged forward, the last words accompanied by a spray of something unpleasant smelling as he closed the gap.

Susie clamped her eyes shut and winced.

Then there was a noise — something that sounded like an "oof".

Someone screamed.

Susie opened her eyes.

Max was spread-eagled on the floor, Tara sitting on his back. 'Call the police,' she said. 'I heard him threatening you. You can get an injunction, then if he comes anywhere near you, he'll end up in court.'

'You're the one who'll be in court,' Max spluttered. 'You've hurt me. I am going to charge you with GBH.'

Tara got up. 'Yeah, right. You can prove that, can you? You were so far out of control you tripped over, then face-planted the flowerbed. Didn't he?'

Susie was too astonished to answer.

Tara cracked her fingers. 'Oh, and by the way, I recorded you making your threats.' She pulled her phone from a pocket and held it in front of Max. 'Anything else you'd like to say that we can use in court.'

Max pushed himself up. Susie had been about to help him, but Tara put a restraining arm on her shoulder. Max picked up the letter and looked about to say something, but Tara was still holding her phone in front of her, so he turned and marched down the drive.

'I've always wanted to try that move,' she said as Max's car kicked into life, and he disappeared up the road in a puff of smoke. 'Are you okay?'

'I have no idea what all that was about,' Susie said weakly. It was far too late to ring Fairchild's solicitors, but she'd have to in the morning.

'You look like you could do with a drink. Come on.' Tara put her phone back in her jeans' pocket and walked indoors. 'Maybe I could teach a women's self-defence class as well as pole dancing — what do you think?'

* * *

Norman Fairchild looked over his desk at Susie. 'Really, there is nothing to worry about,' he said. 'Terry was clear in his will and instructions. It would be ridiculous for Max to even think about contesting it.'

'His argument is that his father wasn't of sound mind when he made his will.'

'Terry's will is dated twenty years ago, well before his dementia was diagnosed. He wrote it about the same time he paid Max and Jodie's mortgages off. The power of attorney was only registered eight years ago. Seriously, Susie, Max hasn't got a leg to stand on. I will write to him again. A sort of cease-and-desist letter. Not that contacting his stepmother is illegal, but it is certainly causing you a degree of distress. I will warn him that should he continue to make threats, we will be looking to take out an injunction and reimbursement of all legal fees you incur as a result of his claims.'

'Max seems to think Terry should have made provision for his grandchildren.'

'Families.' Norman shook his head. 'I see this so often. Now, forget Max for a moment and tell me how you're doing.'

Susie twisted her hands in her lap. 'Good days and bad days,' she said. 'I forget an anniversary or some event and feel guilty when I remember it. His birthday is—' Susie twisted the gold ring that she still wore on her ring finger — 'was, in April. I don't know how I should spend it. Or how I should feel.'

'Are you keeping busy?'

'Please, Norman. What is this all about?'

Norman sighed. 'At this stage, all I can tell you is that Terry was always pretty certain he wasn't Max or Jodie's biological father.'

'No way. He'd have said. We didn't have secrets from one another.'

'My understanding is that he didn't mention it during his life because he was aware of the issues a revelation like that could cause, and he thought one day his ex-wife would be honest enough to tell them the truth. However, he said that if either child did make a fuss, bearing in mind he'd been more than generous during his lifetime, then he expected them to prove they were his children. He had DNA tests done. I have the results of those and details of who I need to contact to compare them with either Max or Jodie's results, when and if they have their tests done.

'If they insist on challenging the will, they have to, because they need to prove they are his biological children, and if not, he wants his name removed from their birth certificates. I have instructions to do that.'

Susie frowned. 'He never said a word.'

All this time he'd kept a secret from her.

That hurt. She didn't think they kept anything from one another. She wondered whether there was anything else she was about to discover.

Her head shot up. 'I'm not going to suddenly find out he was married to someone else, am I? That our marriage is bigamous? Or that he was born Theresa or something?'

'Those were the only instructions he left me,' Norman said. 'But in the event that DNA tests are carried out, I have letters for all three of you.'

'Can't I have mine now?' Susie asked, feeling for a moment like a naughty child asking her father for sweets. 'If whatever he's written can't surprise me any further, then it might help me understand this uncharacteristic move.'

She turned away to avoid watching Norman shake his head, just as her father would've done. He'd have banged on about ruining her appetite. At least Norman couldn't pull that one — he'd already killed it.

It was like some sort of gut-wrenching clamp had tightened about her. She and Terry had complete trust in one another because they knew they'd always been totally honest. Didn't they? And if he'd kept one secret, what else had he been hiding?

Susie resisted the urge to shout "*Pl-e-e-a-se*" and pout, a childish reaction usually reserved for circumstances where she

71

knew she wasn't going to get her own way, because if there was one solicitor unlikely to break a client's confidence, it was Norman Fairchild. She got up and left. She needed to get out and have a good cry. She could feel the tears building behind her eyes.

Norman's words were muffled by the heavy door closing behind her.

* * *

Bob stared down at the document he had printed out at the library, or rather the librarian had. It was a bloody stupid idea, he knew that. Even the librarian had looked surprised when the document emerged. Although, not as surprised as he was to find he now had a library card for the first time in his life.

The dozen or so pages in front of him represented his dream. The application form covered every angle. It was blunt. He needed to be fit, certain medications weren't allowed in Asia, and it wasn't going to be a luxury holiday.

Thirteen weeks on the bike.

He hadn't ridden bikes seriously for a long time. Thirty-five years ago, he wouldn't have thought twice about applying for a place, now he felt like a sad middle-aged, if not old, man who was letting his dream slip away. He shoved his hands into his jeans' pockets. 'Stupid idea,' he said aloud.

He'd promised Elaine he'd never ride a bike again. He'd never broken that promise while she was still alive. On the other hand, she'd promised him several times she'd give up drinking — she never had.

He was vaguely aware of a woman standing outside the solicitor's office as he came out of the library. She had her back to him and was rocking. It sounded like she was hysterical. Wailing rather than crying. People were giving her a wide berth. Should he stop and ask if she was okay? As likely as not if he did, he would be given a mouthful and told to mind his own business.

Except, there was something familiar about the woman on the corner. Bob's feet seemed incapable of moving away. As if she knew she was being watched, she started to turn.

* * *

Bob put down the tray on the café table and watched as Susie read the twelve pages of tightly printed text through red-rimmed eyes.

She'd hesitated fractionally when he suggested a cup of tea. She'd turned away and wiped her eyes. He'd thought she was on the verge of making an excuse, so added, 'I have this idea that I'd really like your advice on.'

She hadn't said anything on their way to the lorry park, so he'd filled in the gaps by talking and explaining his idea. She'd jerked occasionally and there seemed to be another tear or two building up that he pretended not to notice.

The man behind the café counter was cleaning down the griddle as he approached.

'No hot food at this time of day,' he grunted, before Bob could ask.

Susie muttered something which sounded like 'thanks' as he set a mug in front of her, but she was concentrating so hard, that she didn't look up.

'Pastries today,' he said. 'You look like you need sugar.'

'Uh-huh.' Her forehead was slightly creased. Was that a frown? What had he missed? She rubbed an eye, still red-rimmed, and turned a page. She reached for the mug, so he turned the handle slightly towards her. He only took his own hand away when she'd gripped the handle and seemed to have a firm hold. She lifted the tea to her mouth and took a sip but didn't take her eyes off the page she was reading.

A dimple at the corner of her mouth twitched occasion-ally. She was clearly lost in thoughts he couldn't fathom.

'It's quite comprehensive.' Eventually, she tapped the pages on the table to straighten them, laid them down and looked straight at him. 'They recommend you look at some off-road training courses if you haven't got up-to-date experience.' She didn't look up. Instead she got her phone out, typed something in and stared at the screen. 'The company they recommend seem to run at least three, two days each, in Wales or Spain. Wales is not a huge commitment, although Spain might be nice. Why don't you try the first one, to see how you feel about spending all day on a bike again. You might hate it and then you haven't lost anything, but if you love it, you could sign up for the other two.' She handed him her phone.

His stomach fluttered these days whenever she looked at him, and it did again now as she watched him read the page she'd loaded.

'It says bikes available to hire for the duration. It doesn't even sound like you have to take your own. Looks like a no-brainer to me. I think you know that too. You have an itch, and you need to scratch it. Go for it. Will you mention it to Josh or Poppy?'

'No,' he said firmly. 'They'll try and talk me out of it.'

'What are you going to tell them about spending a weekend in Wales? Won't they think it a bit strange you just going off like that?'

'They think everything I do at the moment is a bit strange.' Bob sighed and handed Susie back her phone. 'What about you? Do you think I'm being ridiculous? Am I just a silly old man? Would I be better off sitting in front of the fire, slippers on . . . ?'

'Wearing handmade cardigans and reading gardening magazines while watching daytime soaps or renovation programmes. Absolutely—' she swiped something on her phone — 'not. One, you're not old.' She held the phone out again.

And two? He wanted to ask.

'They are doing the level-one course next month. And according to their website, they are still accepting bookings. Why don't you fill in the application form and see if there are still any spaces available. Then you can pay the deposit, do the level-one course and see how you go from there? We just need to think up a cover story for Poppy and Josh.'

Bob grinned. He liked the sound of the "we". It felt good. 'Do you think we can really pull it off?' he asked.

Susie's nod was emphatic. 'It's your dream,' she said. 'We have to try.' She took a bite out of the cherry-and-chocolate pastry and closed her eyes. When she'd swallowed the mouthful, she opened them and smiled at him. 'This is good, thank you. You're right — I needed it.'

She'd started to look brighter. He was pleased. It gave him a warm feeling in the pit of his stomach.

'I should think you want to know why I was standing in front of Norman Fairchild's office, sobbing like a baby.' She took another bite.

To be fair, his children had never made that sort of noise even as babies. Probably best not point that out.

'I'm sure—' Bob tried to sound more concerned than horrified. Of course he wanted to know, but he wasn't going to tell her that. 'I'm sure you had your reasons.' Okay, he couldn't think of any. 'I assume it wasn't because he'd just played you the guitar riff from "Hotel California". Maybe it was. If I'd been forced to endure that, I'd have probably sobbed too.'

Susie stared at him as if he'd completely lost the plot.

'We go way back, Norman and I. We were in the same band.'

Susie's confusion seemed to lift, if only a little. 'At Maddie and Josh's wedding, you said it had been a while since you'd sung in public . . .'

Bob nodded. 'But for future reference, if he ever tries to tell you that "Stairway to Heaven" was Led Zeppelin's greatest song, I hope you'll point out that it's not a patch on "Kashmir".'

Susie stopped chewing. She put the pastry back on the plate and looked at him.

'Sadly, "Stairway to Heaven" was one of our most popular requests,' Bob said, as nonchalantly as he could. 'Most wedding receptions, usually somewhere between "Bohemian Rhapsody" and "Stuck in the Middle With You".'

An odd sound came from the other side of the table.

Susie was laughing. 'Please don't tell me "Stuck in the Middle With You" was ever a popular request at a wedding,' she said.

'Good song for the first dance. Great rhythm.'

'You mentioned a guitar riff?'

'He was bass. I was rhythm.'

'We are talking about the same Norman Fairchild?'

'There could only be one Norman Fairchild. They broke the mould the day he was born, but let me tell you, those tweed jackets that make him look every bit the country gentleman are nothing more than a disguise. Under that tweedy exterior is a glam rocker just waiting for shiny flares and platform soles to make a comeback.'

Susie tilted her head. 'Now, I know you're teasing me.'

CHAPTER TEN

'Sorry, it's Mothering Sunday and we're drowning under seas of daffodils.'

Susie was helping at Treetops. She took a couple of bunches from George, but he still had arms full of them. 'You do the doors,' he said. 'I've got these. Trouble is, you can find them everywhere and they're cheap. Suddenly, every Tom, Dick or Harry remembers that his mother likes flowers. We need to split them into vases and spread them round.'

Susie suggested he leave them on the side in the laundry room and she would try and find homes for them all. 'Which residents don't have visitors? I'll make sure they all have some in their rooms,' she said.

'We can't,' George said, with a horrified expression. 'I've looked online. They are poisonous. Health and safety and all that. Any substance known to be poisonous shouldn't be anywhere near a resident.'

'You're not seriously expecting them to eat a daffodil?'

'I wouldn't put anything past that lot.' George smiled. 'Seriously, though, it's just not worth the risk. Let's put them in vases in public places, but out of reach.' He muttered under his breath, 'Although it is tempting to boil them up for some of our trickier residents.'

'Reggie still causing problems?' Susie asked, slipping an apron on.

George raised his eyes. 'It's Cheltenham this week, so the betting scandal continues. The whole place is glued to the sodding racing. Thursday was St Patrick's Day and he taught them the words and tune to "Danny Boy" and made them sing it during the presentations after each race while he worked out who'd won. Oh, and they made green bow-ties and green hats out of the soft furnishings. Now we're two bed quilts down. Don't laugh. It wasn't funny. I blame Julie Andrews.'

Susie did laugh. '*The Sound of Music*, the one where she made all the von Trapp children summer play outfits out of curtains!'

'Yep. Which is why *The Sound of Music* is now on our banned film list. And any suggestion that someone might like an outfit made from curtains, well . . . And then there's "Danny Boy" — if I never hear that song again that will suit me just fine. Even now, three days on, every time a horse comes on to the TV someone starts singing it and they all join in. It's like some sort of weird flash mob, but in high-riser electric recliners.'

Susie grinned. 'Sounds like he's making an effort and clearly everyone's having fun.'

'Yep. Our residents love him. He's got a nice voice, I'll give him that. He offered to help with our summer concert, and in a moment of madness, I agreed. His plans have taken off, possibly a bit grander than anything I had in mind. Now he's got them auditioning for a musical.'

'I look forward to coming to see it. What's he planning on putting on?'

'*The Best Little Whorehouse in Texas*.'

"You're teasing" had been on Susie's lips, but the expression on George's face suggested he wasn't.

One of the assistants walked in with another two bunches of daffodils.

'Vases,' George said. 'I'll get them for you.'

Susie removed the cellophane and trimmed up the bunches, leaving them all standing in a sink full of water. A concert or opera was on her list of things to do this year. Did *The Best Little Whorehouse in Texas* count?

She hadn't told anyone yet, but she had a concert ticket in her emails. An actual concert ticket. It wasn't until much later in the year, but she was going to see Donny Osmond in December. Ideally, it would have been earlier, so she could get the Christmas letter written before she went, but then, was a Donny concert something she'd boast about in her letter? She'd chosen it because she could be reasonably sure the audience would be of a similar age and she wouldn't feel out of place. She could remember the words to several songs and would probably sing along. Then there was the fact that a large percentage of the audience would be female, and she'd got a reserved seat, which she hoped meant that she wouldn't be expected to rush forward or stand in front of the stage all night waving a lighter or probably these days, her phone in torch mode.

George came back with a tray full of vases. 'After this, we're going to need to resort to milk bottles,' he said. 'Can you put them around the main lounge? I ought to go and help Fiona with lunch service.' He didn't wait for a response.

Susie sorted the daffodils among the vases and arranged them as best she could, cutting the stems at various lengths. The tray of full vases was heavy, and it took three trips to the lounge to get them in. After what George said about them being poisonous, she worried about leaving them on one of the coffee tables in the middle of the room, but the only occupant at the time looked to be fast asleep in an armchair.

It was a nice and light room, with plenty of windows set high enough up the wall so the chairs placed under them didn't obscure any of the light. Susie figured that one vase on each sill should be safe. They weren't particularly high, but the residents would have to wrestle the heavy chairs out of the way to get to them, or do what she was about to do and clamber over them. She slipped off her shoes and climbed onto the first one positioned under the window nearest the door. She dusted the windowsill before putting the daffodils in what she hoped was roughly the middle and went to climb down. There was a hand stretching up to her.

'Here, allow me,' a voice said.

Susie took the hand and allowed herself to be helped down.

'Thank you.'

The man with the hand was Reggie. Him of the betting fiasco and St Patrick's Day fame.

She took a step back and viewed the window. There should be enough for three on each sill. 'If I climb up again, could you pass me two more vases and make sure they're equally spaced.'

'Reckon so.' Reggie looked at the tray on the table. 'All of them?'

'Well, yes, all the windows round the room,' Susie said. 'If I can do it without getting in anyone's way.'

'You're okay. They'll be a while. They've just been given the early lunch warning and are speeding to the dining room as we speak.' He coughed and when he started speaking again it was in a much faster paced voice, as if he was commentating on a race. 'It was pandemonium at the starting gate this lunchtime. Violet cut straight in front of Gladys as soon as the door opened and overtook her on the first corner. But once in the hall, Bernard, with clever use of his walking stick, took the lead by the conservatory.'

Susie laughed. 'What about you? Aren't you hungry?'

'I'll give them a chance to sort themselves out before I wander in. I can help you for the next ten minutes or so. I'll leave the clambering over the assault course to you, but I'm happy to hand up the flowers and make sure the position's okay.'

Susie nodded and climbed onto the second chair. 'I've just spoken to George. He says you're putting on *The Best Little Whorehouse in Texas* this year. Isn't that a bit ambitious?'

'Possibly.' Reggie made a face. 'Six of them have already expressed an interest in playing Miss Mona. Edna wants to be Melvin P Thorpe and Eric wants to be the sheriff. What about you? Staff as well as residents — we need all the help we can get.'

'Seriously? Me, sing?'

Reggie handed up another vase. 'Well now, that's the thing about musicals — someone has to.'

'Why that one?'

'Limited amount of dancing required. I toyed with the idea of *West Side Story*, but a bit too energetic for most of them. We'd need a hoist on standby, a team of paramedics and probably the local undertakers. I can't see the management here agreeing to the expense. Those that made it through the first number without a hitch would probably need a lie down before the second. We do only have a limited amount of time between lunch and afternoon tea.'

Susie and Reggie worked their way around the room until every vase had been placed suitably out of reach.

'Thank you,' she said. 'The room certainly looks brighter.'

Reggie sniffed. 'Easter's coming. You'll need to take them down again next week, ready for baby chickens and rabbits. And I should probably tell you that if you're planning on extensive decorations using eggs, you might have enough grannies in here to suck them, but the kitchen gets a bit funny when their supplies get raided.'

'Thanks, I'll warn Fiona.' Susie smiled. 'Aren't you worried they'll forget the words?'

'We'll give them songbooks and have a screen behind the audience with the words on.' Reggie flicked his head at the back wall. 'All they have to do is open and close their mouths. I'll sort out a backing track. That way, if they do all fall asleep, or worse, Dolly and Burt can finish it off for them. But the funny thing is, people always seem to remember songs.'

'You sound like you've done this before.'

He checked his watch. 'You could say that. I used to teach. Children, not geriatrics, but similar issues. I should get going. Roast today. Stan's probably seated by now and I don't want him stealing my potatoes. Have a think about the Miss Mona part.' He wandered off without looking at her. 'You'd be good.'

Susie thought she could hear him singing "I Will Always Love You" until he was halfway down the corridor.

CHAPTER ELEVEN

'It's crab linguine.'

Bob looked round the table. They were all there. The Wednesday morning continental cookery class. Eight weeks learning the basics of Italian cookery, and today the class had been allowed to cook a dish of their choice for the last day. Then there was to be a sharing lunch so they could all try each other's food. There was a mouth-watering assortment, from pizza through to risotto, with pasta and Bob's crab linguine in between.

The noise levels were up there with the start of a bike race. All the women seemed to be talking at once. Most of the conversation Bob couldn't fathom at all. Not that he was trying — he didn't care what the price of butter was, or that Sylvia was knitting outfits for a new grandchild. Or that Irene had won on the Grand National and then blown the whole lot on a fish supper.

He nodded when he was complimented on his crab. It was good. No, actually, it was bloody excellent. He tried to be as generous with his comments about the others' food.

He liked Karen's arancini and said as much. He had his eye on some of Lesley's lemon-and-cream-filled cannoli for dessert. He kept an eye on the plate — they were going fast and he didn't want to miss out. Lesley was talking about the new bookshop's monthly book club and trying to encourage them all to go to the next meeting. He wondered if Susie was a member. Then he heard that this month's choice had been *Superwoman* by Shirley Conran, and he listened to a couple of the group complaining about how difficult it was to find a copy. He remembered Elaine had read that one years ago. He might even have a copy at home. Potentially, he could read a few pages and see if he enjoyed it, then maybe he would turn up. Of course, given the choice, he'd prefer a good murder mystery, or perhaps the art of motorcycle maintenance. Maybe he could suggest one of those when it was his turn to choose.

The college refectory was full. The cookery course was now extolling the virtues of another endless night of TV. He switched off. One of those things he didn't like in a woman or anyone else was endless chatter for chatter's sake, but tell that to Michelle and Lou.

A young boy with a tray was hovering at the edge of their table, looking at the two vacant seats. He was joined a few seconds later by Mike, Bob's apprentice, who grinned when he saw Bob.

'Hey, Mr D,' he said. 'Okay if we squat on your table.'

Bob smiled at the lad. 'Fill your boots,' he said, gesturing to the free chairs.

The boys nodded their thanks and sat down.

'This is Rick,' Mike said. 'We had the same lecture this morning.'

The kid had black under his fingertips. Bob wasn't psychic, but if he hadn't been told, it wouldn't have been too hard to guess that Rick had been doing a mechanical course, something with oil.

Rick nodded at him and sat down. He looked about the same age as Mike, so probably straight out of school. He produced a book and a Tupperware lunchbox from a black rucksack. He opened his lunchbox to reveal a solitary sandwich. Rick looked first at the sandwich, then the food on the table and sighed. He didn't pick up the sandwich until he'd opened the book and was staring intently at the page in front of him.

From the way his lips were moving, Bob thought he was probably reading under his breath. He used to do the same. The kid didn't look happy. Instead of turning the page, he took a mouthful of his sandwich and sighed again.

'Tricky subject?' Bob asked, as he finished his plate of linguine. There was still a lot of food left. The sharing lunch was a nice idea, but who really wanted a full Italian at midday? He'd already split the crab mixture, so he could take some home for Poppy. He'd cook her some pasta to go with it. She'd polish off anything that was left. And if the last few nights were anything to go by, Tony would probably be there to help too.

The boy looked up, his eyes glistening. 'I just don't get it,' he said. 'And this is only Level 1 Motor Vehicle Maintenance.'

'You're doing a diploma?'

The boy nodded. 'My dad said I'd never amount to anything. Looks like he was right.'

'Want to try some linguine?' Bob pushed the serving plate towards the boy.

'Please,' the boy said, tucking in hungrily.

'I made it this morning. Tell me what you think.'

'Are you a chef then or what?'

'Me. God, no.' Bob laughed. 'I'm a mechanic.'

'He's my boss,' Mike added proudly.

'So why is he cooking?'

Obviously, the linguine had gone down well — the kid's plate was clean. He was looking around the table. Out of the corner of his eye, Bob saw Sylvia swoop in for the last lemon cannoli. Shit! He was too late to stop her. He pretended not to notice. Narrowing his eyes and throwing her death stares wasn't a great way to end a friendly meal.

He had enjoyed the Italian course. The crab linguine was not only delicious but there was something satisfying about making and cooking fresh pasta, and he'd enjoyed the dough making last week. He wondered when he might get the chance to show Susie the results of his labours. Next term it was Indian, and he'd readily signed up for that eight-week course.

The kid was still staring at him, clearly waiting for a response.

'Because a good friend of mine earlier in the year,' Bob said, 'told me we shouldn't just hang around waiting for things to happen. Life's too short, and then suddenly we get old and find there's still a lot of things we want to do. So . . .' Bob hoped Susie didn't mind, being sort of paraphrased, 'we should get out there and kick arse.'

The kid looked confused and looked down. He was slumped in his chair. Something was up.

Bob looked to Mike for help. 'What's going on?' he mouthed.

'Rick's course finishes today because they haven't got anyone to help out next term with the practical sessions, and he can't transfer to mine because he hasn't got a work placement.'

Rick nodded but didn't look up. Around the table, the women from the Italian cookery class were starting to get ready to leave. Bob stood up and gave a few of them a hug and waved at a couple more. They promised to see each other again after Easter. He waited until the group had left before he sat down again. Rick had gone, but Mike was still finishing off a bag of crisps and a doughnut.

'Rick's got a theory test this afternoon,' he said. 'He doesn't think he's going to pass. He was talking about not bothering to go, because there's no point.'

Bob tidied the plates onto a tray and took them to the nearest rack. The dining hall was busy with another influx. Judging by the number of people queuing at the counter, another course had finished its morning session.

'You finished?' he asked Mike. 'What class have you got this afternoon?'

'It's a practical, in the garages.'

Bob cleared Mike's plate and can onto a tray, too, and stood up. 'Good,' he said. 'Then take me to your leader.'

* * *

It had been Tara's idea to go clothes shopping in Templeton. Susie had a rare weekend off and Tara had found her that morning crying over a cup of tea in the kitchen.

Tara had joked about no use crying over spilled milk, but clearly realized something was seriously wrong.

Only it wasn't. It was just one of those ridiculous photo memory pictures on her phone that had caught her unawares. "On this day . . ."

Susie studied the picture of the local park's flowerbeds. Up until that point she hadn't really given any thought to the date, so had forgotten its significance. Today would've been Terry's eightieth birthday. Nobody told you how you were supposed to feel on anniversaries, or when you would ever stop feeling guilty that you'd forgotten one. Would it get easier?

They hadn't done big celebrations in recent years. There had been no point in expecting the family to visit. They didn't, so Terry and Susie made a point of always going out. In later years it had been local gardens or the park, where they could walk round and not get in anyone's way. Last year's trip had been a miserable experience. Terry hadn't wanted to go. They'd walked as far as the churchyard, but every five minutes he said he wanted to go home. And when he got to the lychgate, he refused to go any further and clung to the wooden upright. She'd tried to interest him in some flowers that were starting to poke through, but he didn't appear to understand what she was talking about and shouted about going home.

They'd been out for less than half an hour.

She'd baked a cake, but Terry refused that too and somehow it ended up on the floor. She'd cried then as well.

Tara put her arms about her and pulled Susie in for a hug. Susie sobbed against her chest while Tara gently stroked her hair. Neither said a word and Tara made no attempt to quieten her. It was a while before Susie had cried herself out. She was just blowing her nose when Tara said, 'Let's get out of here. I'm taking you shopping. Retail therapy — that's what you need.'

The ladies' section of Templeton's only department store was huge. Signs hung from the ceiling to indicate the different brands. Susie didn't know where to start. But now she was there, perhaps she could find something suitable for the meal that Maddie and Josh had invited her to. It had been years since she'd been shopping for clothes for anything other than work. She wanted something she felt special in. The first rail at the top of the escalators was full of evening gowns.

Nothing too shiny. No sequins. Understated. Elegant. Something to make her feel confident that she was looking her best.

'What kind of impression are you trying to create?' Tara asked, breaking into her thoughts.

'What do you mean?'

'Femme fatale? Casual sexy? Casual? Formal? Formal sexy?'

'I don't know.'

'Okay, material type? 'Silk, PVC . . .'

'PVC?'

'You know — alluring or fetish?'

'No!' Susie squeaked. Oh God, this was such a mistake. 'I shouldn't have let you talk me into this. I don't want to look outrageous. I just want to feel comfortable. I'm going out for a meal with friends, that's all.'

'One of whom, you are hoping will take things further. You need to make it clear you fancy him.'

'I so don't. Maddie is a colleague and Bob is Josh's father. End of. Neither of us want or need a new relationship.'

'Yeah, right. The first time I met him, he had his arms around you. The next, you were sitting either side of the worktop feeding each other ravioli. I think that moves your whole relationship up the scale into being more than just friends.'

Susie blushed. There was an element that she did want to impress Bob.

'You go a real pretty shade of pink when you blush,' Tara laughed. 'Maybe we should think of a complementary colour, like blue.'

'I like green,' Susie said belligerently.

'You might, but I'm afraid it might not like you. With my skin type and colouring it might suit me, but I think you should consider something a little less conspicuous and obvious. Obviously, orange would clash with your cheeks if you're anywhere near Bob. You'd probably suit black or white, but that's not really party enough.'

'It isn't a party.'

'Course it is. You're being fed and plied with alcohol.'

Susie watched as Tara expertly skimmed the rows of dresses. Within minutes her arms were full of a selection of outfits that would have been perfect for anyone heading to Ascot or a wedding. A shop assistant appeared and asked Tara if she wanted to try anything on.

Tara handed over her hoard and pointed at Susie. 'No, but she does. She's got an important date and needs to make a good impression.'

There was no point arguing. The sooner Susie tried the outfits on, the sooner she could get out of there. It was her day off and she wanted to relax. The new Jim Broadbent film was showing at the cinema — maybe they could catch that and plough their way through a bag of pick-and-mix.

Susie followed the shop assistant into the changing rooms and waited until she'd hung all the dresses up.

'Is any of this what you're looking for?' the woman asked.

'I guess.' Susie shook her head. 'No. Sorry, not really. Tara's idea.'

'I thought as much. What sort of thing are you after?'

'Elegant, understated. It's for a dinner out with friends. Nothing fancy. Something I'm comfortable in, that I can wear afterwards.'

'Right.'

Susie allowed herself to be led by the arm out of the changing rooms and across the shop floor. She imagined the woman was trying to get rid of her. She could see two men in suits standing by the tills. Security. Clearly, she was going to be asked to leave. *Could the day get any better?*

The woman stopped by a rack just in front of the lifts. 'These came in this morning. I think the colour would suit you and with your figure . . . What size are you?' The woman pulled a royal-blue dress from the rack. 'This one's machine washable. Perfect for any occasion.'

CHAPTER TWELVE

Susie stood up and stretched her arms above her head as Cynthia Bailey's email popped up in her inbox. She'd been sitting down all morning. Instead of switching her computer off, she sat down again and opened the email. Another five minutes.

Exciting news, the subject line read. She was being invited to a school reunion. An Egyptian meal at Hosni's Palace in Templeton. There was a menu attached. It looked good, and they were assured entertainment from whirling dervishes and an invitation to try their hand at the dancing.

She reread the message, hardly able to believe Cynthia Bailey had only gone and bloody arranged it.

Fifty years . . . how did that happen?

Thirty-eight of them she'd spent married to the same man. Now, she was a widow — a bit of a conversation stopper, that. She rarely checked social media posts and didn't understand how anyone could be glued to it for so long each day, but today she signed into Facebook as the email directed her to.

A private group had been set up for her year. There was a button to click to join. Another box popped up asking the name of your favourite teacher. That was easy, it was the

French teacher she'd had for the first three years. Susie hit send and within what felt like seconds had a notification back to say her application had been successful. Then a message from Cynthia popped up: "Good choice, look forward to catching up with you properly next month." Several emojis and a row of Xs followed. "I wondered about a WhatsApp group, but this seemed easier, now that we've all got to a certain age!"

Cynthia explained that the reunion should ideally be later in the year, but she'd figured there was the likelihood of people being away in June before the school holidays, and there was a possibility she'd be off on a cruise in September and away for six weeks. The date she had suggested was only a month away.

There were lists of people in the year who'd been invited and of those she'd been unable to contact — she hoped others could provide contact details.

Susie had registered the death recently of Simon Farringdon. She ought to drop a line to Cynthia and let her know he wouldn't be coming. Within minutes of the email arriving, the reply-alls started appearing: "Great with me. Look forward to catching up" or "Super, see you soon".

There were fourteen members of the group so far. At the top of the page was a request that everyone give a brief summary of their life since school. Jeez, this was worse than the bloody Christmas letter.

Duncan sent greetings from Mauritius where he was in the diplomatic service. The post didn't say any more than that. No mention of whether he would be home for the reunion, or what he was doing there. Presumably something important that was covered by the Official Secrets Act.

One girl waxed lyrically about being a nutritionist. She was looking forward to catching up with everybody and hoped they were eating sensibly or else they'd have her to deal with. Lucy *bloody* Miller. Oh yes, Susie remembered her. Lucy had spent most of their first two years at school giving Susie a hard time because she was only the reserve on the hockey team, while Susie always got a place. It all changed with the new games mistress, then Susie didn't even make the reserves but Lucy was always right up there. The snide remarks and her gym kit going missing on a regular basis only to turn up in the showers wet through stopped about the same time. Nothing Susie could prove, but she was perfectly sure Lucy *bloody* Miller was responsible.

Why was Cynthia doing this? She hadn't seemed to particularly enjoy school at the time. Susie would be amazed if her school days registered as the happiest in her life either. In her own case, not even close. Probably down there somewhere between glandular fever and the accident in chemistry with sulphuric acid.

She scrolled through all the notifications as people, whose names she barely remembered, reminisced about things she had no recollection of.

Susie checked her diary for the date next month, although there was little point — it was empty. It wasn't even a weekend she'd agreed to work. Susie scanned the "invited" column.

Two sets of her classmates had married one another. It looked like one couple were still together, but Nadia's surname was different from Archie's — she was using her maiden name. Susie guessed that hadn't been one of the school's successes. Presumably they'd sit at opposite ends of the table and hopefully not resort to flinging food or insults at one another. She wondered how many others were widowed, or how many had managed nearly forty years together. There were a couple of doctors there too.

In the last paragraph Cynthia suggested everyone post a message if there was anything they wanted to get out of the way before they met up that was likely to generate an "I'm sorry to hear that response". "I'll start," she wrote. "I'm a recovering alcoholic. It's been nearly three months and I'm taking it one day at time. If you see me looking longingly at a bottle of wine, then please say something interesting to take my mind off it. If you see me heading to the bar with a determined look in my eye, you have my permission to do whatever is necessary to stop me getting there." Susie doubted that could be used as a defence for murder.

There had been no hint of any of this in Cynthia's Christmas letter. Jeez, Susie hadn't expected that. She went to make a cup of tea. By the time she got back to her computer there were more notifications: a suicide at university, five divorces, another death apart from Simon Farringdon's, which someone had also mentioned. Two had emigrated — one to Australia and one to New Zealand — and wouldn't be able to make the reunion. Irene had five kids by five different fathers, and Heather, who'd had a child while still at school, announced that she was now a great-grandmother. Sounded like the sex education hadn't improved since her day. She wondered whether the biology department still had the "too embarrassed to ask" box. Three other alcohol or drug-related problems. Two nervous breakdowns, four redundancies, one dead teacher.

Someone asked whether anyone had heard the rumours that one of the school's teachers had been arrested for murder. One of the invitees was back at their old school as an English teacher, and confirmed that, yes, another teacher had been arrested, but it was attempted murder and they were nearly halfway through a fourteen-year sentence. Someone asked if the school was holding his job open for him, with lots of laughing emojis.

Alan Wheeldon replied, "It wasn't a him, it was a her. It was my wife who was arrested".

Susie stared at the screen, open-mouthed. Clearly, she wasn't the only one. The replies weren't immediate. Then came a flurry of various emojis depicting shock or hugs.

Alan Wheeldon, that was a name to remember. Mr Personality himself. She'd been partnered with him for dancing lessons in their final term at school. Exams were over and it seemed that the most important lesson they still had to learn was how to dance in preparation for the end of school ball. He hadn't been her choice, or she suspected she his, but they'd ended up the last two left once everyone else had been paired up. She dreaded those lessons. Alan had no sense of rhythm, and when he wasn't standing on her feet, felt the need to grab her in inappropriate places or leer at her. It still made her shudder to think about those last few weeks of school. There had been a rumour flying about that they were an item, and someone had caught them making out behind the cricket pavilion. She couldn't believe anyone would take it seriously but kept getting strange looks from her classmates. She wondered if Lucy Miller had been behind it and had pleaded with Cynthia to tell everyone it wasn't true.

Cynthia had refused and told her there was no point. Everyone would believe what they wanted and if she protested too much they'd think she was lying anyway. She was better off ignoring it. They'd all be going their separate ways soon enough.

After a particularly trying dance lesson that resulted in them colliding with two other couples and the gym bars, the instructor had pushed Alan aside and told him to watch as he'd whisked Susie round the dance floor. That had been an astonishing experience. Susie had such confidence in her partner's lead that she went wherever he asked and fell instantly in love with dancing. She didn't go back to school once her exams were finished. She never went to the end-of-school dance, but within a week she *had* signed up for a dance class.

A line of flashing dots suggested someone was typing. Alan's name popped up again. One of the replies said: "You married a teacher?"

Watching while someone composed a message and typed was like watching paint dry. Presumably he was writing an essay. It couldn't have been just Susie waiting for a reply. No new messages flashed up.

And finally, there it was. He'd married the school's French exchange student. Susie couldn't remember her, but a number of people did, judging by the replies.

Someone asked when they got married, and Alan said ten years ago. They'd lost touch for a while — he went off to university and then trained as a pilot with one of the major airlines, during which time she'd been working in a French school. They'd met again by accident when she'd travelled on one of his flights. They married in the Caribbean. She'd come back to this country with him and got a job at their old school in the French department.

Alan, a pilot — this was getting stranger by the minute. Like one of those horror movies, where you had no idea what was going to come next. His sense of steering was shit in dance lessons, yet someone let him take charge of a plane — really? Susie was glad that when she and Terry had travelled anywhere it had nearly always been by car.

Several more surprised-looking emojis popped up. Then came a few more messages. Two more said they'd also trained as teachers but were working out of the area. And one had gone into the church.

Was this normal? In her year there had been, what, sixty pupils? So probably no more than the average number of problems in that number. It just felt somehow intense when you saw it written like that on the screen. More messages popped up.

Susie wondered whether the English teacher would report back to the school, and based on that, would they feel that their aspirations for her year had been met. She typed a brief message explaining about Terry. Cynthia's instructions about no one saying, "Sorry to hear that" seemed to have been taken to heart. The only reply she got was a heart-shaped emoji from Alan.

CHAPTER THIRTEEN

Susie pushed open the door to TOTU apprehensively. She'd only ever been in this restaurant once before. It didn't appear to have changed much — its grey and pink décor looked the same. She and Terry both enjoyed food but had rarely eaten out in the last ten years or so because Terry always found it too traumatic.

She could count on the fingers of one hand the times she'd dined out since Terry had died. Come to think of it, they'd all been with Bob. First, Maddie's wedding. Then the Lorry Park Café. Did a sausage sandwich and a Chelsea bun or a cherry Danish constitute dining out?

Twice, she'd taken herself to the cinema. She wasn't quite ready to go out for a meal on her own. Part of the enjoyment of any meal for her was the company and tonight it promised to be good. She smiled at the thought.

The restaurant was packed. The first Tuesday in each month at TOTU was billed as Country and Western Night with their resident singer, Lily Brooks. A waiter appeared by Susie's side.

'The Diamond party?' he asked as he took her coat.

Without waiting for a reply, he indicated she should follow him, although she could see everyone already seated at a large table in the middle of the restaurant.

She wasn't late, but she was last to arrive. There was only one seat left and that was between Maddie and Bob. Her heart did a little excited jump. He was there and looking good.

The only time she'd seen Bob in anything other than black jeans and a leather jacket had been at Maddie's wedding, but tonight he'd opted for a linen blazer, crisp white shirt and chinos.

'Hi,' she said, smiling and trying to sound as if she was greeting everyone, not just one man in particular.

Everybody called something back. She thought she could detect Luke's slight Midlands' twang but couldn't make out what he said. She smiled in his direction, hoping that was the right reaction.

Bob stood up. He probably would have pulled out the chair for her if the waiter hadn't beaten him to it.

She'd hoped he'd be there, but hadn't wanted to question Maddie too closely. It was just lovely to have been included along with Charlotte and Luke. They'd both worked with her for a lot longer.

'Of course you're invited. You're part of the team and it's our way of saying thank you to everyone involved with our wedding,' Maddie had insisted.

'Please don't tell us you'll be thinking of us workers while you're away,' Luke joked. He would be standing in as interim superintendent registrar while she and Josh went on their extended trip to the States. 'I'll have this place running so efficiently by the time you're back you won't recognize it. I'll crack the whip and these two won't know what's hit them.'

Susie had laughed with them. In the nine months she'd been at the Register Office she'd never met anyone as laid back as Luke, but she knew the three of them would work together and make sure the place ran efficiently. Maddie would be missed, but they'd already figured they could share her workload between them, which meant they had so far dodged any suggestion from management about getting a temp in.

One of the things that Susie loved about the Register Office was the way they always pulled together whenever there was something to be done. She'd agreed to work three extra weekends over the next two months. It meant it would be even harder to fit in any pole-dancing lessons. But now she had her own pole as well as a live-in tutor, she hoped she'd at least be able to continue with the exercises and level of fitness she thought she was starting to achieve. She winced as she sat down.

'Okay?' asked Bob, his brow crinkled with something she hoped was concern more than the realization she was middle-aged and so were her hips.

'I overdid the walking yesterday. I misjudged the distance.' She smiled back. It wasn't a complete lie. Her daily walking distance on her phone indicated she'd done eight miles. It had been lovely, but a lot of it had been uphill and hard work. And she'd had to clamber over a wall and under a gate to stick to the footpaths indicated by her Ordnance Survey app. She'd already planned to scale down her ambitions for the next one. 'I think I'm probably going to have to put off the Three Peaks' Challenge and London Marathon for a year or so.' She grinned. 'Or maybe indefinitely.'

Bob's expression looked as if he were poised on the brink of a funny comment, but he held her gaze for a little longer, then turned away. He reached for his glass and gulped down some water.

Gone was the humour on his face when he turned back. 'I should have said earlier, but you look stunning. That blue really suits you.'

Susie couldn't remember the last time anyone had complimented her like that. A burning sensation swept up her neck. She hoped Tara was right about the colour of her blush working with blue, because the square neckline meant there would be a lot of pink skin. And the blush was still rising, threatening to erupt onto her face.

His eyes were fixed on hers.

Hers were fixed on his.

'Thank you,' she managed eventually.

The spell was broken by the waiter who arranged plates with several small canapés on each around the table. He carefully explained that the small gougères contained taramasalata, while the biscuit-looking ones were blue stilton and date.

'And so do you,' she murmured to her place setting without looking up.

Another waiter filled their glasses with water. Around the table came several appreciative noises as canapés were sampled. Susie went for the gougères first and was surprised at how the flavours exploded in her mouth. She sighed.

'Good, eh?' Bob was still watching her.

'Amazing,' she said. She would be completely flushed by now, more tomato than anything more subtly coloured. She quickly turned away.

Seated opposite was Josh's colleague, Tony Longworth. Susie recognized him from her days with Latton Data. When Terry had had to move into Treetops last year, she'd suddenly found herself with time on her hands and taken a job working for Josh briefly as an admin assistant, before he went back to the States and she became a registrar.

Tony caught her eye and reached over to shake her hand. 'Good to see you again, Susie.' His expression suggested he meant it. 'I was sorry to hear about your husband.'

She was saved from answering by the woman next to him who stretched her hand across the table too. 'Poppy. Josh's sister. We met at my brother's wedding. I was one of the bridesmaids,' she said.

In the corner of the restaurant a blonde woman strummed a guitar and started to sing a country-and-western number that Susie recognized. There were several claps from around the room. She obviously wasn't the only country fan. After forty years with Terry she probably knew most of the popular songs, word for word. She could have sung along. The woman's voice was clear and beautiful. Susie closed her eyes and let the music flow over her. *Terry would have loved this.*

As the woman paused, Susie heard Bob's voice. Her eyes snapped open and found the waiter staring at her now.

'Do you want another minute?' the waiter asked.

'No need.' Bob squeezed her arm. 'Will you trust me on this one?' he said quietly. 'Why don't you go for the lobster starter and the partridge main course? It tastes as good as it sounds.'

'Thank you. Lobster and partridge, please,' Susie repeated.

The waiter wrote something on his pad. 'Good choice,' he said.

'What do you think about those two?' Bob asked, once they'd all given their orders, jerking his head towards Poppy and Tony, who sat together with their heads almost touching, seemingly lost in conversation. 'Do you think I'm about to lose my daughter?'

'Think of it as gaining a son-in-law?' Susie teased.

'It's early days for heaven's sake. Leave them alone,' Maddie said from Susie's other side. 'Has Susie told you she's started a life-drawing class?' she asked, looking at Bob.

He kinked an eyebrow. 'And how's that going?'

'It was my second session yesterday, but I think I'm more of an abstract painter.' She laughed. 'More Rothko than Reubens.'

'You're going to have to put me on your Christmas-card list,' he said. 'I can't wait to see how you call this one — *spent April surrounded by naked men.*'

'It's only the model who gets undressed,' Susie said. 'Although it's taken Mrs Ogbourne St George a while to understand he is supposed to be naked. Both weeks now she's offered to bring in clothes because he looks cold, and yesterday she thought he would look good in a hat and plans to bring in one of her husband's next week.'

Bob's laugh was low and deep and warmed her. She was having a lovely time. The food was awesome, but so was the company. It was the sort of occasion you never wanted to end.

The singer sang most of the old favourites and every now and again asked for requests. Luke collected suggestions from their table. Poppy asked for "Jolene" and Susie for "Could I Have This Dance?".

'Interesting choice,' Bob said, when Luke had gone to negotiate with the singer.

'Terry and I had it at our wedding. It was always one of my favourites.' She sighed, and a heaviness settled on her chest.

Bob looked concerned. 'Any more problems with Max?' he asked.

'I haven't heard anything. It's up to him and Jodie now to decide what they want to do. Norman Fairchild said he'd contact me as soon as he had the results of any DNA tests.'

'Is there nothing you can do in the meantime?'

'What like? A voodoo-doll-making class?'

'Redford do one of those?'

'No, but there are lots of YouTube episodes on the subject, so if Max becomes a problem, I should be able to create something to stab quite easily.'

'Don't tell me — you used to bite heads off jelly babies,' Bob chuckled.

'Only the red ones.'

The wine and conversation flowed freely round the table. The singer sang both their table's requests and they cheered enthusiastically. Josh made them laugh as he explained the route he had planned for his and Maddie's American trip. The places they'd be staying in, if he was to be believed, would give *Psycho*'s mother a run for her money, but Maddie hadn't looked concerned. Her trust in her husband was evident.

Susie enjoyed being part of the table. She relaxed, occasionally throwing in the odd remark. Bob teased Josh about his bike. Soon, mid-lemon meringue soufflé, the singer announced the next song would be her last. Someone asked for "I Walk the Line". She laughed and said she'd give it a go. She strummed a few chords and started singing about keeping a close watch on her heart.

'You're not the only one doing odd things this year. Has Dad told you about his blacksmith's course?' Josh asked. 'He went with the intention of making a gate. Apparently, that wasn't possible in a day, but we are now the proud owners of a metal key ring, a bottle opener and a poker.'

'Pokers are always so useful.' Susie nodded slowly. 'Underrated, but I couldn't do without one.'

'Yes,' Poppy laughed. 'But maybe you have an open fire.'

Susie was saved from having to reply by Josh's next question.

'What are you doing next term, Dad? Sheep shearing?'

'Don't mock me. I'm just trying to keep my mind and body active.' Bob looked petulant. 'It's good to keep busy.'

'So, what then — conversational Latin?'

Bob shrugged. 'The college is starting a geriatric ballet class on Thursday afternoons.' He didn't look at Poppy, but Susie could see the corner of his mouth curve into a smile as he stretched for another piece from the cheeseboard. 'So Indian cookery in the mornings and straight into ballet classes after lunch. I'll be out all day unless you feel you can't cope without me at the garage.'

'Geriatric ballet classes?' Susie whispered as soon as the conversation had moved around the other side of the table.

'Nah. The college have asked if I'll help with their basic automotive maintenance course. I'm going to do a couple of hours a week.'

'Indian cookery too?' Susie was amazed.

'I've taken a leaf out of your book. I'm broadening my horizons. Italian last term — you really should try my crab linguine. Indian next term.'

'Crab linguine.' Susie was stuffed, she probably wouldn't need to eat for the next few days. Still, the thought of it made her mouth water. 'One of my favourite foods.'

'I make it with tomatoes and chilli. A touch of garlic and lemon.' Bob kissed his fingers. 'Bellissima.'

'I'd like to try it. Sounds wonderful.' Susie smiled.

Bob looked as if he was about to say something. She hoped it would be an invite to do just that, but at that moment, the singer finished singing.

'Thank you, ladies and gentlemen,' she said as everyone clapped. 'You've all been a great audience. Enjoy the rest of your meal.'

Suddenly, a scuffle broke out at one of the tables on the other side of the room. A table full of middle-aged men, who'd clearly been drinking steadily. Someone got up from the table and made their way to the singer.

'You asked for requests earlier,' he said loudly. 'I made a request. I want to hear, "Islands in the Stream".' It was one of those one-sided conversations pitched at a level that was difficult to ignore, with lots of finger-pointing.

The singer tried to back away. 'No,' she said, 'I can't. I won't.' She unclipped her guitar.

The man started to argue the case. He stabbed a pointed finger at her chest, his voice getting louder with every syllable.

The bistro went silent. The singer stood in the corner of the room, looking lost and upset. Suddenly, a Bob lookalike was by her side. Susie swung round. She hadn't heard him get up, but his chair was empty.

He signalled something to the approaching waiter and moved between the singer and the man. 'You're spoiling everyone's evening. That song's a duet.' He crossed his arms in front of him and stood on the stage, daring the guy to argue. When he pulled himself up to full height, he towered above the man, who took a step back. 'What Lily meant is that she couldn't do it justice on her own,' he said.

The man looked about to say something.

Bob raised a hand. He tapped the microphone and then lifted it off the stand. 'Shut up and listen. If Lily doesn't mind, and providing you sit down, pay your bill, leave a frigging enormous service charge and you and your mates promise to go as soon as the song is finished, we will sing "Islands in the Stream". I will take the male part.' He looked at Lily.

Her movement was slight, but she must've agreed, because the man moved away and went back to his table. The restaurant stilled. There was a bit of a kerfuffle at the table and the waiter rushed across with what looked like their bill.

The chef came out of the kitchen and the rest of the waiting staff gathered in a line either side of him, their arms crossed over their chests.

Bob stood next to Lily while she selected a guitar. 'Come on, we can do this, girl,' he said. 'After three.'

The first chords of the song started. Susie put down her spoon and watched, amazed, as Bob started to sing. A flush of warmth crept up her body. She wished it was her he was singing to. By the time they got to the chorus, a few people had joined in. Susie found herself singing along too. Lily and Bob were grinning at each other. He reached out and took her hand.

'He's got a lovely voice, hasn't he?' Maddie said. 'According to Josh, he used to be in a band.'

'He told me,' Susie nodded, staring at Bob and Lily's hands.

As soon as the song finished, the table of middle-aged men got up and left. Bob and Lily looked deep in conversation. As the door closed behind the men, Bob and Lily turned to face the restaurant. Lily signalled for him to give her the mike.

'Thank you, ladies and gentlemen,' she said. 'I am sorry about that, and I am sure we wish them well on their walk home. Let's hope they are walking home.' There was a ripple of laughter round the restaurant. She nodded then handed him back the mike. 'Bob, over to you.'

She took a step back and played as he sang "Friends in Low Places". The line of waiters and the chef looked far more relaxed and clapped along with the rest of their customers in time to the music.

The atmosphere felt electric. Bob put the microphone back on the stand as he finished the number, and everyone stood and applauded. He grinned, bowed and turned round to acknowledge Lily.

'I've got one final number,' she said, 'then I really must go. It's well past my bedtime, but I couldn't leave without saying thank you to my friend here. She turned her back on the restaurant and ruffled her hair. She played one note on her guitar then turned, and in a breathy voice, sang, completely unaccompanied, "Diamonds are a Girl's Best Friend".

'Wow,' said Susie, as Bob slipped back into his seat next to her. 'She was amazing and so were you.'

There were so many questions she wanted to ask. She was feeling things she didn't think possible. Surely, she couldn't be jealous of the singer.

'What have I missed?' Bob asked, picking up one of the petit fours.

'Susie telling us about her felting workshop, school reunion and possibly a zip-wire experience. Although she hasn't booked it yet,' Josh said getting up.

Apparently not the sort of thing you should tell someone about to eat another petit four.

'If you're thinking that's not a good idea at my age,' Susie said, 'then please don't. The others have already said as much.'

'Last thing on my mind. I heard they've got some decent ones in Wales.'

Josh came back to the table, putting his wallet back in his pocket. Susie asked if she could pay her share, she'd had such a lovely time, but he shook his head and told her to put her money away.

'This is our way of saying thank you,' he said, looking down the table at his wife, who was standing between Luke and Charlotte, an arm on each. She was bent talking to them and they were all laughing.

'I am a very lucky man, and I wouldn't be here today if you hadn't all come to my rescue and pulled strings to make sure our wedding happened.'

Three waiters appeared with a pile of coats as the singer walked past. As Lily Brooks reached Bob, she put an arm on his shoulder and handed him a piece of paper. 'Call me,' she said. 'It would be good to catch up properly.' She looked like she was about to leave, but Bob turned and stood up.

Susie followed Maddie and Josh out of the restaurant. When she turned, she saw, through the open doorway, Bob still talking to the singer.

Josh and Maddie insisted on walking Susie to her car. They set off down the high street, promising they would WhatsApp occasional photos and made Susie promise that she'd come for a meal as soon as they got back to hear all about the trip. It wasn't far. Susie hoped that Bob would free himself of Lily and catch them up and was disappointed when they reached the parking bay.

'Of course I will. We've heard Maddie talk about nothing else except this trip since Christmas.' She half-raised her eyebrows as Josh held her driver's door open. She slipped in and clicked her seat belt into place. 'I need to know how it works out.'

There was still no sign of Bob. 'Say goodbye to your father for me,' she added as she closed the door.

She started the engine and pulled away. Tears were threatening at the back of her eyes. 'Pull yourself together, woman,' she said out loud.

The traffic lights in the high street turned green as she approached.

'Jealousy is not a good look on anyone.'

CHAPTER FOURTEEN

'You're back on the bikes, then,' Freddie Brompton said. He'd walked down his front steps even before Bob had brought Josh's Ducati to a stop on the gravel outside the house. He was either psychic or had a good early warning alarm system.

'Trick question, right?' Bob laughed as he pulled off his helmet and ran a hand through his hair.

Freddie stuck out his hand. 'So, to what do I owe this pleasure? Don't tell me, you've managed to find me a Pagani within my budget?'

'Okay, I won't.' Bob laughed. The two men shook hands. Freddie slapped his back.

If Bob had had something stuck in his throat, the force of the slap would've probably dislodged it. As it was, it just knocked him off balance.

'You've timed it right,' Freddie said, as Bob straightened up. 'I've had a clear out of one of the sheds and rearranged things a bit. Before you come in, want to have a look?'

Jenny stood in the open door looking down at them. Bob raised a hand in greeting and made a face that he hoped indicated he had no choice in the matter. She laughed and retreated indoors as Freddie pointed to the side of the house.

Bob didn't doubt they'd be in the kitchen soon enough. He'd catch up with her then, because no visit to Freddie's would ever be complete without a trip to see his car collection, or a cup of tea in their kitchen accompanied by one of Jenny's cakes. Freddie might refer to his outbuildings as sheds, but that was an understatement. The house was built on an old airfield. Most of it down to the river was laid to lawn, apart from two old hangars that Freddie had refurbished over the years.

'Do you miss the band?' Bob asked as they wandered round, and he spotted Freddie's drum kit covered by a dust sheet in the corner. '"Flash Sticks" Freddie Brompton?' he added.

Freddie raised his arms above his head and rotated a full 360 degrees. 'The one and only.' He moved behind the drum set, pulled back the dust-sheet and sat down. 'I still practise. Like to keep my hand in. Never know when a new band will come calling. I want to be ready.'

'Yeah, right.' Bob never really knew what Freddie did for a living. His house on the outskirts of Allingham was huge and he had a collection of cars to die for. The rumour during their school years had been that his father had won a fortune on the football pools.

Bob never asked.

Freddie never said.

They'd always kept in touch, but mainly because of the cars. Bob had sourced most of them and made sure they were regularly serviced, which was a bit ridiculous really — money for old rope, seeing as they did so little mileage.

He couldn't imagine Freddie sticking with anything for long. How he'd stayed married to Jenny was an enigma. Freddie was an ideas man but didn't seem to have the staying power to see them through. Although, it was an attitude that had served him well in the eighties. He'd worked in the City for a while but got out before the stock-market crash. He said it was because he got bored and wanted to run a drum school, but it did mean he hadn't lost everything overnight like several of his old colleagues.

The drum school never really got started. It wasn't a venture he'd thought through properly. He advertised for a while but then it seemed to die a death. Bob had thought at the time that a drum school in Allingham would probably be as popular as a recruitment campaign for the Brownies in an old people's home. Looked like he was right.

Freddie bent down behind the drums and reappeared with a pair of drumsticks that he knocked together above his head before he started playing. Big, extravagant moves, just as vigorous as when the band were together. Presumably the hangar or house was soundproofed. Either that or Jenny was more long-suffering than Bob could possibly imagine.

'Yep, I miss those days.' Freddie held the cymbal still to stop the sound. 'But then I never wanted the band to break up. It was you lightweights who made that decision.'

'If memory serves me right,' Bob said, 'I was in hospital at the time and not consulted.'

'You were in a bloody coma, so we couldn't ask you. And Norman had moved to London when he joined that law firm.'

'He wasn't consulted either, then?'

'He was only available to play on the odd weekend when he was home. I heard he joined another group for a few months. Never heard of them, though.'

'To be fair, they'd probably say the same about the Brothers in Boxers,' Bob joked.

'It's funny, isn't it? We all live close together, bump into each other from time to time, and no one has ever suggested a reunion. Maybe we should give Norman a call — see if he's up for a session.'

'Yeah, right. We couldn't agree what to play when we were youngsters. What makes you think it would be any easier now that we're all getting old? And if I remember correctly, back then it wasn't just the songs we couldn't agree on. We couldn't even agree on the type of music we should be playing.'

Freddie came out from behind the drums and covered them back over with the dust-sheet, tucking all the edges in carefully as if he were putting a baby to bed. He patted the sheet before turning to Bob and making a tsk noise. 'That's all in the past,' he said with a wave of his hand. 'Hatchets have been well and truly buried. Maybe we could do a reunion tour. Imagine it. Let's call it, "The Brothers in Boxers are back in town".'

'When you say "reunion tour", can I remind you that the scout hut never got rebuilt after the fire and is now a fast-food drive-through. The pub at the end of the high street has been converted into flats, so that just leaves the Badger and Fir Tree, which I have been led to believe has become something of a gastropub these days, whatever that means.'

'No billiard table or dartboard and a room full of tables. Menu chalked on the wall.' Freddie shrugged. 'And it'll have been Farrow & Ball-d into a nice sage colour with a fancy name. There's at least one in every town these days. The go-to place for posh burgers and multi-cooked chips.'

'That's as maybe, but while the last thing I want to do is pour water on your parade, what I am trying to say is that we don't have any venues.'

'You must start thinking bigger. "Outside the box", isn't that the expression? We could headline at the Redford Festival. I know the guy who runs it, or perhaps . . . an illegal rave.'

'I can't see Jenny being happy about that. By the way, I saw Lily Brooks the other night,' Bob said. 'She's still singing. She has a regular country-and-western set on Tuesdays at the bistro in town.'

'Still as gorgeous as ever?' Freddie asked. He pulled the cuff of his jumper down and polished the wing of his E-Type with it. He stood back and checked the car before he let go of his cuff. 'She had a good voice. I heard her husband left her.'

'That must be easily thirty-plus years ago, and before you get any ideas, she's loved up at the moment with her yoga master — Geoffrey.'

Freddie held his hands against his chest. 'As if. I've never looked at another woman since I met Jenny. You still got a guitar?'

'Two.'

'Bring them over one night, and we can jam together. No one can hear us out here.' Freddie gestured around the hangar.

'Funnily enough, I got the guitars out this morning. The acoustic one could do with restringing, but still sounds good. It ought to, it cost me a small fortune at the time.'

'They say guitars are like men,' Freddie chuckled. 'Get better with age.'

'Really! Someone should've told my electric one — that's had it.'

'Do you know what I heard on the radio the other day? On one of those request shows.'

'Not "I Wish I Was Heaven Bound with You"?'

'The one and the same.'

'Do you know what happened to "The General"?'

'Reggie? Probably dead.'

Bob sighed. 'No way. He could have been only what, ten, twelve years older than us at the most. He probably made the big time and is living it up in LA.' Clenching his right hand, Bob held up it up to his mouth and pretended to use it as a mike. 'And now, for all you romantics out there. After three, boys. Take it away. One, two, three . . .' He pointed to Freddie, who launched into an elaborate miming routine to suggest he was drumming. After a second or two, Bob pretended to strum a guitar, then tapped his foot. And as if that was the cue, they both started singing together, *I wish I was heaven bound with you.*

'I hate to think how many wedding receptions he had us play that at.'

'I guess The General, if he is alive, must still be getting royalties.'

'Probably him who requested it. I can't imagine any sane person doing that.'

'As music teachers went, he was brilliant. I was chuffed when he asked me to play the guitar in this band he was pulling together. I thought I'd made the big time.'

'Me, too.' Freddie clapped Bob on the back. 'Come on, let's go and find Jenny.'

'That one hit changed him. Suddenly he thought he was an overnight sensation. Then Elvis only went and bloody died and he wanted us to become a tribute band.'

'Maybe we should have. Punk music was on the up. We were being squeezed out anyway.'

'There was no way he was getting me into a one-piece white jumpsuit, with or without a cape and flares,' Bob frowned.

'Shame. I'd have paid good money to see that,' Freddie laughed. 'I heard he did okay for a while as a solo performer.'

'Do you remember his affair with the MP's wife?'

Freddie whistled. 'Not something anyone's likely to forget.'

'It was all the papers wrote about for weeks.'

'Word to the wise,' Freddie laughed. 'If you're going to do something bad, make sure it's not on a quiet news week.'

'He had a bad time. I felt sorry for him. His wife left him, and his daughter, Caroline, disappeared too. Do you remember the emotional appeal he made on television for any news?'

Freddie nodded. 'It was sad. I wonder if she ever turned up.'

'Who knows. He went completely off the radar after that. Rumour had it that he ended up in the States.'

'*Sweet Caroline*,' Freddie hummed.

'We had some fun in those early days, didn't we?'

'Did quite well with our wedding and pub bookings. And whatever you say about them, the Badger and Fir Tree have monthly karaoke sessions — we should go one evening. Ask Norman. It might be fun to see if we've still got it.' Freddie looked thoughtful for a while. 'You asked me if I miss those days. Yes, a part of me does. I don't think it was the applause, or that side of it.'

'Which to be fair was never a huge part of our act.'

'But somehow it never felt real. The band wasn't cohesive. It always felt like it was just waiting for the first opportunity to fall apart.'

'Sometimes we were lucky if the audience were still awake at the end of our set, or the whole party weren't in the car park having a good old-fashioned fist fight.'

'Emotionally charged events, wedding receptions. Reggie always insisted on full payment up front for anything where families and alcohol were involved. He always asked the manager to give us the heads-up the minute the police were called.'

Freddie laughed. 'Give us time to pack up and get our kit out intact. Do you remember that wedding when one of the bridesmaids started showing the pictures on her phone of her having sex with the groom the night before the wedding?'

'I thought it was hard enough work at Josh's wedding, keeping the bride's father from singing a bastardized Barry Manilow version of "Mandy".' Bob rubbed his hands through his hair.

'How did it go, Josh's wedding?' Freddie asked.

'Beautiful. They make a lovely couple. In America just now. He's finally riding the Pacific Coast Highway.'

'That's how come you're on his bike, I suppose.'

'Just keeping it ticking over.'

'I know you, Bob Diamond. That'll have a lot more miles on the clock by the time he gets back. You say you met Lily the other night. How was she?'

'Good, apart from a spot of bother with some drunk wanting her to sing "Islands in the Stream".'

'That's bad! Isn't that the one she used to sing with her husband, before he dumped her. How did she take the request?'

'She got upset. He started getting lippy, and I ended up singing it with her. That's what got me to thinking about the band.'

Freddie set the alarm and locked the hangar before he turned. 'I miss the adrenaline rush before a gig, however small it was. You?'

'Music, singing and the guitar were a form of release for me. I needed that. If Reggie hadn't taken me under his wing,

I wouldn't have done as well at school. Probably got into a lot more trouble. The funny thing is, there's so much I know I learned at school, but it didn't go in. But every song I ever sang or played, I'm pretty sure I'm still word- and note-perfect. How does that bloody work?'

'Don't know, mate, but you and me both.' Freddie pulled a flash-looking mobile from his pocket as he walked towards the house. He seemed to be reading something on the screen, then he tapped it and held the phone up to his ear.

They'd just reached the back of the house as Freddie said, 'This is Mr Brompton. Does Mr Fairchild have a moment to speak to me?'

CHAPTER FIFTEEN

Having not been in the Register Office since collecting Elaine's death certificate, Bob hesitated before pushing the big wooden door open. The place hadn't changed much. That day had been a blur. He couldn't even remember why he'd needed a death certificate. Everything had been sorted out long before the coroner had held the inquest and he'd given Bob an interim one to use to sort out the bank, the tax office and her pension.

There weren't any "No dogs allowed" signs that he could see, so Bob reasoned it was okay to take Miss Phyllis in. He stroked the dog's head, and she trotted in happily with him.

Susie sported a surprised look when he rang the customer-service bell, and she looked up to see who it was.

'I was just walking past,' he said. Was there a hint of a smile? He hoped there was.

'I've got a change-of-name appointment coming in any moment.' Susie looked down at her watch.

'Sorry, I should have . . .' *Should have, what?*

It had been three weeks since Maddie and Josh had left for the States. She'd probably been working extra hours to cover Maddie's absence. He knew that. She'd said as much at their last meal.

But he'd hoped she might ring him. She had his number.

Okay, there was no reason why she should have. Still, it would have been nice to hear from her. Hear her laugh again. Hear what ridiculous thing she'd taken up next. He'd hoped to bump into her at the Lorry Park Café a couple of times, but the industrial unit she'd danced in gave no indication it was being used on Saturday mornings anymore. If she was still pole dancing, it certainly wasn't there.

He could have rung her too. He had her number. He'd been sad when he'd turned round after saying goodbye to Lily at the restaurant to find she'd gone. He'd watched as she'd hurried from the restaurant, Josh opened her car door for her and then waved her off, and felt a rush of jealousy. He was just being foolish, and it made him feel like the old man he was.

'After that I've got lunch. If you were still around in about half an hour's time, I'd be happy to join you.'

It was Bob's turn to smile. 'My friend here and I were considering walking to the bakers in the high street. Would you be happy to join us there for a sausage sandwich and a cup of tea?'

She was most definitely smiling now. 'Lovely,' she said.

'It's a date, then.' Bob blushed. 'Well, you know what I mean.' He turned and left without waiting for a reply. That was a daft thing to say. Of course, it wasn't a bloody date. If it was a date, he'd take her somewhere special, not just turn up on the off chance because he still felt unhappy about not saying goodbye in a restaurant three weeks earlier.

Poppy had intimated the other day that Susie might've got the wrong impression about his relationship with Lily. He'd laughed at the time — it was ridiculous. No one could think . . . Could they?

Lily Brooks had been a couple of years younger than him at school, but Reggie, their music teacher, had singled her out as someone with talent and introduced her to the band.

When requests at weddings and their other gigs in those days came in for the popular country numbers, which they often did, Lily would step forward and take centre stage. She had an exceptional voice, but she didn't want to be a backing singer and would moan loudly and at length, when asked, to the point the band would often leave her out of other numbers.

She left the band when she met a Kenny Rogers lookalike. It didn't surprise anyone. As splits went, it wasn't major — the band carried on. Bob or Reggie would sing the country numbers even though Bob considered himself more of a heavy-rock musician. Their playlist had always been eclectic. Reggie maintained their audience weren't welded to one artist or another, they just liked a good song. Bob too. He was happy as long as no one suggested platform heels or make-up would be a good look for him. Reggie wore enough of that for all of them. He'd tell them it was what his public expected. A one-hit wonder, with one of those earworm songs that had made number one in the UK charts. It had earned Reggie a place on *Top of the Pops* before he'd joined the school as music master.

Even now, walking around the rose garden at the Register Office, Bob could remember every chord, every word of the song that he'd heard and played so bloody often.

'*Driving down double yellow lines*', he hummed.

Shit, now "I Wish I Was Heaven Bound with You" was going to stay in his head all day. It had a guitar riff that always got people up and dancing at weddings and parties, but the more he tried to make sense of those lyrics, the more his head hurt.

> *Those double yellow lines,*
> *Helps my chakras realign.*
> *I'm ready to make a move, girl.*
> *Want to make my energies whirl?*

No wonder Reggie had struggled to come up with a second hit.

There had been a suggestion at the time that he had been heavily influenced by the Bay City Rollers, something about the road number he'd used in a later verse. Personally, Bob and the band thought it had more to do with heavy drugs.

It was April, and the rose garden to the side of the civic building looked empty. The arches over the path were still naked. The roses had clearly been pruned back in early spring, shoots starting to emerge, but there was no suggestion that any rose blooming was imminent. In a couple of months' time, Bob was sure it would look amazing.

Bob hoped that any brides would check out the colours of the flowers before their big days. He remembered a story he'd heard from Poppy about a wedding she'd driven the bride to. It had been at the local church. The vicar had come out and apologized that the walkway was no longer lined with pink hyacinths, as they'd been vandalized. All the flowers had been annihilated one night during the previous week. He was distraught — it had never happened before. The bride had put her hand on his arm and said, 'Don't worry, reverend.'

'What sort of person would do that?' Poppy had whispered as they watched the vicar retreat to the church door to wait for the bridal party.

The bride had turned to Poppy and said, 'Maybe a bride who loathes pink hyacinths and whose mother-in-law knows it. That's why she gave the church a huge donation and a bag full of bulbs the previous autumn and even supervised the planting.'

'*We could hit the road to forever, take the A5 to paradise,*' Bob sang.

'*Make love together and drown in each other's eyes,*' came back, sung in a higher register than he could manage.

He snapped round to find Susie grinning at him. 'Don't tell me this place has made you go all soppy.'

'No,' he spluttered, as she bent down to pat Miss Phyllis. 'You know that song?'

'I hear it often at weddings. I'm never sure what's worse, One Direction or that one. Did you know a recent survey showed that seventy-five percent of those who chose "Little

Things" for their wedding, got divorced. Not a great track record.'

'Absolutely,' Bob said solemnly. 'If they're too young to like decent music, they're too young to get married. Can't you insist people have to be at least — I don't know — thirty before they get married.'

'Decent music — says the man I've just found singing, "I Wish I Was Heaven Bound with You".'

'I'm impressed you recognized it. I must be getting better.' Bob turned. She was teasing him, and he liked it. 'Sausage sandwich?' he asked, and then added, 'I think we should discuss your music preferences.' He indicated the high street with a flick of his head and lifted an arm. She slipped her arm through his and they walked off. It felt good. Like it was meant to be. Like a switch had been flicked on.

'We used to make up "Bingo" lists,' he said. 'Back in the band days, we'd all choose five songs that were bound to be requested at any gig we were about to play. The one that got the fewest selected had to buy the food on the way home. Even back then there were certain requests that made us wonder if the marriage would last. Do you remember, "You're So Vain"?'

'Oh God, yes. How about, "D-I-V-O-R-C-E"?'

'"White Wedding".'

'"Suspicious Minds".'

'"Release Me".'

'"I Wish I Was Heaven Bound with You".'

'You win. I'm sure things have changed.'

'Nope. Maybe in a generation's time.'

'What makes you say that?'

'The cynical side of me predicts that expensive weddings will become a thing of the past, because the wedding couples, having discovered that doing away with present lists and asking the guests to cough up for a honeymoon, is starting to wear a bit thin and then they'll start to ask them to contribute to the actual do itself. I figure at some point, the guests will realize the hire of a morning suit, a room in an expensive hotel, as well as a large cash sum for a wedding present is more than they are prepared to pay and start making excuses not to attend.'

'You think that will happen?'

They'd come to the high street. Bob pushed open the door to the bakers. It was lunchtime and all the tables were full, but as he was about to say so, Susie pointed to one at the back where everyone was starting to gather up their things.

'I was being facetious,' she said, once they'd sat down. Miss Phyllis settled under the table. 'Having said that, only last week one of the guests at a Register Office wedding was publicly dumped by his partner when she discovered the gift he'd given the bride and groom for their honeymoon fund was more than he'd coughed up for her last Christmas present. By a sizeable amount, according to her. What was the name of the man who sang that song — Captain something?'

'The General.'

'He never had another hit,' Bob said as the waitress came across to them. She made a fuss of Miss Phyllis first, before she wiped their table and put down a pot full of utensils.

'What can I get you?'

'Sausage sandwich, and a mug of tea, please,' Susie said, putting the menu down.

'That's for two,' Bob said, smiling.

'How did you know about the sausage sandwiches here?' Susie asked as the waitress walked away. 'Do you come here often?'

Bob grinned. 'The most clichéd pick-up line ever, and from the woman who called my song choice corny.'

Susie flushed. 'I wasn't . . .'

'Not as often as I used to,' Bob said. 'I'm supposed to cut fatty food out following a heart scare last year. According to my dietician, I'm allowed to suck on the occasional lettuce leaf when the hunger pains get too bad.'

Susie's eyes twinkled.

'I have to limit my intake, check calorie contents of all ingredients on any food that passes my lips.' He looked down and arranged a serviette on his lap. 'I shouldn't have come.'

'I'm glad you did.' Susie reached across and squeezed his hand.

'Me too.' Bob fiddled with the utensils, passing Susie a knife and fork and a paper napkin. 'I'm sorry I didn't get the chance to say goodbye last time we met.' He didn't look up. 'I had a lovely time, with great food and company.'

The waitress put a plate with a sausage sandwich and a small pile of greenery in front of each of them.

'I didn't realize it came with a side salad,' Bob joked.

'Would you like my side salad too? I could swap it for your sausage sandwich if that would keep your dietician happy.'

'In your dreams, lady.'

The waitress came back with two mugs of tea. 'Any sauce?' she asked.

They both laughed and Bob shook his head.

'You met a friend, I understand.' Susie cut off a small piece of her sandwich.

'Lily's just that. A friend. Nothing more, and absolutely head-over-heels in love with Geoffrey.'

Susie was concentrating on her food, but she was listening, Bob was sure of that.

'She used to sing with the band and then with her husband — they were popular on the country-and-western circuit. It helped she could do great Dolly Parton impersonations and he looked a lot like Kenny Rogers, but he left her for another singer. I didn't even realize until three weeks ago that she'd started singing again.'

'You don't need to explain.'

But Bob did. It had hurt to see Susie walk away. More than he'd expected. They'd had a good laugh through supper. He'd enjoyed the evening and that was mainly down to her. The thought that he didn't know when he'd see her again had kept him awake most of that night and a number since then.

'You do have a lovely voice.'

'Thank you.' He'd enjoyed singing again. A part of him still wished they hadn't given up so easily on the band. But they were young, and all had lives to get on with. Norman Fairchild had gone off to university and chambers or wherever you go to become a solicitor. Bob went through an apprenticeship with his father and was doing well racing bikes.

Competitions took him away from home a lot. Consequently, he missed rehearsals and then he'd had his accident.

Racing to the hospital to be with his wife for the birth of his daughter, he had been wiped out at a roundabout by a van. He made it to the hospital before Poppy arrived, but had been in theatre, undergoing life-saving surgery while Elaine, three wards away, gave birth on her own.

He'd been put in an induced coma until the doctors figured he was stable enough to be brought around and meet his daughter.

The first thing Elaine did was to make him promise bikes were consigned to history or she would leave him. His racing career was over.

Then there were multiple operations to get his leg pinned. He'd been in hospital for a while, learning to walk again.

At the time he hadn't given singing another thought, and by the time he next saw Freddie, he discovered the band had folded and The General had thrown his toys out of his pram and decided that life as an Elvis impersonator was more lucrative.

CHAPTER SIXTEEN

Susie parked in the car park behind Hosni's Palace. She'd briefly toyed with the idea of driving straight off again. What on earth was she doing here? She hadn't seen most of these people for years. School days weren't the happiest of her life, and in her experience there was usually a reason why people didn't keep in touch. Luke had laughed at her this morning and said much the same thing.

She watched a couple of people walk towards the restaurant. They were dressed in skirts and high heels. It was hard to judge their ages from their backs. Susie realized she was holding her breath. The sensation of cold sweats, the same as she used to have at school, swept over her. The same as when Lucy Miller was nearby. Lucy Miller — could that be her?

If it was, her hair colour had changed. Susie gathered up her keys and bag and climbed out of the car. Then, across the chilly evening air, came a laugh that seriously hadn't changed. Susie wondered what Fuck-Off-Lucy was amused by this evening.

She should have arranged to meet Cynthia somewhere beforehand. They could have arrived together. Even if they'd met in the car park, they could have walked in together. Safety in numbers and all that. You ridiculous woman, she practically shouted out loud. She had gained a lot of confidence over the last year as a registrar. She could walk into any room and address one hundred people these days. A few more cars entered the car park and parked, their occupants setting off in various directions. Susie took a deep breath.

Luke had suggested a few comments she could use this morning. Okay, practise: "*Hello Lucy, nice to see you. Still bullying the underdog? You've had an entire life to be an idiot. I really thought you'd be ready for a day off.*"

There was a knock on the passenger's side window that made her jump. She looked over the bonnet to see a bearded man in a baseball hat looking in.

'Can I help you?' she asked.

The man straightened and looked at her from the other side of the car.

Alan *sodding bloody* Wheeldon.

'Susie, I thought it was you. Long time, no see.'

Her mouth opened. She shut it again.

'Don't break my heart and say you don't recognize me.'

'Course not,' Susie said quickly. 'But you might have had less facial hair last time I saw you.'

He laughed. 'Shall we walk in together? That'll get them talking. It will be quite like old times.'

No, it flaming won't. He stuck out an elbow which Susie pointedly ignored. If he thought she was going to walk in arm-in-arm with the man who'd made the last few weeks of her school life hell, he had another thing coming. She made a show of checking her car was locked, putting her keys away and set off towards the restaurant.

Have your meal and go. Just a couple of hours — you can do this.

'Cynthia suggested there will be dancing tonight.' She tried to inject some brightness into her voice. 'Have you spent the last month channelling your inner whirling dervish?'

It won't be as painful as the felting workshop. At least your thumbs shouldn't bleed.

Alan kept up a steady stream of chatter as they walked across the car park about the weather, his drive to Templeton, how much petrol cost.

Get through this and do something nice tomorrow. Book a zoo-keeper experience.

'We have something in common,' Alan said as they reached the restaurant courtyard.

'Do we?' Susie asked.

'A dead relative.'

Not a statement Susie was expecting. She stopped and frowned at him.

Alan didn't seem to have noticed. 'My mother died last year,' he went on. 'Like your husband. Difficult times, but we get through them, don't we?'

Susie wished she could conjure up a witty comment designed to put him firmly down. Her mind refused to play and went completely blank.

Why on earth would a sixty-something-year-old man think that those two things were in some way related. He had no insight into how she felt about anything, let alone her husband.

Alan was talking again. Her refusal to engage with his last announcement hadn't pushed him off track. He didn't like pets, but didn't mention his wife or ask any questions about how Susie was or what she had been doing.

'I've always wanted a dog,' she said as they entered the restaurant. 'I always thought there was something wrong with people who don't like animals.'

A great noise erupted. Cynthia charged across the reception and threw her arms around Susie, who allowed herself to be dragged into the restaurant, glad to get away from Alan.

'You came,' Cynthia said. 'I wasn't sure you would. Lovely to see you.'

Over her shoulder, Susie could see Alan follow them in. He took off his jacket, but his cap stayed firmly on his head. He looked a bit put out as he looked around.

Cynthia guided her to the other side of a large table where there were just two spaces free. 'I've saved you one,' she said, and then dropping her voice, said in a slightly conspiratorial manner, 'Don't look, but Fuck-Off-Lucy is at eleven o'clock.'

"Don't look." Wasn't that one of those things people say when what they mean is turn round and look. Susie got the message and turned. She tried for a casual 360-degree turn, taking in everyone on her way round. Cynthia was right. Lucy was there, and not only that, she appeared to have got to Alan on his way in. Her hand rested on his arm, and they were talking animatedly together.

'We really must do lunch one day,' Cynthia said, as Susie finished her rotation. 'We have so much to catch up on. Did your lodger tell you I'd phoned?'

Tara had left a message on the side to say that someone had rung while Susie had been on her felting course. But she couldn't read the name Tara had written. Not Bob, Max or Norman, so she'd more or less ignored it, figuring they'd ring back if it was urgent. Besides, she had more important things to do, like find a home for the March hare she'd spent three hours of her life needle-felting while puncturing her thumb in the process. Repeatedly stabbing a pile of wool had been very therapeutic until it was covered in blood. But the hare did have all his required features — tail, legs, nose and eyes — and so far hadn't fallen flat on its face.

'I thought she said you were at a felting workshop.' Cynthia squinted at her and picked up a large glass of cloudy liquid with a parasol stuck out of the top. 'I must've misheard . . .'

'You didn't. You're not drinking, are you?'

'No way.' Cynthia waved her glass dismissively. 'But there is free booze during the meal.'

'Are you sure that's a good idea? You know, with your . . .' *Condition — was that the right word?*

'I'm fine. Don't worry about me. Feel free to fill your boots. I'm on the mocktails.' Cynthia squinted again. 'Really,' she added, 'I'm okay to be with other people drinking around me these days.'

'Good, and mocktails sound good.' It was difficult to tell from the cloudy, odd-coloured drink in Cynthia's hand what it contained. 'I might join you. I'm driving after all.'

'No hangovers for us in the morning.' Cynthia reached for a jug in the middle of the table, poured out another glassful for Susie and topped her own up in the process. 'Why aren't you staying the night here in Templeton? Didn't you get the message with the hotel details on it? There's quite a crowd of us staying.'

'I only live half an hour away and like my own bed. I'm sorry. I could've invited you to stay but just didn't think of it. It's so long since anybody who has come to visit needed a bed for the night.'

Cynthia squeezed her arm. 'I'm not much further, but a night in a hotel, and being away from being a wife or mother is just what I need right now. I don't care how hard the bed is, I just need time alone.' Cynthia might still be smiling but there was a cold quality to her words that made Susie shiver.

'Is everything okay?'

Cynthia's smile looked like it had been drawn on by a child with far less talent than any artist.

'Everything always sounds so brilliant in your annual Christmas letters.'

Cynthia gave a small snort. 'Let's do lunch soon, yes? We can talk properly then. I think we have a lot to catch up on. Especially if you've taken up needle-felting.'

No point in mentioning felting was probably not something Susie was likely to feel the need to return to anytime soon, even if she could take a picture of her little felt hare and use it in her own Christmas letter.

On the other side of the room there was a lot of laughter, one laugh pitched higher than all the rest. Someone was trying to make a point. Susie didn't need to turn, but as if one, they both turned, looked, then turned back and giggled at each other. 'Do you really think she's making a play for Alan?' Susie whispered.

There was lots to talk about. In the intervening forty-something years between school and now, everybody had done something they wanted to share loudly and at the same time. The volume was high. Cynthia had decided that after every course, everyone should change places. She'd numbered each place and in the centre of the table was a pot filled with numbered squares of paper. Everyone had to take a piece of paper and the number on the seat was where they should be sitting for the next course. She wiggled the other pot and made sure everyone put their numbers back in. 'Just take your glass,' she said. Susie was impressed by the way everyone did what they were told, but it meant for the main course she was sitting beside Alan.

'Enjoying it?' he asked.

'More than I thought I would,' she said, putting down her glass. 'So far, so good.'

'Oh, me too.' He nodded enthusiastically, taking a large mouthful of what looked like some sort of punch.

The volume inside the room seemed to rise with each course as more and more alcohol was consumed.

'Any plans for this year?' he asked without turning his head. A slight slur to his words probably meant that glass of punch wasn't his first or probably not his second.

'What, you mean like a zip wire across the slate mines of Wales?'

'Yes,' he said dreamily, clearly not listening to a word she was saying.

'Well, I've applied to become a test driver for space hoppers.' She took another mouthful of her main course. The food was good. She just wished she was sharing a meal with Bob, or Tara, even Max, just not Alan-bloody-sodding-Wheeldon and her former classmates.

'Right,' he said, his eyes firmly focused on Lucy Miller.

'Then I'm thinking of becoming a clairvoyant,' she said nonchalantly.

'Oh, that is good.' Alan was openly staring across the table. His eyes bulged and his mouth hung open. Lucy, opposite, was laughing with a bald man wearing a small goatee. Clive. Back at school, Clive had been practically strawberry blond.

Susie had sat next to him during starters. He'd been good company, telling her how, having left at the end of the fifth form, he'd joined his father's company. Something along the lines of swimming pools and hot tubs. It had taken him abroad and he now divided his time between Spain and England with his wife. Then he'd started moaning about Brexit and the problems that had caused him, and Susie had been glad when the plates had been cleared until she realized who she'd be sitting next to for the next course.

Alan had hardly touched his meal. People were still helping themselves to seconds. There was no chance this course would be over anytime soon.

Susie reached for her handbag and wiggled her chair back to give herself enough room to stand up. Suddenly, Alan lifted his baseball cap and scratched his head. She stood very still, hoping he wouldn't turn and notice her. He didn't. She must've stood still for at least a minute before she dared to move.

Okay, look casual.
Everyone will assume they know where you're going and won't ask.
Walk slowly.

The narrow corridor was well lit and thankfully empty. She passed the toilets, hoping no one was on their way out, and without looking back, left through the back door. Everything had been paid in advance, so she wasn't leaving anyone in the lurch. She realized she'd been holding her breath as the door closed behind her. Never had any service yard looked quite so appealing.

CHAPTER SEVENTEEN

Susie was engulfed in a hug, first from Maddie and then Josh as soon as she'd walked through the front door to Bob Diamond's house.

'You're back,' she said. 'Silly thing to say, of course you are. You're cooking supper this evening.' They laughed and took the bottle of wine she held out. There was a sparkle in both their eyes. Susie didn't think she'd ever seen two people as much in love as these two.

'Come along,' Maddie grinned. 'I'm dying to know what's happened in the last six weeks . . .'

'Seven,' corrected Josh. 'And before you ask Susie about the office, remember we agreed we're not talking about anything work related until Monday.'

Maddie led her back into the kitchen and Josh went over to the hob where a large bowl-shaped dish was cooking, full of what looked like yellow rice. 'Jambalaya,' he said, by way of explanation.

'Hardly a Los Angeles delicacy.' Poppy waved from the other side of the kitchen. 'According to your recipe book it's a Louisiana favourite,' she said. 'I thought when you said "American evening" we'd be having cheeseburger and fries, or pizza.'

'We're saving the Los Angeles speciality for dessert.' Josh laughed. He took a small spoonful of the dish and handed it to Maddie: 'Try this.'

'Ice-cream sandwiches,' Maddie mumbled as she tried the spoonful. 'That's really good.' She waved the now empty spoon at Poppy. 'Don't knock them until you've tried them. Your brother introduced them to me when we were over there last year, and I haven't looked back.'

'Take a seat.' Josh pulled a stool out from under the worktop. 'Dad's just walking Miss Phyllis. He'll be back shortly.'

'He better be,' Maddie said. 'The jambalaya is so almost ready.'

'Has he mentioned yet that he has a woman?' Poppy asked, walking across to the cooker.

'No,' all three of them said at the same time.

'How can you be certain?' a voice asked from behind Susie that sent a tingle careering up her spine.

If Poppy hadn't been so intent on tasting the pot, she might've heard Bob enter the room or realize it wasn't Josh speaking.

'He's turned really weird lately,' she said mid-mouthful of the rice mixture. 'He's never here and if he is, he goes all soppy as soon as his phone rings. If I ask him about it, he makes some excuse about wanting to talk to a man about a car. He won't even tell me what car.'

'Pot, kettle, black.'

Poppy spun round. 'Dad.'

'How this young lady has any idea as to what is going on with me, is frankly beyond me.' Bob slipped on to a stool next to Susie. 'Her head these days is so high up in the clouds. Do you know one of the mechanics the other day asked me if she was all right because she's started singing at work.'

'Poppy singing at work — now you have got me worried.' Josh removed the spoon from Poppy's hand before she could use it as a weapon or take another spoonful of food. 'We don't want you ruining your appetite.'

'Don't change the subject,' Poppy laughed. 'We're talking about Dad, not me.'

'You were talking about me, but we're all far more interested in what, or should I say who, is going on in your life. By the way, I've just let Tony in.'

Poppy blushed scarlet.

'Touched a nerve, have I?' Bob asked.

'Tony. Not Tony Longworth? Why is he here?' Josh looked genuinely confused.

'I'm guessing, but I suspect he's been invited to supper.' Susie looked at Poppy for confirmation.

Poppy's slight movement of her head, Bob clearly took as a nod. 'Good,' he said. 'I've opened the gate to the yard for him, so he can park up. He'll be through in a second.'

Susie remembered Tony from the meal at TOTU. He and Poppy had seemed quite infatuated with each other then. Clearly, things hadn't cooled since.

'Great, I could do with a catch-up,' Josh said.

Bob poured the wine into two glasses on the worktop and slid one across to Susie with a smile. 'I didn't see your car. Did you walk?'

Susie nodded. His dark eyes held hers for a second. 'It's not far. I enjoyed it. It's a lovely evening.'

'In that case, Miss Phyllis and I will happily walk you home later. To make sure you get back safely.'

'Or Josh and I can drop her off,' Maddie said. 'It's not far out of our way.'

Bob frowned momentarily. For a second Susie thought he might argue. 'I'd love the walk, if that's okay,' she said. 'It'll do me good to walk off supper.'

'I'll go and find Tony.' Josh looked at Maddie.

'Remember, no talk about work until Monday,' she said. 'I hope you're not going to spend all night making Tony relive every last minute since we went away.'

'What do you take me for?' He gave the pan on the stove another stir and handed the wooden spoon to Maddie. 'Five minutes, that's all.'

Susie couldn't tell from the look on Poppy's face whether she was pleased or not.

'Well, if he's going to talk about work,' Maddie said, 'then so am I. What's happened at the Register Office since I've been away?'

'Don't you want to wait for Luke?'

'He rang earlier — one of the children has an ear infection, so he's not coming. It's just you,' Maddie said. 'And Tony. So come on, spill the beans.'

'Well, obviously we missed you and fell completely apart the moment you left the country. The council had to call in the army to help with the backlog of work that we created in those first three weeks, while we were all lying on the floor waving our legs in the air and throwing tantrums and moaning about being directionless.'

'I'd have paid good money to see that,' Bob muttered from behind his glass of wine. Susie was glad the others were laughing and appeared not to have heard, otherwise there was every danger she would flush the same colour as Poppy.

'How's the Christmas letter coming on?' Maddie asked, handing Poppy placemats and Bob crockery, and telling them to set the table.

Susie told them about the disastrous school reunion.

'You ran away?' Maddie laughed.

'Not ran exactly,' Susie said. 'And I have made my peace with Cynthia.' She'd rung the next day and apologized for not saying goodbye. 'And I'm going to Bath for a shopping trip and lunch with her the first Saturday in June,' she added. 'We have a lot to catch up on, so it will be good to do it properly.'

She didn't add that she'd been left feeling that Cynthia, although still an attractive woman, seemed to be juggling a handful of neuroses with Prozac, and, until recently, alcohol. She didn't know whether it would be appropriate to ask, but it didn't sound as if life was quite as rosy as it was painted in the Bailey's letters.

Cynthia had done incredibly well at university. Then gone on to get a doctorate in wastewater before teaching at the same university. For a while, Susie had the impression she'd been the go-to expert in her field. She hadn't married until she'd been in her mid-thirties.

Something she'd said at the reunion suggested she'd stopped work when she had the children, which surprised Susie. Cynthia had made light of it, but an expression that passed briefly over her face suggested that might not be the whole truth.

'You never had children of your own?' Cynthia asked.

'No,' Susie said. 'Terry already had two when we met.'

'And I suppose he'd already had a vasectomy?' Cynthia pushed. 'He was that much older than you, wasn't he?'

'Something like that.' Susie shot her a fake smile over her drink.

'Didn't you want your own children?'

'I never really considered it,' Susie lied, wishing Cynthia would drop the subject. Of course she'd wanted her own children. Most women did. But they didn't happen. Max was eleven when she was first introduced to him. And Jodie thirteen. She'd been warned about the terrible teens, raging hormones, pushing boundaries, and tried to be tolerant. A weekend with them in the early days had been more than enough. She was always glad when they could hand them back on a Sunday night, and she could get back to work on a Monday morning and deal with adults again. People told her that they'd grow out of it. They were wrong. As Max and Jodie got older they seemed to get even more bolshy and unpleasant, treating her more as an unpaid hired help than anything else. Life became ever more expensive with increasing demands for driving lessons, help with student loans, holidays, cars, wedding presents, deposits for houses, grandchildren. Neither of them had had invites to Max's last two weddings. And only Terry was invited to his first.

She wasn't surprised that Max was giving her a hard time about Terry's will. In his fifty years he'd never missed an opportunity to tap his dad for cash, even if that was often the only contact they had. Susie had always made sure to send cards and gifts for every birthday, but in the last twenty years they'd rarely visited. It hadn't seemed to bother Terry. He didn't seem to recognize either of them when they did. He'd be polite — he always was. Smile and ask them how they were, but with the same sort of interest he'd show in passing strangers rather than beloved family members. Susie sighed.

'Everything okay?' Maddie asked.

'Yes, sorry. I was miles away. Anything I can do?'

'Perhaps . . .' Maddie glanced up at the clock. 'Could you round up Josh and Tony . . .'

'I'll do that,' Poppy said and shot out of the room before anyone could stop her.

'In that case . . .' Maddie watched Poppy go, 'can you stir this, and I'll finish laying the table?' She grinned at Susie. 'That's a girl in love!' She stopped. 'So, no problems at work?'

'None.' Susie frowned. 'As I keep telling you, woman.'

Maddie laughed. 'I know, I know.'

'Except we all missed you and are glad you'll be back next week. Luke has blocked out an extra hour for Monday morning's meeting so we can hear all about the States. And don't have breakfast — we've all been tasked with bringing cake.'

Josh came back, closely followed by Tony and Poppy who seemed to be sharing a joke.

'Come on,' he said, 'let's sit and eat.'

It was a lovely meal. Susie laughed a lot. Josh and Maddie relived their journey and when one of them stopped for breath, the other carried on the sentence. Sometimes a memory would make them giggle and it would be difficult to understand exactly what they were trying to say, but the more they laughed, the more everyone else did too, so it really didn't matter. It felt like Susie imagined family meals should feel. Good food, great company. She helped Bob clear the table between courses and Josh's ice-cream sandwiches were a huge hit.

By the time Bob helped her into her coat and she'd said goodbye to everyone, she was totally stuffed and her sides ached from laughing so much. It had been a lovely evening.

Maddie and Josh were still chatting to Poppy and Tony. Bob slipped on a jacket and whistled Miss Phyllis, who appeared instantly.

'Did you ever do anything about the off-roading courses in Wales?' Susie asked as they walked back to the town centre, companionably side-by-side. The evening was warm despite it being May. The threatened overnight low temperatures hadn't materialized yet.

'My first one's in a couple of weeks' time,' Bob said. 'Then the other two are about a month apart. All booked and paid for. Not quite sure how I'm going to explain them to Josh and Poppy.'

'You'll think of something. You're definitely going?'

'Deposit paid, so all being well. What about you? Busy weekend ahead?' Bob asked as they crossed the main road, Miss Phyllis walking obediently between them.

'I'm helping out at Treetops Nursing Home on Sunday,' she said. 'And I'm doing an Introduction to Mediumship course tomorrow morning at the college.'

Susie felt Bob falter slightly next to her and stuck out a hand to help.

'Are you going to tell me you believe in life after death? Spirits telling you what to do, and where to find their missing millions.'

'It's all in the interests of research, and I'm keeping an open mind,' Susie said. 'Well, until after tomorrow anyway. What about you? I understand you're on a dating website. Any interesting offers?'

When Poppy had mentioned the dating website at supper, Susie had been surprised by the sudden burning sensation in her chest. Not heartburn. The evening had been lovely up until then. She'd enjoyed the easy banter and the teasing, but the thought of Bob on a dating website had been painful. She hoped she'd disguised it well, laughing along with the others, but her feelings were mixed. If this was jealousy, she didn't like it.

Bob was an attractive man. She felt things for him that she hadn't felt for a long, long time, but they were both hurting, and she was racked with feelings of guilt every time her insides did a little jump or performed some sort of intricate gymnastic manoeuvre because she'd seen him, heard him or even, these days, just thought about him. She should be in mourning. Queen Victoria had been in black for the rest of her life, although if the film on telly the other night had been anything to go by, then she did have other liaisons. Susie shuddered. Terry had only been dead seven months.

Towards the end of last year, Susie had attended a bereavement course. Not because she was incredibly sad, but just because she wasn't sure how she should be feeling.

'Grief can be a heavy weight to carry around,' the counsellor had said sympathetically when Susie had rung to talk about counselling. 'Think of it as a rucksack you're taking on a journey. Then one day you'll feel like you've maybe left it somewhere — you're no longer overburdened with it.'

Susie wasn't sure that would be a comfort. She'd left a handbag once in a restaurant and had been frantic until they were reunited.

The counsellor explained patiently that Susie and Terry's relationship had changed dramatically from married couple to that of carer and patient. Susie hated that thought. She'd loved Terry, always had. They'd been partners. Lifelong friends.

'All marriages change over time. Friendship replaces passion. Lust can develop into love,' the counsellor said. 'Yours just changed more significantly and earlier than most.'

There had been six of them on the course. Five of them had lost someone recently, although one of those was a dog. The sixth woman appeared to have got mixed up between bereavement and poetry. When it was explained to her that she was on the wrong course and could swap, she'd said, 'No, you're all right. I'll stay. You seem like an interesting bunch.'

When Susie and Terry got together, their age difference had worried him. He was sure he'd go first, but neither of them had expected he'd go so soon. His retirement from work had coincided with the beginnings of his dementia, so they never had the chance to travel the world or explore. Or at least he didn't. She owed it to him to make the most of the rest of her life.

Occasionally, in the last few years, he'd remembered her name and would smile at her. On those occasions she'd convince herself that he did understand, but then he'd say something completely off the wall, often referring to some event in his distant past that she had never been a part of. His smile still melted her heart, and in those last few months a smile felt like a prize. A real honour, as he bestowed so few. Those days were the times that had kept her going. She thought once he'd died she would start to do the things they'd always promised each other they would. Travel more. She wanted to see the world. He told her once that whoever went first, once they had come to terms with the death of the other, they shouldn't stay single for ever unless they wanted to. 'Not actively look,' he added. 'Well, not unless you want to. But be open to opportunities.'

Bob was a year ahead of her in the grieving process and his family seemed to be pushing him to move on by registering him on a dating app. Historically, he was through the black phase and should be embracing purple. Although from his fashion sense, it seemed no one had thought to tell him as much. He was dressed that evening, as usual, in his trademark black leather jacket and jeans.

The bereavement counsellor had asked one of the women what her feelings were about a new partner and she'd laughed. 'I've just got rid of one. I'm not ready to be saddled with another.' Susie had smiled. She felt the same in some ways, but there was something about Bob Diamond that made her feel alive.

'I'm not suggesting any of you rush into anything,' the counsellor said, 'but don't rule anything out. You will go through all sorts of emotions   that's part of the grieving process. Don't push people away and you might be surprised.' Surprised? Susie was bloody amazed.

When she first met Terry, she'd been blown away by his good looks and the way he made life fun. She couldn't believe he'd been interested in her. He'd joined the company as a senior manager with a wealth of experience. She was still young and naive. There was a moment in their first costing meeting, when somebody said something ridiculous but didn't notice. She was busy biting her lip and trying not to laugh when Terry caught her eye — his eyes were sparkling too.

'Excuse me,' he'd said, standing up. 'Another meeting. Let me know the outcome.' And he'd left the room. Two minutes later one of the receptionists came in and asked her if she could take a telephone call that was urgent. She'd made her excuses and left the meeting too. Terry was waiting for her in reception and laughed. 'I thought you might need saving,' he'd said. In the next forty years, they'd laughed a lot.

The laughter and friendship was what she had missed most in those last ten years of her marriage.

Bob made her laugh too. She hoped they were friends. There was nothing wrong with friendship, and maybe a mild flirtation would be okay after all. Neither of them was ready for any more than that. She sighed.

'Penny for them,' Bob said as they reached the traffic lights. He pressed the button, and they stood waiting for the green man.

He looked concerned. Susie smiled. 'I'm not sure they're worth that much,' she said.

He frowned. 'Something was on your mind.'

'Okay. Okay, I was just wondering exactly what your dating profile says?'

'You know, usual sort of thing. Self-made millionaire with a sense of adventure ready to have some fun. Got a valid passport? Then get in touch.'

'What happens now?'

'Hopefully, in a day or two's time, they will have forgotten all about it again. They set it up earlier in the year, but they can't get into my profile anymore. To be honest, I'm not sure I can either. I changed my password. Well, I asked Rick, my new apprentice to do it. The last thing I want is Poppy or Josh interfering.'

'Won't they want to know why you haven't done anything?'

'Those two? No, they're too wrapped up with their own relationships at the moment.'

'Why don't you tell them you've met someone. That it's early days, but you want to give it a go before you go on a dating website?'

Susie didn't see the lights change, but the beeping noise suggested it was time for them to cross the road. They were almost home. She didn't want the walk to end.

'No way.' Bob raised his eyes. 'I'd never hear the last of it. They'd want to know every last detail.'

'How about you say you met her at the heart clinic? You were both waiting for the results of some tests and got talking. It's early days and you're both playing it cool, but you want to see how it plays out before you start looking around.'

'She'd need to have a name.'

'Jean sounds about the right age. And if she came from Wales then you'd have an excuse for visiting Wales for the off-roading courses. After you finish them, just tell them it didn't work out and you decided to go your separate ways. Or, if you love the off-roading so much that you want to do other courses, you can carry on visiting her. Maybe if Poppy and Josh think there is someone, they won't ask too many questions about you disappearing off for a weekend.'

'I wish,' Bob laughed. 'You don't know my kids. Okay, let's say I decide to tell them about "Welsh Jean". How can we make her convincing?' They'd reached the end of Susie's road. Bob stopped. 'Miss Phyllis could probably do with a quick run round the park. I don't suppose you've got time . . .?'

Susie liked the "we" and yes, she had time. She nodded and her smile got bigger.

'Jean would need a back story,' she said. 'Like why she was in a heart clinic in Redford. Maybe she's moved to Wales recently to be with her family, following her heart attack. That's why you hadn't met her before.'

'Wouldn't they have transferred her medical notes up there? It's a hell of a way to come back to get results . . .'

'Her decision. She liked the doctor. And you've offered to help put up some shelves or decorating, that's why you're going up for the whole weekend. She's off dating because she's been ghosted and is fed up of getting pictures of naked torsos. And dick pics.'

Bob looked at her. 'You're teasing me. Men don't really send pictures of their . . . you know . . . to potential dates these days, do they?'

Susie looked at him. 'You should talk to Tara. My pole-dancing teacher. Apparently it's a minefield out there. I'm glad I'm not looking for anyone. I'm much more old-school. I like conversation and face-to-face meetings. Whether or not they've been circumcised comes quite a long way down the list of questions I want answers to.'

Bob chuckled. 'I'd need contact details for Welsh Jean. What can I tell them about her? Even if they don't want to know her shoe size and entire medical history, I'll need to have a mobile number at least to be convincing.'

'Store my number in your phone as Jean. That way, from time to time you can send me a text or give me a call. Just let me know when you're going to be away and I can always send appropriate texts. You know, "Looking forward to seeing you" or "Drive carefully", that sort of thing.'

Bob smiled, but his smile didn't reach his eyes. Susie wished she could read his feelings. Had she gone too far?

CHAPTER EIGHTEEN

Susie walked through the park again the following morning on her way to the college, still buoyant after last night. Bob had made her laugh again. Even with the walk round the park, they'd reached her house too soon, and she'd wished they could have just gone on walking and talking. It had felt good. She'd been about to invite him in for a nightcap when Maddie and Josh had driven up. They were on their way home and wanted their dog back. They offered Bob a lift back to the garage.

He'd dropped a kiss on Susie's cheek and looked into her eyes. 'I'll see you soon,' he said.

She'd put her hand up to stroke her cheek, as she watched them drive away. 'I hope so,' she murmured.

The Introduction to Mediumship course was apparently designed to help unlock her psychic abilities and connect with the spirit world. She'd enrolled on it mainly to upset Max. She looked down at the page she'd printed out from the details the college had sent.

One of the issues Max had thrown at her was that he was sure his father had meant to change his will. She had no doubt that as soon as the DNA results were back, whatever comparisons were made, he'd be in touch because Terry had apparently told him that he'd asked Susie to make better provision for his children, and clearly she was going against his wishes.

With a mediumship course under her belt, even just a one-day one, then perhaps she could look him in the eye and say she was learning how to communicate with the spirits who have passed over, and Terry's spirit came back loud and clear, and said "Bollocks, Max".

It had been listed in the summer-term prospectus as an alternative therapy course. She'd been about to throw the prospectus away. The *Learn how to start to contact the departed, on behalf of others, and channel your psychic powers to enhance and enrich your life and world* had caught her eye. But this morning, the college looked decidedly locked. No queue of people waiting to get in. Only a handful of cars parked outside and, so far, there'd been no need to duck to avoid the incoming covens of witches on broomsticks. In fact, she was the only one standing in the car park. She checked the details on the email again. She was in the right place, or at least within a few metres of the what3words location the email had provided. The date was right. The time was right.

Definitely no one around. Which raised several questions about the competency of the tutor. Shouldn't a true psychic have noticed her standing in an empty car park on a Saturday morning and sent some sort of message. Maybe they had. Maybe Susie just wasn't ready to start receiving them yet hadn't managed to open her channels far enough. Bollocks to Max anyway. She should've gone for an online one. Most of those had been free as long as you didn't mind receiving shed loads of junk email for the rest of your life.

The college didn't look to be closed permanently. There was nothing to indicate it had shut down on the door. She hoped it hadn't because next month she planned on joining the "Make a Dress in a Day" course too, and she'd already sourced a pattern and material for that. As a child, she'd been quite handy with a sewing machine and had made several outfits — most she'd rather not remember.

She set off to walk round the college — perhaps it was in a room at the back.

Secondary school and the wearing of uniform had been a real breakthrough for her. She'd loved it, even if it was grey. It meant that whatever she wore was the same as other children, and she was no longer singled out or laughed at for her homemade knickers. Her mother had let her wear knee-length socks for the first time, although to be fair, they had usually bunched round her ankles by the end of assembly.

She wished her mother hadn't let her go to a teenage party wearing a long lavender seersucker skirt with a frill and a gathered waist that she'd made, which her mother had told her she looked lovely in. She'd spent the evening standing in the corner, sipping Pomagne, while feeling like a fancy crocheted toilet-roll cover.

It had been her father who'd come to her rescue when he'd picked her up, and she'd cried all the way home. He took her shopping for a proper dress and gave her a dress allowance in addition to her pocket money. She missed his wisdom and kindness.

Back at the front, she rattled the door again. Definitely locked, and no one answered when she pushed the bell at the side for a second time.

Face it. It ain't happening, girl. Old Susie would probably go home and do an hour's housework to get over the disappointment, but new Susie now had a free day and was two minutes' walk from the station. She'd catch the first train somewhere and explore wherever it was that she ended up. She stood in the queue at the station for train tickets and wondered how she could put a positive spin on this latest experience.

Mediumship course not as successful as I hoped. Clearly my inner psychic isn't ready to be channelled, or my channels aren't clear enough — no news from Terry.

CHAPTER NINETEEN

'This is what they call a gastro pub these days then,' Bob said.

Freddie nodded enthusiastically. 'At least the food's supposed to be good. Jenny has been on at me for ages to try it.'

The centre of the conservatory area had been cleared and there was a small stage set up, with a mic and what looked like a television screen. 'Apparently, you always have to book on karaoke nights,' Jenny said. 'If you want to eat.'

Bob didn't mind the eating bit, it was the singing bit he wasn't sure he was fully committed to. He glanced down at the large unyielding A3 sheet of paper they had all been given, as Norman Fairchild slipped into the chair opposite.

Freddie slapped him on the back. 'You made it, mate,' he said delightedly.

Norman's expression mirrored Bob's own, but they shook hands across the table and Norman planted a kiss on Jenny's face.

'I was in two minds,' Norman said. 'Part of me kept checking the calendar wondering if it was some sort of April Fool's prank, just a bit later than usual.'

'Sadly, no,' Bob said. 'Freddie was bloody determined.'

A waitress hovered by their table and Norman asked for a lager shandy while Freddie said they'd be ready to order food when she came back.

'Let's get one thing clear from the off,' Norman said. 'I don't care how much money we're offered, I'm not singing "You're the One That I Want" with either of you. No way. Never. Agreed?' He looked up, his hands flat against the table.

Bob smiled for the first time that evening. He recalled that bloody wedding reception too. 'We were an all-male group,' he said. 'I still can't understand why they insisted on that song.'

'Something to do with Freddie Flash Sticks over there, insisting we knew the song from *Grease*.'

'The one about the cars,' Freddie said. 'I didn't say we knew them all.'

The waitress took their orders. Burger and chips in several different ways.

'I couldn't find The General,' Freddie said. 'I tried his place, but it looks shut up. Maybe he's dead.'

'We'd have heard, wouldn't we?' Jenny, his wife said. 'The press like nothing better than a good funeral.'

'Probably,' Norman said.

'He used to be one of your clients, didn't he?' Bob asked Norman.

Norman shook his head. 'Can't divulge confidential information. The law society would have me hung, drawn and quartered. I'd never work again.'

'If you'd been hung, drawn and quartered,' Freddie said, matter-of-factly, 'wouldn't work be the last thing you needed to worry about?'

Norman took a sip of his drink. 'Figuratively speaking,' he said. 'What's this about a reunion?'

'Will you or will you not help us find The General?' Freddie asked.

'Not,' said Norman, firmly.

'If he is one of your clients, can't you ask him to get in touch with Freddie?' Jenny asked.

Their food order arrived, as did the announcement from the barman that the karaoke was now open. Two girls made a rush for the stage and made a passable rendition of a number that Bob recognized as being by Wham!

Norman took a large bite from his burger and chewed it thoughtfully. 'If he was one of my clients,' Norman said, 'and assuming I was in possession of a letter that had been addressed to him and marked personal, I would be obliged to pass that letter on.' He took another mouthful. Freddie looked about to say something, but Bob saw Jenny reach for his arm. When he turned, she nodded at him. 'Don't push him,' she said. 'And shut up. That's Daisy and Vicky up there.'

Once Daisy and Vicky had finished, Freddie, Norman and Jenny stood up and cheered. The women bowed, and seeing as they were still standing there when the next song started, they sang that too. When they'd finished, they passed the table and stopped to chat.

'Daisy's my beautician,' Jenny said, sitting back down at the table. 'The woman completely responsible for my looks and everlasting beauty.' She glanced at Bob who smiled. He might've been widowed nearly two years now, but still recognized when a remark was designed to draw a compliment.

'I hope you're paying her well,' he said. 'She's clearly worth every penny.'

Jenny laughed and forked up her last lump of coleslaw. 'How was your burger?'

'Good,' he said. And it had been. 'Thanks for the recommendation.' Out of the corner of his eye he saw Freddie approaching the stage. 'What's he doing?' he asked.

'Ladies and gentlemen, excuse the interruption.' Freddie was talking into the mic, while the barman fiddled with something below the television screen. 'But for one night only, possibly never to be repeated, you are about to experience something completely original. You may have heard your parents, or in your case, darling, your grandparents . . .'

'Oh, God,' Jenny said. 'Why did I ever think he'd just get on the stage and sing a bloody song?'

'. . . talk about the best group in the world. Well, Redford, they're back. Put your hands together for the one and only Brothers in Boxers — or at least, most of them.' Freddie started clapping loudly, and Bob was amused to see that quite a few others joined in. It sounded like people were stamping their feet. He looked at Norman who was in full eye-rolling mode, but they both rose and walked to the stage, muttering 'I'll kill him' and 'Not if I get to him first' under their breaths.

Freddie did something to the small computer on stage, then stood back as the opening bars of "Hotel California" started.

Bob and Norman nodded to each other. 'Just the one song, then we kill him?'

CHAPTER TWENTY

Bath was a place Susie often considered visiting but had never got around to. She'd taken the train from Redford in the end. The journey gave her time to read through the guidebook. She'd always wanted to see the Roman Baths and the abbey looked impressive. She wondered what Cynthia had planned. It was certainly busy and as she walked through the town centre — she was amazed to see how many people were there. She felt like a tourist, checking the directions on her phone and looking in awe at all the Georgian architecture and the elegant Bath-stone buildings. She wished she'd arrived earlier and had more of a chance to explore, but Fiona had asked if she could spare an hour to help with breakfast at Treetops. She'd sounded desperate when she rang at six that morning. For a moment, Susie had toyed with not answering the phone.

'I wouldn't have called, but the locum agency isn't open until eight and I didn't know who else I could ring,' she'd said when Susie did pick up.

George had been surprisingly cheerful when she arrived, despite that morning's staffing problems.

'The summer musical has been put back to December,' he said. 'Hallelujah.'

'Why?' Susie asked.

'Reggie's request. I guess he realized the enormity of the task, especially as Edna and several others are insisting that if we're doing a musical, it has to be *Oklahoma!* and they won't take part in anything else.'

'Really?'

'Her favourite musical apparently. She saw it in London many years ago when Howard Keel was playing the lead.'

'Reggie's not keen?'

'He's got a point. There are a lot of dance numbers, and the performing rights are restricted this year. Let's just say negotiations are still underway. Edna's not entirely happy, but I've told them they need to reach a compromise and remember it's for everyone's entertainment. Then this morning, out of the blue, Reggie's announced he's planning on going away for the Verona opera season and is likely to be away for at least a month, but he hopes to have reworked the script for *The Best Little Whorehouse*, in line with his discussions with Edna, by the time he gets back, ready for serious rehearsals.'

Susie nodded. 'He told me that trip's on hold.'

'No.' George groaned. 'Please don't tell me that.'

'He can't go without a carer. They don't have enough people to look after him.'

'I go once every ten years,' Reggie had told her, when she'd checked the lounge for stray residents. 'But this year I had to tell them about my medical condition and the wheelchair.'

'Do you need to take the wheelchair?' Susie tidied away a few stray cushions.

'Too damn right. Get priority seating on the plane. Normally it's not a problem. This year, they're blaming Covid and said they can't accommodate me unless I bring a carer. I don't suppose you fancy a month in Verona?'

'Tempting as it sounds,' Susie had laughed, 'I am a working woman.'

He'd nodded but Susie noticed his eyes had dulled and his chin wobbled as he looked down at his hands. For the first time she thought he looked old and had felt guilty ever since, especially when he hadn't appeared for breakfast. She wished she'd had more time to check on him, but she was on a tight schedule this morning. She was meeting Cynthia at quarter-past-ten.

Susie stopped by Pulteney Bridge and admired it. Her guidebook said it was Palladian style. It was stunning. Terry would have loved it. If only they'd had more time to explore together.

She had no idea what Cynthia had got planned for them, but there were a lot of things she hoped they'd have time to stop and look at properly. "Girl's day out" Cynthia had said. That could mean just about anything. In their school days, it usually meant a cinema visit and a trip to the local pizzeria.

There were several museums and galleries she'd like to see. Possibly some interesting shops too. Food was obviously involved — she'd had an email from Cynthia earlier in the week telling her that they were booked for brunch at the Pump Room. She checked her watch. She had five minutes before she was officially late, and according to Google, it was going to take her four minutes to get there. She sped up.

Cynthia was already seated at one of the tables, set for two, when she arrived.

The place was smaller and more compact than she'd imagined. Only a handful of tables, but all of them occupied.

Cynthia waved. Clearly, she'd been watching the door.

The waiter took the folded serviette from the table and pulled out a chair but had to wait until they exchanged hugs.

'How was your night in the hotel?' Susie asked, sitting down. 'You know, following the reunion. Did many stay?'

'Alan was there until late. He kept asking about you.'

'I thought it was Lucy Miller he was interested in.' Susie grinned. 'I hope they'll be happy together. Did he take off his baseball hat?'

Cynthia shook her head. 'Now you come to mention it, no he didn't. Do you think he's got some sort of disease?'

It was Susie's turn to shake her head. 'Only if comb-overs can be classified as a disease.'

'You are joking?'

'I wasn't drinking, and I know what I saw when he lifted his hat to scratch his head. I'm telling you, I saw that he had a good foot of hair, wound in a coil on top of his head, before he put his hat back on. Thankfully, he was too busy ogling Lucy to see that I'd noticed.'

'Do you think he takes his hat off when he has sex?'

'That's something I'm thankful I'm never going to be able to answer.'

'I don't know.' Cynthia raised her eyebrows and started to read the menu. 'I think he'd like to hear from you.'

'I don't care. He gives me the creeps.'

'He could get a haircut. Maybe I'll ring and suggest it.'

'Doesn't reduce the creepiness. Don't bother.'

They giggled, and as if they'd pushed a call bell, the waiter suddenly appeared back at their side to take their order.

'Tell me about you,' Susie said, once she'd ordered a cheese scone and a cup of English breakfast tea.

Cynthia took a deep breath before she answered. The sort of deep breath that heralded bad news. 'Not great. Giles is planning on becoming an architect like his father. He's doing well at university and Kelly's got a place at Oxford Brookes next year, depending on her results. She's in a long-term relationship with Neil and they were talking at one time about a civil partnership, but I think they've decided to wait.'

'There are differences between marriage and a civil partnership,' Susie said. 'If they do decide that's a possibility, I'd be happy to talk to them. Just tell them to give me a ring — you've got my number.'

'Thanks.' Cynthia nodded. 'I forgot you're a registrar these days.'

'If it's not the kids making you look unhappy, I guess it's you and Alfie. Things not so great?'

'We have nothing in common,' Cynthia said, quietly fiddling with the edge of her beautifully crisp white serviette. 'He rarely comes home from work before eight-thirty or nine these days, and when he does, he goes straight into the office. And he doesn't even fold the towels in the bathroom once he's used them anymore. Do you remember that film with Julia Roberts years ago, where she had to disguise her appearance to escape from her husband because he was obsessed with straightening the towels in the bathroom?'

'I think there was slightly more to it than that, but yes, sort of.' Susie smiled.

Cynthia was still recognizable from their school days so she figured she wasn't just about to be told that she'd undergone extensive surgery so that Alfie wouldn't recognize her.

'He used to be a bit like that, but now, well, it's like he's had a complete personality change and it's the reverse in our house these days.' She was still fiddling with the napkin. 'It's me who folds the towels. We celebrated our pearl anniversary last year and this year we can't stand being in the same room together. I think he's having an affair.'

'Oh, God. I'm sorry.'

'I gave up everything for him.'

A career in sewage — everything.

'I can't ask him, because what if he says it's been going on for years and he's not going to give her up. Or worse, what if he says we're finished. What will happen to me then? I'll end up on my own, alone, and at only sixty-one, through no fault of my own. I haven't had an affair and it's not even as if I'll have a body to mourn.'

'Is that so bloody awful?' There was a steely undercurrent to Susie's tone. She was fighting very hard to keep her temper.

'Yes, of course it is. I wasn't born to live alone.' Then something registered. The penny dropped. The lemons lined up. 'Oh God, I'm sorry. I've put my foot in it haven't I?'

'Yes, I'd say.'

'I didn't mean . . .'

The cheese-and-chive scone arrival was timed to perfection. Or it would've been if Cynthia hadn't chosen that minute to burst into tears. She pushed her seat back and fled through an archway on one side of the room. Susie hoped she was heading to the loos and that she hadn't just been landed with the bill for two cheese-scone brunches.

The waiter's face remained expressionless as he poured her a cup of tea. She ate half her scone while she listened to the resident piano player.

Cynthia was back before she embarked on the second half, full of apologies. Her eyes were red. 'I just forgot,' she said, through sniffles. 'You're always so composed and lovely. And I do know how special Terry was to you. I used to be envious. Maybe I just need some time away from Alfie.'

'Where will you go and how long for?'

'I don't know. Nothing permanent. Just long enough for us both to realize that we've taken each other for granted for too long. What we've got should be great. I mean, it's not like money's an issue.'

'Glad to hear it.'

'We've just got stuck in a bit of a rut and need to climb out.' Cynthia finished her scone and pushed her plate to the centre of the table.

'How about a month away as a carer for a man in a wheel-chair who wants to visit the Verona opera one last time.' Susie forced a smile.

It was a joke. Just a throwaway comment. She hadn't really considered it worthy of conversation, but Cynthia wanted to know more. Apparently, a month in Italy might be just what she needed.

'I can afford to pay my own way,' she said, 'if you're worried about me taking advantage of him.'

That hadn't been on her mind — Susie couldn't imagine Reggie letting anyone take advantage of him. She remembered last weekend's nuclear-war practice. She'd arrived at Treetops to help on the Sunday, only to find George and Fiona run ragged.

In the lounge, the residents were watching the government's *Protect and Survive* instructional film from the 1970s telling them what to do if some foreign power announced they'd just launched a nuclear attack. There had been a government alert the day before. That had been what started it. Most peoples' mobiles had sounded at the same time. The alert had come with no instructions as to what to do if it happened for real, which Reggie did not think satisfactory.

'Four minutes,' he'd complained. 'In four minutes, we'll all be dead if we don't practise.' He'd set up a working party as soon as they were allowed back in the lounge.

Most of the residents seemed to have signed "Do Not Resuscitate" forms. They were all in the small office by the front door. But, far from agreeing that dropping dead was an option, now they all seemed determined to survive a nuclear attack.

According to Fiona, she and George had managed to stop the residents unscrewing the fire doors to make their refuges, only to find, subsequently, the minute they were left to their own devices they'd loosened all the screws again, so "it wouldn't take so long in a real emergency". The fire doors now needed to be checked daily and the storeroom checked for baked beans and tin openers, which the previous evening had to be retrieved from behind the chairs in the lounge.

'If that lot think they are going to sit under ripped-down doors in the lounge and eat baked beans for a fortnight . . .' George rubbed his head and sighed. 'I'm out of there at the first sound of any sirens.'

Susie had chuckled, but she'd been right with him. 'Is that why Violet is insisting on being wheeled around on a commode today?' she asked. 'It's quite a fancy one.'

'Arrived this morning. Another credit-card purchase. Her family will kill me. And that's why we've now added news reports to our banned television programmes list.'

This morning, he'd looked much happier at the thought of Reggie's extended trip, until Susie had mentioned it had been put on hold.

'Quite honestly, if there was seriously any way that man could go away for a month, while we get things back on an even keel, I'd contribute to his carer's costs. Are you sure you can't take the time off work? Didn't you say that your boss has just had a sabbatical? Doesn't that mean you can take one?'

'I've only been there a year. And it's coming up to our busiest season, so no, absolutely not.'

They finished their brunch and Cynthia slipped her hand through Susie's arm and asked if they could have a look at one of the dress shops that she'd read about in one of her women's magazines. She steered them through the crowds.

There was a brief lull in Cynthia's questions about Reggie while she tried on two outfits. Susie waited outside the changing rooms.

'What do you think?' Cynthia asked, pulling back the curtain and doing a quick spin.

Susie nodded at Cynthia. 'You look astounding in it.'

'Do you think it would be any good for Verona?'

'Verona?' Susie's phone vibrated with a new text. Her heart skipped.

J, Can I ring — 5 mins? Bx

Bob.

Please. She typed back. She didn't care if that sounded too eager.

'Something wrong?' Cynthia asked.

'Sorry.' Susie tried to maintain a serious face. 'Looks like a problem's come up back home. I'm going to have to call it a day.'

'What about Reggie?'

'I'll be at Treetops tomorrow afternoon. Why don't I find out if he's serious, and if he is, I'll ask him to give you a call?'

'Tell you what,' Cynthia said, 'why don't I meet you there? Then I can meet the man myself.' She stopped when she saw Susie staring at her. 'That won't be a problem, will it?'

Susie gave a quick shake of her head. 'No, it's fine. Look, sorry, I have to go.'

She practically ran from the shop and didn't look back. She'd come back to Bath another day to explore when she wasn't in danger of turning the corner and being caught out in her lie by Cynthia.

'Hello, darling,' Bob said. 'Have I interrupted something?'

'Bit over the top with the greeting,' Susie giggled. 'I hadn't realized our relationship had reached that stage yet. But no, you've got me out of a difficult situation, for which I'll be for ever grateful.'

'Glad to hear it.' She thought she could hear a smile in his voice. 'Where are you?'

'Bath — as in Somerset, not the bathroom.'

'Phew, thank goodness for that.'

'I'm fully clothed and making a speedy beeline for the train station. I'm guessing you're in company?'

'Great day, thanks,' he said. 'I'm really looking forward to next weekend.'

'Does that mean your off-roading course is happening soon?'

'I thought I'd head off about 10 a.m. It's a five-hour drive. I'll probably stop somewhere for a spot of lunch, but I should be with you by five, latest.'

'Sounds perfect,' Susie said. 'Should I ask you questions about your diet?'

'I don't think there's anything I won't eat.'

She smiled. He sounded like he was walking up and down. She wondered who was there. Probably Poppy. 'Drive carefully.'

'Thank you.'

'And Bob?'

'Yes, Su— Jean.'

'I hope it goes well.'

CHAPTER TWENTY-ONE

'Susie Keane, you are seriously the answer to all my dreams,' George said, walking across the Treetops lounge to meet her.

Susie laughed. 'I bet you say that to all the women.'

'He does.' Violet sniffed. 'Except Maisie, but she's got a UTI.'

'I didn't realize you were so shallow.' Susie grinned at George. 'Nice greeting, by the way. Was there something you needed me to do today that's particularly unpleasant and you're just trying to butter me up?'

'No,' he said. 'You've done everything I could possibly ask. Well, not you. Your friend. Reggie is going to Verona — hallelujah!'

'My friend . . .' Susie's voice tailed off as she realized what George had just said. There was only one person she'd mentioned Reggie's trip to Verona to. She'd told Cynthia where he lived, and vaguely mentioned meeting her here this afternoon. It was more an offhand remark than a considered conversation or a firm arrangement. She hadn't really expected Cynthia to turn up. 'You do mean Cynthia? Cynthia Bailey?'

'The one and same.' George squared up an untidy pile of magazines into the middle of the small table in the centre of the room. 'She breezed in like a breath of fresh air this morning. By the time tea was served, it sounded like all their plans were well and truly in place. Reggie won't be with us for nearly six weeks. In an ideal world, he'll realize that communal living isn't for him and return to his own house at the end of the trip. But we will keep his room for him until the end of September, just in case he misses us too much.'

Susie felt used. Cynthia had just gone behind her back and arranged it. What did she think her reaction was going to be? She didn't give a stuff who Cynthia went travelling with.

The aborted Bath trip had been difficult. She'd sent Cynthia a text afterwards, apologizing for having to dash off and thanking her for arranging things. She'd got one back immediately saying, "Must do it again sometime". She deleted it. She'd rather spend three hours felting another flaming March hare than listen to Cynthia telling her how lucky she was to have a dead husband. She couldn't remember why they'd lost contact before. They'd seen each other regularly through university whenever they'd been home. She supposed life just got in the way.

'Reggie thinks he's died and gone to heaven. A woman is accompanying him to Verona and paying her own way. She told him she could do with a break, and it was somewhere she'd always wanted to see.'

'Really.' Susie wouldn't have put Cynthia down as an opera lover. She remembered, even as a young girl, Cynthia had a thing about action movies. The bloodier, the better. She was the first one in their year to go and see *The Exorcist*. Cynthia's usual movie companions were boys. She rarely asked Susie if she wanted to go, knowing Susie was far happier with a group of the other girls who liked the gentler films. Even *Jaws* had been a step too far. She'd spent most of that movie with her eyes shut and her breath held and experienced sleepless nights for weeks afterwards.

Operas were usually depressing, weren't they? Didn't quite a few of the main characters expire in the arms of their beloved, or alone, after a particularly poignant lament?

Hardly the psychological thrillers that Cynthia enjoyed. Susie couldn't remember her ever being in the choir or the orchestra. She certainly didn't get involved with any of the school plays or musicals they put on. She was at a loss to know where Cynthia's sudden love for opera came from.

There were probably things that Cynthia didn't know about her as well. Like her longing to travel the world, or the zip-wire experience she had on her list of things to do. It wasn't just there because she wanted to impress her Christmas letter list.

These were things she wanted to do for herself. Maybe everybody understood that the Bailey's letter was just a sham. She'd certainly look at it in a very different light this Christmas.

She'd book the zip-wire experience when she got home. Cynthia may be going to Verona, but she was going to fly over the slate mines of Wales at over 100 mph.

'By the way. The battle of the musicals. Reggie won. We're putting on *The Best Little Whorehouse in Texas* at Christmas.'

'Edna gave in?'

George shrugged. 'She says they've come to a compromise. She's going to play Miss Mona's assistant at Christmas. We're going ahead with the original idea of a garden party at the end of this month. The local school are coming along to sing to the residents while they demolish cream teas outdoors, providing the weather's good enough, otherwise it will have to be in the conservatory.'

'The Christmas musical sounds fun.'

'Yes, but I've already received some comments about whether I think it is appropriate and I suspect I'll get more. I don't suppose you'd help me draft a letter to send out.'

George certainly looked a lot more relaxed.

'Okay. Talking of Reggie, where is he?' Susie asked.

'Cynthia took him out for lunch.' George blew her an air kiss. 'You really are the answer to all my dreams.'

'You sure you don't have a UTI?' Violet said, tugging at Susie's sleeve. 'Have you checked recently? Only, he'll go off you if you have.'

CHAPTER TWENTY-TWO

I've just hit reset on the Christmas letter fiasco. I should let you know that Cynthia's will be very exciting this year. She's headed off for the opera season in Verona, as carer for one of Treetops' residents. I volunteer there. Lovely bunch of residents and staff and we always have a great time. I hope that she'll take care of him. Reggie has a low boredom threshold and frequently gets himself into some amusing scrapes with the other residents. Victor has just discovered that Reggie's idea of editing all his old Super-8 movie collection was to splice them together. A serious collector of such things, Victor is currently distraught, but only at the nightly rum-shot stage, not tranquilizer stage yet. Still, it would probably be beneficial to the blood-pressure levels of all concerned if Reggie stayed away for at least six weeks.

The Introduction to Taxidermy course wasn't quite what I expected and probably not something I'll take any further. For a start, I don't know when I'd find the time to scour roadside verges for fresh roadkill. One of my relatives many years ago used to collect butterflies and mount them. I was reminded of this on the first evening when the tutor showed us a picture of a cat that he'd been fond of before death. And another after. The minute it popped off the mortal coil, he stuffed the thing. The trouble with giggling is that once you start, you can rarely stop – it becomes almost hysteria. Apparently, he found that upsetting.

I got a refund from the college when the Introduction to Mediumship course didn't happen. I was the only person booked on it and they hadn't foreseen the lack of interest.

My life-drawing tutor described my efforts as cubist. The model wasn't too pleased with my picture either.

The wedding season at the Register Office is underway and I'm tied up most weekends, although not in any kinky sort of way. Last week's wedding couple told me about the ballroom lessons they'd had in preparation for their first dance. There's a dance lesson that goes on at the local sports centre – ballroom for the over-fifties – and I've got my first session on Monday evening. I miss dancing and thought it might be fun. The week before, one of the weddings was a Comic Con-themed event. Really strange to see five Doctor Whos in the same room at the same time as a giant lobster, a Princess Leia lookalike and a Tardis. The Tardis was the best man.

School reunion was interesting, and it was fascinating to hear how everyone was doing these days. Someone did point out our next fiftieth reunion was unlikely to have the same number of attendees. Always look on the bright side!

CHAPTER TWENTY-THREE

'I've just had a bloody fantastic weekend,' Bob said, ruffling his hair and putting his gloves into his helmet. 'I wanted to say thanks and tell you that I'm definitely booked on the next two courses. Are you okay to continue the pretence?'

Susie looked at him blankly from her doorway.

'As my Welsh Jean?'

'Yes, that's fine.'

He knew he probably wasn't the sharpest tool in the box, but something wasn't right. He moved round until he stood in front of Susie. Her arms were crossed in front of her chest and she'd either been chopping onions — a lot of onions — or crying, judging by the state of her eyes.

He took a gentle hold on both her arms and pulled. She released them and let him lead her back into the house, where he sat her down on a chair and bent down until their eyes were on a level. 'What's wrong?'

She sniffed and he pulled a tissue from his pocket, hoping it was clean. She didn't check but dabbed her eyes. Tears were coming again.

'Right, don't move,' he said. He'd only been in her kitchen once before so it took a moment or two to locate the things needed to make a hot drink. He knew she drank tea. People say sweet drinks are best for shock so he added two heaped spoons of sugar and, as an afterthought, added another, then handed her the mug.

'I don't take sugar,' she said.

'You do now,' he said, adopting the same tone he used to use on the kids when he needed them to do something they didn't want to. She didn't argue but took a sip and winced.

'Now,' he said quietly, when the tea was half-drunk. 'I could tell you about my fabulous weekend, but I don't think until you get whatever it is off your chest, you will be fully engaged with that conversation. Why don't you tell me what's wrong — is it Max?' He felt his chest tighten. What on earth could he have done to make her react like this?

She shook her head. 'Not this time. It's Norman Fairchild.'

No, he couldn't imagine Norman upsetting anyone like that, not deliberately. Okay, his "Stairway to Heaven" riff might but Susie didn't look like she'd been subjected to that.

'The results are in from the DNA tests. I went to see Norman today. He gave me a letter from Terry.'

'Oh.' Bob waited — in these situations, silence was usually best.

'Max and Jodie aren't Terry's children,' Susie said. 'I knew that he had mumps as a child and there had been talk at the time that he might have problems later in life, but when Jodie and Max came along, he didn't think any more of it.'

'Until he met you,' Bob said.

'We tried, but children didn't happen,' Susie said.

'And you didn't consider . . . I don't know, medical help of some sort?' Bob was way out of his depth when it came to talking about gynaecological problems. Even thirty-seven years of marriage didn't prepare you for conversations of this sort with attractive women. Give him an engine and he could get to the bottom of any problems with that and happily talk about them, but this . . . He stared at his mug.

'We decided we liked each other's company, and having Max and Jodie alternate weekends was difficult enough without any more. Terry was in his forties by the time we married. Max was eleven and Jodie in her teens. So we never pursued any treatment or seriously considered other options.'

Susie sighed and Bob looked up. Her arms were clutched around her waist again. He mirrored her body language to avoid reaching for her.

'I hit my early thirties and perimenopause about the same time. Then it became clear that children were even more unlikely to happen. By then, Jodie and Max were adults and the last thing they wanted was a half-sister or brother. The doctor said we could consider IVF treatment, but it was one of those offhand comments. In the same way that if you go into a sofa showroom, the sales representative might say, "you could consider leather" or "have you considered a corner unit?". You know what I mean?'

Not entirely. Bob tried for a reassuring smile.

'I suppose what I'm trying to say is that I don't remember any conversations around the subject. It wasn't an elephant in the room. Not a topic we both avoided. I thought it was done and dusted and we'd made the decision to get on with our lives. I assumed Terry felt the same, but he must have gone for tests at some point.' Susie straightened her arm and clenched her fist.

Bob took Susie's hand in his.

'His letter says he was sorry for going behind my back, but our GP suggested that because of his childhood mumps and the age difference, he should be tested, in case we did decide to go for IVF at some stage. Tests would mean that we would've at least ruled out infertility on Terry's part. They probably thought they were being kind, as my hormones were all over the place. Terry's letter said it was the doctor's surprise when he told him that he already had two children that pushed him into having the tests done.

'When the results came back, he didn't take the matter further at the time. Max and Jodie were adults, he'd looked after them financially all their lives, treated them as his own, and there was no point upsetting the applecart. He hoped that, although they could be difficult, as time passed, they would respect him as their father, if not their biological one.

'His letter went on to say that if I am reading this, he is dead, the children have already or are about to contest his will and are probably causing me grief.'

Susie's eyes filled up with tears again. Bob handed her another tissue.

'And that by now I will know that he lodged his own DNA profile report with Norman. Norman will have requested test results from Max and Jodie. These have arrived and show they are not his biological children and can have no further claim on his estate. In which case, he has asked Norman to contact the Register Office to remove his name from their birth certificates and tell them they are not entitled to another penny — blah, blah, blah, etc.'

'He never said a sodding word about any of this. He kept it all a secret from me. He lied. That hurts. Really hurts. Why? Did he think I was so shallow that I'd want out of the relationship because he couldn't have children?'

'I imagine it would have been a lot more complicated than that,' said Bob. 'It sounds like you weren't the only one being lied to. His first wife must have been some pretty hard-nosed bitch to let him believe that they were his children and keep up the lie all that time. He'd have had to come to terms with that.'

'I could have helped him. He should have told me,' Susie whispered.

Bob rinsed out a dishcloth and wiped the worktop. Not that it needed doing — Susie's kitchen was sparkling — but he needed to keep busy. He just wanted to hold her and comfort her, but he wasn't sure that was what she needed right now.

He had absolutely no doubt he was the father of his two children. Elaine's drinking had been an issue in later life, but as far as he was aware, the only lies she'd told him had been related to hiding booze around the house. To find out he wasn't Josh or Poppy's father would have been devastating. Maybe Terry's relationship with his children hadn't been as good as theirs, but surely he must have suffered too. It must

167

have hurt like hell. As a parent, aren't you supposed to be responsible for teaching your child the difference between right and wrong? Truth and lies. If they suddenly discover that you've lied to them over something as huge as their parentage, then everything they've ever believed about your relationship with them is a lie — that must have a shocking effect on them too and be pretty difficult to deal with.

'He didn't actually lie to you.' Bob hung the dishcloth back on the tap and bit his lip. 'He just didn't tell you.'

'Same thing.' Susie's eyes blazed. 'Terry lied by omission. I thought we told each other everything. Now it transpires our relationship was based on a lie. What else did he lie or just not tell me about? You can't just not tell somebody something because it might upset them. What if he didn't like bacon-and-leek pudding?'

'Would that have been a problem?' Bob frowned so hard, his eyebrows must have joined in the middle, but he couldn't work out where this line of conversation was going. 'There must have been things you didn't tell him or let him believe you felt differently about.'

'You mean like curry?'

'Curry?'

'I like curry, but he didn't, so whenever he said, "Do you fancy going out for a meal?" I never said, "Oh, I'd kill for an Indian". That's hardly the same though, is it? If he'd been allergic to nuts, I wouldn't have eaten nuts either. That's unlikely to have sabotaged our relationship, is it?'

'Have you eaten today?' Bob asked.

Susie shook her head. 'Not hungry.'

'Well I am.'

'Sorry,' she said, sitting upright. 'I should've asked.'

'No, you shouldn't. I turn up on your doorstep on a Monday evening uninvited. But now, come on, get your coat. We're going out for a curry.'

For a moment, it looked like she might refuse, but then she stood up and nodded.

They walked together towards the town centre.

The Indian on the high street was busy, but the waiter picked up two menus and led them to a booth at the back. He made them comfortable and put a large jug of tap water and a plate of poppadoms on the table, promising to return to take their order soon.

Considering fifteen minutes ago Susie had professed to being not hungry, her order, when the waiter returned, was substantial. Then finally, she turned, faced Bob, and giving him a blistering smile, asked, 'Can we share?'

'Goes without saying.' He added another curry and a keema naan to the order, and waited until the waiter had repeated their order back to them before he said, 'I'm going to ask this, although I probably shouldn't. And it is none of my business. So tell me to butt out if you want.'

'Just ask the question.' Susie dolloped a spoonful of what looked like mango chutney on a corner of her poppadom.

'Okay. Were you the cause of his first marriage breakdown?'

'No, I bloody wasn't.'

Said more forcibly than Bob expected.

'Sorry, sounds like I touched a nerve.' He held both hands up. 'I shouldn't have asked.'

'But you have, and I wasn't.' She snapped another pop-padom in two and piled one half with pickles and relish before she spoke. 'You're not the first to suggest it. Everybody assumed that because I was so much younger than Terry, I was a siren on the lookout for a sugar daddy. But Terry and his wife had been living apart for nearly five years before I met him. He'd joined my company as a senior manager and was working on one of the projects I was assigned to.

'The trouble was, his marital status wasn't common knowledge and people like to gossip. Our first year wasn't easy. He'd get panicked phone calls from his wife because one or other of the kids had injured themselves, or in Max's case, someone or something else. He even considered going back to her. He called our relationship off on one occasion. On another, I called it off. It wasn't because we didn't love each other, just that we were trying to be fair to the kids. There were always tears. Then he came round one night holding a piece of paper — it was his divorce absolute. We didn't get out of bed for two days. When we did, the first thing we did was go to the Register Office and book our own wedding. He moved in with me the same day, and we were never apart again. Well, until he had to move into Treetops.'

'How were the children back then?'

'I didn't meet them until after we were married. His wife wouldn't allow it. She thought I was some sort of temporary squeeze that Terry would soon get fed up with and she didn't want the kids' lives to be disrupted because he was having, and I quote her here, "a mid-life crisis".'

'Was Terry happy with that?'

'No. He wasn't that old.'

Bob smiled, despite himself. 'I meant about the children.'

'Oh.' Susie looked as if she was starting to relax. 'He didn't have much choice. She had full custody of the children. He was allowed to take them out one evening a week and for one full day at weekends, but he had to pick them up and drop them off at her house at specified times. He didn't want to upset things, and the only way he could have got her to change anything would have been to take her to court and challenge the custody arrangements. Once we were married, he did. And the court allowed us to have them to stay alternate weekends. They came to us on Friday nights and had to be back at their mother's by 6 p.m. on Sunday.'

The hot plates arrived first, then the food and they watched as the waiter explained each dish and handed them each a plate.

'Right from the start, they were bloody awful,' Susie said, spooning at least half of the mushroom fried rice onto her plate.

She handed the oval plate containing the rest to Bob. 'The worst thing is, if I'd even thought for just one minute that they weren't his and he'd just invited them round for all those years as some sort of sick joke, I'd have had to bloody kill him if he wasn't already dead.'

Bob reached across and squeezed her hand, and when she didn't immediately pull away, he left his there stroking hers. He hoped it was comforting.

'Max blamed me for the divorce. I think he still does.'

'Maybe, but he'll have to reconsider that now he knows the result of the DNA test.'

She picked up a fork with her free hand and began to spike bits of meat.

Bob was impressed — she really did like curry. The funny thing was, it wasn't just Terry who hadn't liked it — Elaine had never been that keen on curry either. She was always happier with a pizza or fried food rather than any "foreign muck". Her limited tastes defined their diet over many years. They knew which day of the week it was by what was served up for dinner. Unplanned meals out created havoc, to the point Bob had given up suggesting going out for a meal. He couldn't remember the last time they had. Elaine would have needed to make up her face, probably have a drink while she was getting ready, and then spend the evening moaning about why he had ever thought this was a good idea, especially as she'd probably got chops, a pie or fish out of the freezer already.

Should he have argued more? If it was the other way round and she was sitting there now, would she be saying their relationship was built on a lie because she never knew he preferred cauliflower bhaji to chips?

No, probably not. If Elaine was sitting there, she'd have ordered the English option, probably chicken and chips, and then moaned all evening about the smells while consuming vast quantities of wine. Susie's eyes were still red, but pinker rather than scarlet now, and that could have something to do with the strange lighting in the restaurant. She looked less angry even if it didn't look like tears were too far away.

Susie looked as if she enjoyed every mouthful of her meal. By the time she'd put down her knife and fork, they'd even shared a joke or two. She looked relaxed. Bob smiled. 'Good?' he asked.

'Bloody delicious,' she said, stroking her stomach. She nodded towards the one samosa left on the plate. 'Do you want that?'

'Yes.' He grinned. 'Half each?' He took a knife and carefully cut it in two. She smiled as she took half from the plate.

'My favourite.' She visibly savoured every mouthful. There was something about the way she ate it that made him feel warm inside.

When she'd finished, she opened her eyes. 'Now, tell me about Wales. I'm sorry, I should've asked. I really do want to hear about it.'

He was pleased to talk about it. She asked lots of questions about the day and bikes, and Bob was in his happy place. He extolled the virtues of different bikes most of the way home, and by the time they turned in to her road he was clear in his head which bike he intended to buy. 'The new Triumph Tiger,' he explained. 'It was a dream to ride, so manoeuvrable. You'd be amazed.'

Susie smiled at him. 'I've never ridden a bike before,' she said. 'I'm probably not the best person to try and impress. To be honest, I'd probably be amazed with an electric skateboard.'

'Please don't tell me you've got one of those on your list,' he said. 'Dangerous little bleeders.'

'More dangerous than motorbikes?'

'Definitely. Motorbikes are different. I can't explain why. Just that it's a good feeling, the wind rushing past. You feel on top of the world — well, I do anyway.' He stuck his hands in his jeans' pockets. 'If ever you wanted to ride a motorbike . . .'

'Thanks,' Susie said. 'Not something on my list, but that's changing daily. It won't be for a while yet. Did I tell you I've booked to do a zip-wire experience? Then there's the Most *Wuthering Heights* Day Ever coming up. Tara and I have tickets for that.'

Bob wondered whether he'd just been turned down for a Kate Bush experience. That had to be a first.

'I've decided that I need to start doing things for me, not to impress others. Don't get me wrong, I've loved everything

so far. Well, apart from the taxidermy and the mediumship.'
She had a faraway look in her eyes. 'I don't suppose you fancy putting on a red dress and taking part in a mass dance event.'

Bob exhaled. 'I don't dance,' he said.

'You know, there's a ballroom course at the college for the over-fifties, on Monday evenings.' Susie smiled. 'You could always go along. I'm sure they'd be delighted to see another bloke. Usually, the women have to rotate — there are not that many men. If you're a woman, you're lucky if you get a man every three dances.'

CHAPTER TWENTY-FOUR

'Well,' Bob said, looking around the site, which was filling up worryingly fast. There was still a large queue of cars waiting to get in. 'Looks like we've brought the average age round here up a bit.'

Freddie had a purple sticker on the windscreen of his car and had driven them through the VIP channels to the entrance, so they weren't subjected to what the travel news was saying was a two-mile queue.

Bob stepped backwards as two girls chatting to each other were in serious danger of colliding with him. 'I'm feeling bloody old.'

'You should have worn sunglasses, like me.' Freddie moved an expensive pair of designer glasses up his face until they were clear of his eyes and winked at Bob. 'I'm travelling incognito.'

'Don't be ridiculous. We don't blend in. We'd have been better off wearing fluorescent jackets and saying we're security. Seriously, you must feel out of place too?'

'A man is as old as the woman he feels,' Freddie said.

'You and Jenny are the same age,' Bob sighed. 'You were at school together.'

People seemed to be setting tents up as close as they could to one another. Bob had never cared much for camping, and the waterlogged site and the slightly stale smell of chemical toilets did nothing to persuade him a night under canvas would be fun. Even in the days when he was competing, if they couldn't get a bed and breakfast place, they slept in the back of the van. He still didn't quite understand how Freddie had managed to source three tickets — Redford Music Festival had been sold out for months. People came from miles away to enjoy a weekend of music. Most of them didn't look old enough to be out without their parents. He'd gone to see Led Zeppelin at Knebworth many years ago. He tried to pin a date on it — it would have been late seventies. A strange concert, with moments of brilliance, and moments when they sounded rusty, but the atmosphere was good. And it was the one and only time he'd seen John Bonham play. The drummer was dead a year later.

'Lily's set is scheduled for 4 p.m. on the country stage.' Freddie was studying a sheet of paper. 'She's on for an hour. I think it's that area over there behind the crystal tent.'

'I can't believe that you talked me into this,' Norman said. 'What the hell are we doing here? Remind me.'

'We're telling the world Brothers in Boxers are back,' Freddie grinned.

'Hardly. We've had one karaoke night and two sessions in your hangar so far. The sessions have been fun but hardly focused. You couldn't call them a rehearsal.' Bob shrugged. 'And can I just point out that we can't find our lead singer. We can't even agree on a set list.'

Norman came across, his face a picture of disgust. 'I've just seen two clients, and been offered drugs, and we've only been here half an hour. How much longer do we have to stay?'

'I've already made enquiries about next year's lineup,' Freddie said proudly. 'They're interested in a Brothers in Boxers set.'

'They haven't heard us play,' Bob said. 'If they did, that would soon change their mind.'

'I'm not sure whether to push it as "The Final Tour" or the "Reunion" — what do you think?'

'I think you're flaming mad,' Bob said. 'Norman, did you ever hear anything from The General?'

Norman shook his head. 'I sent your letter to the last address he gave me, but I've heard nothing back, so I'm guessing he's not interested.'

'We could advertise for a new singer.'

'And say what? That a group of ageing men want someone with a good voice to join them for a last rock concert?'

Bob had never really got the festival vibe. It had to be nearly forty-five years since he'd sat in a field listening to Led Zeppelin. That was different — it was one concert. He'd never been anywhere like Glastonbury, Reading or Leeds. Forty-five years. Bob didn't think he'd changed that much. Certainly his outfit was still very similar — black jeans and leather jacket — although he'd filled out over the years, and his T-shirts had long since been replaced by open-neck shirts which conveniently hid the fact that his six-pack had doubled in number and now settled round his waist.

Freddie had always been the more extravagant dresser and into his fashion, experimenting for a while with caftans, then army uniforms. Adam Ant had a lot to answer for. Today he'd opted for fitted straight-leg trousers that were way too short and showed off a pair of white socks, highly polished shoes, a V-neck T-shirt, checked braces and a porkpie hat.

Norman was wearing cords and a Schoffel gilet over a checked shirt. More country than casual, and the wellies he'd insisted they all wore — but which Freddie refused to — could have gone to any engagement and not looked out of place. Well, anywhere except here.

Bob rolled his eyes — they were like some sort of bad-taste fancy-dress party. But having said that, looking around, there were some very odd sights.

Redford had never attracted the international bands which rocked up up at Glastonbury every year, but a lot of new bands on the verge of making a name for themselves seemed to jump at the gig, and it had always been popular.

There were two stages, each offering different music during the day, while at night, the focus turned to the main stage and the headline acts.

For the last thirty years, one weekend a year, the Castledown Estate had been turned into a festival. The country's great unwashed turned up on a Thursday and left again the following Monday. Residents could hear music from most places in the town — they didn't need to attend. Shops did a lot of business, and the hospital had a few drug cases to contend with.

Years ago, he'd known of a way in where the boundary fences weren't great, but now it was such a commercial event that high steel fences were erected everywhere for the duration.

Bob was glad Norman had insisted wellies were the only sensible footwear. A lot of people, mainly girls, were wearing stilettos or shoes unlikely to survive the weekend.

The *Redford Chronicle* was bound to be there, and next week's edition would be full of images of abandoned tents and the aftermath. At some point in time, it seemed that it had become the done thing to buy a cheap tent and then just leave it when you left. Tents, these days, were for a weekend, not for life. They would be gathered up as soon as the coast was clear and handed over to a charity.

There were a variety of odd-looking shopping stalls where potions offering treatment for all things could be bought. A pop-up tattoo parlour, a photographer and a painter each had stalls.

The three men walked towards the smaller of the three stages in silence. The other two were probably as fascinated as Bob was by the goings on, until they reached the edge of a large crowd.

Bob was surprised to see the age group in front of this stage was older than elsewhere. They were all sitting waiting.

A large shack on the other side of the field offered hog-roast sandwiches with the one next door to it offering meat-free alternatives.

There were craft stalls offering everything from umbrellas to needlepoint pictures. Bob smiled, remembering Susie's reaction to her felting workshop animal and briefly considered buying her a small panda cross-stitch kit as a joke. A sort of "just in case you're at a loose end one weekend", sort of thing.

But one person he couldn't imagine being at a loose end was Susie. She took up quite a lot of his thoughts recently. When Freddie had suggested the festival, he'd been in two minds as to whether to ask for an extra ticket or whether he'd get more pleasure out of laughing about it with her later. She laughed a lot, and when she did, her eyes sparkled. He liked making them sparkle. In his last cookery lesson of the term, he'd made samosas. They'd turned out well. He wanted to experiment a bit with the spices and taste, but hopefully he'd master it soon. Then he'd take her some and watch while she tried them.

He wondered whether she'd booked her zip-wire experience. She'd sounded determined when they'd gone for their curry. He'd considered offering her a lift to Wales. He could take the car, but he'd got an agreement with one of the local garages to lend him a bike for his three course weekends. He needed to get some serious mileage in if he was going to do the ride next year. They'd put their foot down at him using it for the off-roading. He'd still have to use one the course provided.

He wondered how Susie would feel about being a pillion passenger. He'd been halfway, more than halfway, to suggesting he took her out for a ride after the curry and then bottled it at the last minute when she'd thrown a Kate Bush experience into the mix.

What would she have said if he'd suggested it? Would she think that would be moving their relationship into a different phase?

He'd only ever taken one woman, Elaine, on the back of his bike and that was before they got married. As soon as they were married, she decided she preferred the comfort of a car.

It had been okay with Elaine — they were in a relationship. It didn't feel odd saying "Hold on tight" and having the feeling of her sitting behind him. Bob wondered how it would feel with Susie on the back. Would she trust him and be happy to lean with the bike? Maddie loved riding pillion on Josh's bike — would Susie enjoy the experience?

She was still struggling with grief. It was early days. Terry hadn't been dead a year yet. Bob hated how upset she'd been at finding out Terry's secret and remembered when, following Elaine's death, certain things had come to light for him. Things he hadn't even told the kids, because he didn't want them to think badly of their mother.

'Come on,' Freddie yelled above the noise. 'There's a free *Mamma Mia!* dance workout class before Lily's set. Let's go and show these youngsters there's life in the old dogs yet.'

Bob noticed Norman gazing wistfully at the hog-roast sandwich van. 'Come on,' he said. 'Let's go and dance with Freddie. I might even spring for burgers at the Badger and Fir Tree on the way home, if you can get us out of here as soon as Lily's finished.'

'Has he told you the organizers have sent a contract through for next year?' Norman asked Bob. 'He wanted me to check it, but it looks like he's about to sign us for next year. Dust off your flared jeans — we're back in business. I'll need to practise "Stairway to Heaven".'

'In that case, I get to play "Kashmir",' Bob said. 'You know the rules. We always agreed we wouldn't play one without the other. Then what do you say, we finish the set with "Sweet Caroline" and "Born to be Wild" for an encore?'

'Sounds good to me,' Norman said. 'Although at some point we're going to have to let Freddie do "Hotel California", you realize that, do you?' he laughed.

'Still need a lead singer and a keyboard player.' Bob shook his head. 'We need to find The General.'

CHAPTER TWENTY-FIVE

Bob was halfway across the car showroom when a sudden pain in his chest stopped him mid-stride. He clutched his chest. For the first time in quite a few months there was a ripple of tightness that felt oddly familiar, unpleasantly so. He straightened up, took a deep breath.

'Everything okay?' Poppy asked, getting up from her desk and walking across to him.

'Fine,' Bob said.

She stood in front of him and shot him a concerned look. 'You're clutching your chest. Is there a problem?'

'Just a touch of heartburn.'

'You looked shattered when you got in this morning, and you remember what your doctor said about watching out for fatigue.'

'I've had a busy couple of days.' That wasn't an entire lie. He'd ridden up to Wales on Friday. The motorway had been stationary. Bikes on slow motorways were great unless the police closed an entire carriageway. They'd been held up for about an hour until they were allowed past, one lane at a time. He'd taken the next turning and a diversion through the Welsh countryside. Yesterday's course had been a one-day affair, but a long day with some evening riding. On top of that, he'd opted to drive back first thing this morning to try and beat the traffic. 'I'm fine.'

'Fatigue and now chest pain.' Poppy ramped up the outrage, the arms crossed in front of her chest, just like Elaine used to do when she was cross. 'I'm not taking a chance. Get in the car.'

'Don't be ridiculous. I'll ring the cardiologist tomorrow.' He tried to walk past her, but she sidestepped him and effectively blocked his way before he managed a step forward.

'Josh,' she screamed. It was an ear-piercing noise and Bob winced as Josh appeared at the door to his office, Tony standing beside him. Mike and Rick, his new apprentice, who'd come in on a Sunday morning to polish the cars, looked up too. Great, now he had a flaming audience.

'Dad, Poppy, what's wrong?' Josh asked.

'He's having a heart attack,' Poppy announced through gritted teeth. 'Tell him to get in the car — we're taking him to hospital.'

Josh frowned. 'Do as she says,' he said firmly. 'But Poppy, you're going to have to take him on your own. Tony and I are off for Sunday lunch with a potentially big client. I'll get to the hospital as soon as I can afterwards . . .'

'Look, it's fine. Probably just heartburn.' Bob smiled and turned to walk towards the house.

'Car,' they both shouted together.

The nurse who triaged him made it all sound so simple. They'd do some ECGs and blood tests, to see what the problem was.

'How long is that likely to take?' Poppy asked, walking behind him. The nurse shook her head. 'We're quite busy this morning, but don't worry — we'll record his observations and ask a doctor to have a chat with you both.'

'What is it?' Bob asked as the nurse left the cubicle.

'Dad, it's August. You know how busy things are with weddings this month. I've got another one in . . .' she checked her watch, '. . . just under two hours. Everyone I know who could help is either driving or on holiday. I can't find anyone else who can cover at this short notice. Even the funeral director doesn't have a spare driver.'

'I was asked by Treetops to accompany him,' somebody on the other side of the curtain said. A woman. Bob recognized that voice, or at least his body did. It reacted with a flutter that pleasantly warmed him.

'The paramedics wouldn't take him without someone with him. And I've got his red bag.'

'Is that Susie?' he asked Poppy.

'How the hell should I know?' she said.

'Stick your head out of the curtain and have a look. I would, but I'm connected to this machine.'

She growled, stood up and viciously pulled the curtain back. He had expected her to come back and tell him instead of going out into the corridor. He could hear women's voices, but they weren't close enough or loud enough for him to hear what they were saying. He desperately wanted to pull the stickers off his chest and go and see for himself. It didn't sound like Susie was ill, but she was with someone. Who?

'Good news, Dad,' Poppy said, coming back into the cubicle. 'I'm leaving you in the capable hands of a friend of yours, Susie Keane. She's here with a patient from Treetops and said she's happy to be your sensible person or whatever they call it, and keep an eye on you too. She'll be in as soon as the doctors have seen the guy she's with.'

Good news? He was lying on a bed, looking pathetically like an old man with a heart problem. He really didn't want her to see him looking like that. 'I don't need babysitting.' He tried to sit up, but as he did, one of the wires became detached and the bloody machine started beeping loudly. One of the young doctors came in and told him to lie down. The doctor pushed a button on the machine and reattached the wire. He waited for a minute or so, until all the readings were showing.

'Doctor,' Poppy said, 'just to let you know, I have to go, but one of Dad's friends is here with another patient and said she'd be happy to take over looking after Dad as well. Could I introduce you? Only, I do have to get off. I'll be back as soon as I can, and my brother will be here this afternoon.'

* * *

'Exactly what happened,' the doctor asked, looking at Reggie's chart.

'He was found unresponsive in his chair by George during morning coffee service,' Susie said.

'Any problems before that?'

'He came back from Italy yesterday afternoon and was apparently on great form. He had a healthy appetite at supper time and spent the evening regaling most of the residents about his trip and the various operas.'

He'd come back in a taxi from the airport on his own. There had been no sign of Cynthia, but George said that when he told Reggie this morning that Fiona had a message for him from Cynthia to say that she needed to talk to him and would be visiting later in the day, he went pale. George had served coffee and biscuits to the others. By the time he got back to Reggie, he was slumped in a chair being talked at by Violet.

Violet said Reggie had moaned a bit when she was telling him about Eric's death a couple of weeks before. She'd not been worried — her husband used to make a similar noise before he farted — so she turned away and held a lace handkerchief over her nose until Reggie stopped groaning. When he'd been quiet for a minute or two, she'd turned back and assumed he was asleep, so went back to playing Cluedo with the others. As far as she knew, he hadn't opened his eyes or made any noise since.

'His test results look to be normal,' the doctor said. 'We haven't had the results from toxicology yet, so is there any chance he's been given sleeping tablets or any other drugs?'

'Absolutely not. The home has a robust drugs policy — everything is double-checked and there's nothing missing. Fiona checked this morning. Reggie is not on any prescription medicine, and he was fine at breakfast this morning I understand. I have his red bag here.' She gestured to the bag on her lap. Maybe he had been upset by Violet's news of Eric's death. Apparently, Eric had been cast in the Burt Reynolds role in the Christmas musical. It sounded like Reggie had done quite a lot of work on it while he was away. It was now mainly narrative with a few songs. No fancy acting required. He was going to play the piano and narrate. Before he left for Italy, he'd talked George into the dancing governor role. They'd had a great evening last month. Fiona and Susie had watched the "Sidestep" song time and time again and then tried to teach George the accompanying routine, which resulted in him hiding behind doors and then popping out, singing a line from it every time he entered or left a room.

'Does the red bag contain anything more useful than a pair of underpants?' the doctor smiled. 'You'd be surprised how often that's all we find in them.'

'His paperwork and DNR form should be there.' Susie passed the bag across to him.

'Jesus, the home hasn't been kind to him.' The doctor was looking at one of the papers and then at Reggie and then back at the page he was holding. He held it out so Susie could see a picture of a young man who looked vaguely familiar.

'If that was his admission photo and he's deteriorated that much over the last nine months, I'd say he probably only has hours or minutes left.'

Susie had to agree. Reggie had aged considerably since the photo was taken, but judging by the outfit, which she assumed was some sort of fancy dress, she thought the photo must be at least forty years old. These days he had much more of a "lived-in" face.

'My problem,' the doctor added, 'is that it looks like he's in a very deep sleep and I don't know why. I think the best thing is if we send him for a CT scan, just to check we haven't missed anything.' He nodded and looked up. 'I understand you have your hands full today with two patients in your care.'

Susie smiled. 'Yes.'

'Another Treetops resident?'

'No. Just a friend.'

'Okay, well he's waiting for some blood test results. How about I put them both in adjoining cubicles in the observation bay? It's going to take at least an hour. Why don't you take yourself to the canteen and get some lunch?'

At the thought of food, Susie's stomach rumbled. It was almost 2 p.m. If she'd been at Treetops, lunch would have been served and cleared by now and she would probably be sitting down to a full three-course Sunday roast with George and Fiona. It was one of the lovely things about volunteering there — the food was good. She considered ringing them with the news, but there wasn't really anything she could tell them until they knew the results of the scan.

She followed the doctor's directions to the canteen. There were three options for a hospital Sunday lunch: meat, vegetarian or vegan. She opted for the tomato-and-feta tart with a salad, took a table by the small courtyard and had just sat down when her phone rang.

She answered without checking the number, thinking it might be Poppy or Josh ringing to find out how their dad was, but it was Cynthia Bailey.

A clearly aggrieved Cynthia. 'I don't think I've ever met such an unpleasant man,' she said. 'Do you know, he made me pay my share of everything? He insisted we went "Dutch" on everything, and he wouldn't have been there at all if I hadn't agreed to go as his carer. You could have told me what he was like. And then he dumped me at the airport. Went off without a word. Do you know how much the taxi home cost? Well, the least he can do is pay for that.'

Susie stabbed a tomato and put it in her mouth. Cynthia was on a rant and unlikely to require a meaningful response anytime soon, so she figured she might as well enjoy her lunch. It took the best part of forty minutes before Cynthia had wound her neck in, long enough for Susie to make an excuse as to why she couldn't talk any longer and say goodbye. She immediately went and got apple pie and custard for pudding and put her phone deep into her bag, determined to enjoy the food before she had to do anything else.

It was almost spot on the hour later when she arrived back in the Emergency Department and found the obs bay. There was Reggie still on his bed, but Bob was sat next to him on a visitor's chair.

'All clear and good to go,' Reggie said. 'Just keeping my mate here company.'

'Your mate?'

'We knew each other years ago, not recently,' Bob said. 'Do you remember that day we talked about hearing The General's song on a radio request show?' He started singing "I Wish I Was Heaven Bound with You". By the end of the first line, Reggie had joined in.'

'Yes,' said Susie slowly, unsure where this was going.

'Well, this is him. This is the one and only — The General.'

'No way.' Susie was aware her mouth had dropped open. But it made sense, the picture the doctor had shown her. Now she remembered where she'd seen that man before. Probably *Top of the Pops* or one of the music magazines going back to the eighties.

'Good news,' the doctor said, appearing beside her. 'Both men can go home when you're ready. We can't find anything at all wrong with Reggie. His scan found his brain's still there. Bob is going home with some medication — he's just waiting for the prescription and then he can go, but he has an appointment scheduled for Wednesday with his cardiologist. There's no point keeping him here.'

'I'm fine,' Bob said. 'Nothing wrong with me either. I have the heart of a lion.'

'Trouble is, that comes with a lifetime ban from London Zoo,' Reggie added and then started laughing. It was infectious. The doctor laughed. Bob laughed and Susie couldn't help joining in.

'Bloody hell, what are you all on?' Poppy said, as she walked down the ward.

CHAPTER TWENTY-SIX

Susie was relieved to find all the residents at Treetops looking well. The unseasonably hot day for late August meant most of them had abandoned the lounge in favour of the garden, and as many doors as possible were open.

It gave her a chance to clean the lounge properly. She pulled out the wing chairs, hoovering behind them as she went. She was on her way to the recycling bins with a pile of papers and a vase of flowers, well past their best, when she saw the one man she didn't expect or want to see in the corridor to the High Dependency Unit. She was quick. She darted out of sight. She couldn't afford to be seen by him, and she was reasonably sure it was him. The baseball hat. She'd never met anyone who wore a baseball cap indoors, except Alan *bloody sodding* Wheeldon.

Edna Oldroyd was walking towards her. 'Want a hand with the doors?' she asked loudly.

'Shhh.' Susie pressed herself flat against the wall. In her panic, she forgot about trying to get into the backyard. Edna came round the corner and stared at her.

'Thanks,' Susie whispered. 'Who's that?'

Edna took a step back the way she'd come and looked down the corridor for what felt like an age. 'Someone who hoped to move into the area and bring his mother with him.

You going out, or what?' she asked, pressing the button to open the door.

'Mother?' Susie muttered. 'Are you sure?' She stepped into the yard. 'Thanks.'

'Apparently, she likes playing card games and loves bridge,' Edna said from the doorway. 'I don't understand how anyone can like bridge. If you're going to play cards, then make it exciting. Texas hold 'em, strip poker even black-jack.' She took the vase of flowers from Susie's left hand, while Susie got shot of the papers, then gave it back. 'It means he thinks she's come to the end of her life.'

'Not necessarily,' Susie argued, thinking of Terry. 'Maybe he just needs more help.' Except Alan didn't.

'I heard it said that if you move house over the age of eighty, the percentage chance of you dying within a year is the same as your age.'

'No.'

'When it comes to the life lottery at the end of the year, you should bear that in mind and I'll split the winnings with you, seeing as how it was my tip.'

'Can you see what they're doing now?'

Edna marched back and stared down the corridor. 'Looking at the communal washing machines. Why doesn't he save his money, and just up her medication if he wants shot of her? Kinder all round.'

'You shouldn't say that. Some of the residents here play bridge,' Susie said, 'I'm sure they'd welcome a new player.' Except not Alan's mother.

'They're not playing bridge,' Edna snorted. 'They're having their afternoon naps.'

She was probably right. Susie grinned. Come to think of it, some of them hadn't drunk their tea last time she looked. 'Edna,' she said, 'before you go . . . If he's who I think he is, his mother died last year.'

Edna stared down the corridor after the retreating party. 'You think he might be here for criminal reasons? Leave it with me.' And she was off.

Susie felt a little guilty as she pushed her way through the kitchen doors. 'Are you okay?' Fiona asked.

'No,' Susie said. 'One of the staff is showing someone round I don't want to see. I think he's here under false pretences. Edna said he was looking for a home for his mother, but he told me she died last year. I don't know, of course, but I get the feeling he's trying to find me. I think an old school friend of ours, Cynthia, might be trying to stir things up a bit.'

'The one Reggie took to Verona?'

'The one and the same. She rang last week while I was at the hospital with him and I wasn't that sympathetic about her Italy trip.'

Fiona nodded. 'Reggie had a good time, though.'

'Edna's onto the man.'

'Good choice. She's like a Rottweiler with a bone. She won't let go until she's discovered the truth. I pity the man. Let's go and find George. We should warn him there might be trouble ahead. When he left here he was heading for the garden to have another word with Reggie.'

'What's he doing now?'

'He's got them making Christmas presents.'

'That sounds positive.'

'Except, he's using old *Blue Peter* episodes as inspiration. 'Last week, there were houses for Sindy popping up all over the place. Violet made one for her daughter because she used to play with Sindy.'

'Hasn't her daughter just retired?'

'Uh-huh.'

'This week it's rocket launchers. Everywhere you go, you find residents on the hunt for plastic bottles. George is trying to crack down, partly because he heard someone mention fireworks and matches.' Fiona put her hand on Susie. 'Is that him?' There was a group of three, led by George, walking towards the conservatory, closely pursued by Edna, who was trying to barge her way in.

'Yep.'

'How long do you expect your mother to live?' Edna's voice rang out down the corridor.

'Look, you better go. If he's stalking you, then it's best you're not here. If he's going to keep up this pretence, he might ask to see the kitchens or hang about and help with the next meal. I'll tell George later that something came up.'

'Thanks,' Susie said. Edna was now walking beside Alan and holding his hand. Susie smiled at the thought he was probably desperate to get rid of her.

As they walked through the lounge, Reggie was sitting in his usual chair.

'Susie, I have a question for you.'

'Ah, Fiona,' she heard George's voice say. 'You'll never guess what. Mr Wheeldon here thinks he went to school with one of our volunteers, Susie.'

'I don't think so,' she heard Fiona say.'

'Could you . . . ?'

'Sorry, Reggie, I've got to go,' Susie said. 'Can't stop. Whatever the question is, the answer's "Yes", but talk to me about it next time I'm in.'

'Oh, I think that' s unlikely,' Fiona said, as Susie practically ran into the hall.

'Why?'

She was straining to hear the conversation now as the group walked into the conservatory. She dared not turn around.

'Well, for a start, Zuzanna's from Poland,' Fiona said, 'and without being rude . . .'

The lounge door closed behind her. Susie breathed a sigh of relief and made for the car park.

CHAPTER TWENTY-SEVEN

Bob smiled. He was feeling good. A morning swim and a dog walk with Miss Phyllis completed. The schools had returned after their summer break and the Early Bird session was back to the regulars.

At lunch he'd narrowly avoided answering Poppy's questions about Welsh Jean. 'Change the bleeding record,' he said at one point. 'Talking of which, I'm off for a session with the band.'

They'd arranged to meet at Lily's. Geoffrey had offered them a yoga session. "Mindfulness" he called it. 'Realign your energies and you'll play much better.' Reggie had started to become a regular at their sessions. Bob was amazed to see that he hadn't lost his ability as either singer, keyboard player or conductor.

Bob always picked him up from Treetops on his way past. He'd hoped they could have arranged a Sunday — he would have liked to see Susie, because he hadn't seen her since the hospital day. He wanted to thank her for taking care of him, maybe ask her out for a meal or offer to cook her one. He'd almost perfected the art of a samosa and his curries had turned into a weekly treat.

Lily led them through to her sitting room. All the furniture had been pushed back against the walls and there were a series of narrow, coloured mats on the floor. 'I'll get you both a drink,' she said. 'We've got ten minutes or so before we need to get started.'

'Great,' Reggie said. 'I'll have a beer, thanks.'

'You'll have elderflower cordial. That's all I'm offering.' Lily shot him a look of despair. 'We're trying to unblock all your energy channels, make you more aware of everything around you — you remember? Mindfulness has been shown to be good for musicians and increases their performance skills, making them less self-critical and likely to be more aware of others around them so they perform better.'

'Your idea or his?' Bob asked Lily pointedly, jerking his head at Reggie.

'Geoffrey's,' they both chimed simultaneously.

'Because he's heard us play and decided we needed help?' Bob didn't think anybody had watched any of their practices since the karaoke session at the Badger and Fir Tree.

At that moment, Freddie must have driven into her drive. Bob couldn't see him from where he was standing in the kitchen, but he could hear his horn. Most of the estate probably could, except Bob recognized the car from the sound of the horn, whereas most of them would have had to twitch a curtain to see what it was. 'He's come in his Gullwing Mercedes,' he announced.

Geoffrey appeared at the kitchen door. He was wearing a fleecy jacket, open over what looked like a skimpy leotard. 'Your other mate has just arrived in a Gullwing Mercedes. He's just making a bit of a meal of parking it.'

Bob tried to maintain eye contact with him. The last thing he wanted to do was look the man up and down and get stuck staring at something he really didn't want to see. 'Great,' he said, turning towards the sink.

Freddie marched through the doors in what looked like a morning suit.

'Jesus, what have you come as?' Lily asked.

'I'm trying to look like a dancer,' he said, giving a twirl. 'Dashing or what?'

'Or what,' Bob, Reggie, Lily and Geoffrey chimed together.

'You can bloody talk,' Freddie said, his gaze settling on Geoffrey. 'What on earth are you wearing? Jenny and I were invited to a fancy-dress party once, where we could only wear one item of clothing.'

'And, you wore a coat,' Geoffrey nodded.

'Don't be ridiculous,' Freddie said, 'I wore a sock.'

'I assume it covered your genitalia,' Geoffrey coughed.

'No. My left foot. And Jenny's covered her right. Those were the days.' Freddie slapped him on the back. 'No Norman?'

'He's in court today. He said he'd be here as soon as he's through,' Bob said.

'Why do you want us to dance?' Freddie stuck his hands in his jacket pocket.

'Not dance, exactly,' Reggie said. 'Just not plant your-selves in a line like zombies. I've asked Geoffrey for help. He's going to help us relax with some yoga, then Lily's going to show us how to move in time to the music. Hopefully, at least then you'll look less like cardboard cutouts, and if you can give an impression of being happy to be playing together again, that would be a winner too.'

'I've told you, I'm not going to do "Stand and Deliver". I'm a drummer.' For a moment Freddie looked like he might turn round and walk straight out the way he'd come.

'He's right. We're men and musicians,' Bob added. 'In case you haven't heard, we don't multitask. Guitar playing, singing, smiling or dancing — you choose, but only one at a time.'

'Nothing fancy. No routines, just a little less like a bunch of old men with cramp. We're going to be playing the soundtrack to a musical for the Treetops residents at Christmas. They're all practically already at death's door. I just don't want you lot looking like you've beaten them there.'

'It worked okay for Debbie Harry.' Freddie took off his jacket, unbuttoned his shirt and surveyed the mats.

But it was Lily's turn to stare in amazement at Reggie. 'Did I just hear you right? This lot are playing in a musical? The one you're putting on at Treetops?' She grinned. 'You must let us know where we can get tickets. I wouldn't miss that for the world.'

'It's cut down, mainly just a narrative now with the odd song,' Reggie explained.

'Fifteen songs by my reckoning,' Bob said. 'We used to do sets with less tracks.'

'Ah, there's been a change,' Reggie said. 'I've had to add three more. And yes, I'm hoping you two will join us. We could do with a xylophone, Geoffrey, and a tambourine, and help with some of the songs, Lily.'

'Can we do that dance from the Gene Kelly musical where they all walk up a settee and it falls over?' Freddie cast his eyes round Lily's room and they settled on her sofa. 'There should be room here — we just need to move it away from the wall.'

'No bloody way,' Lily said. 'You are not walking over my furniture. Even think about it and you can all get lost now. I'm only doing this as a favour.'

Reggie held up a calming hand. 'We know, and we're grateful,' he said.

'How did you go with the consultant?' Freddie asked. 'Did you have to go to the clinic this morning?'

Bob nodded. 'Yeah, good thanks.' He slipped his shoes off and moved to one of the mats.

He should be feeling on top of the world. The cardiologist's appointment had gone reasonably well. The doctor had proclaimed he was happy and couldn't see the stent causing any further problems, provided Bob continue with his medication. 'Keep taking the clopidogrel, you've got the GTN spray if you need it. Just secondary prevention really,' he'd said. 'Stick to your heart-healthy diet, continue with regular exercise and no extreme sports. See you in a month's time unless you have any more problems.'

They all stood on mats and Geoffrey took them through some relaxation routines. 'We're looking to achieve peacefulness in both our bodies and minds,' he said. 'Life is hectic, so we aim to reduce stress and anxiety. Deep breaths and try and clear your minds.'

'No extreme sports. What, you mean like rugby?' Bob had asked the consultant.

'Yeah. Rugby, mountain biking, that sort of thing.' The man had shrugged and wiggled his head from side to side. 'And maybe take a buggy if you're going golfing over the next few months.'

Bob thanked him and left the room before he felt the need to ask about the Ace-to-Ace ride and got an answer he didn't want to hear. The last thing he needed just now was to have his dream whipped from under his feet.

'Are you still with us?' Lily asked.

Bob snapped back to the present. On mats either side of him, Freddie and Reggie were now kneeling, their foreheads touching the floor and their arms stretched out in front of them. Geoffrey had removed his fleece. His leotard, or whatever it was, sported two words across his chest: "Mr Motivator". Elaine used to enjoy the GMTV fitness instructor in the mornings, although Bob didn't remember Elaine ever doing his workouts. He tried not to stare, but from memory, Mr Motivator was probably younger, fitter and had a more toned physique than Geoffrey. And he couldn't imagine he wore sandals with socks.

Bob got down and joined them. He was surprised how relaxing it felt. He enjoyed the session. It was over before he knew it and the mats were rolled up.

They were stood in a line, awkwardly watching Lily.

'We're going to learn a rock-step — simple, just forward and back,' she said. 'The thing is to keep moving, feel the beat,' she said. 'You going to give it a go?'

Geoffrey put on a track, and they all followed Lily's example.

'Never mind middle-aged men,' Freddie grinned. 'We could be mistaken for Pan's People already.'

'Speak for yourself,' Bob said, catching Lily's eye.

'You okay,' she mouthed. She was wearing a worried expression.

'I'm fine,' he whispered and gave her a wink. And he was. That's effectively what the cardiologist had said, wasn't it?

He'd probably put more of a positive spin on it later when he told Poppy and Josh, and it perhaps wasn't the best time to mention that he planned on a motorbiking holiday. And that he'd already paid the deposit and had spent a lot of time considering which bike to buy.

When he saw the doctor again in a month's time, hopefully he'd be able to persuade him the pains weren't heart related, and that he'd followed all his recommendations. Hell, he'd even cut out sausage sandwiches and was eating more fish and vegetables. He planned on continuing to swim and walk on a regular basis.

Lily had them moving for another twenty minutes or so. She'd added in moves, and now they'd gone some way to mastering a side-together, side-together-step, which, when combined with the forward-together, back-together and the clicking of fingers or the occasional clap, was looking more like an acceptable dad dance at a wedding. Lily had put on the *Best Country Album in the World*.

'Sing along, if you feel you can concentrate on two things at once,' she laughed, clapping in time to the music. And they had, until Geoffrey stopped the music and told them they shouldn't overdo it.

'Can you dance?' Bob asked Lily. 'You know, proper ballroom steps?'

She looked at him cautiously. 'Yes, I suppose. Nothing serious, but I was a bit of a whizz at breakdancing for a while. I seem to remember you did a mean moonwalk in your day, Mr Diamond.'

'That wasn't moonwalking.' Freddie clapped him on the back. 'That was his "get out of here quick" move. Back up to the nearest door and then run for it.'

'Speak for yourself,' Bob laughed, and turned away to find his shoes.

'I was wondering,' he said as they were all getting ready to leave, 'whether you'd teach me to dance properly.'

'Seriously?' Lily looked at him. 'What, you mean ballroom dancing?'

Bob nodded, feeling her stare on him. 'Just a waltz, nothing fancy.'

'A waltz can be fancy.'

'I toyed with the idea of a course at the college, but by the time I got round to enrolling, they were full.'

'Okay . . . You've met someone and want to impress her. Is that it?'

'No,' Bob said, but knew as the words came out that Lily didn't believe him.

'Just in case,' he stuttered. 'You know — if I ever do.'

* * *

'Is that Susie Keane?' the voice on the phone asked. There was something familiar about it, that Susie struggled to place. She stared at the number. Not one of her contacts — there was no name. 'Who's asking?' she said, trying to disguise her voice. She tried for an Irish lilt, but even to her untrained ear, she hadn't pulled it off. She winced.

'Susie, it's Alan. Alan Wheeldon. Cynthia gave me your number.'

She did bloody what?

Okay, what did people say about dealing with phone calls she didn't want, on her mobile. Pretend the signal was shit.

'Sorry, you're breaking . . . not here at the moment. Could . . . try after—?'

'Susie, I can hear you fine. I wanted to invite you out for a meal. I figured it would be good to catch up properly. You're single. I'm divorced. We have lots in—'

'Hello, anybody there? Hello?' Susie hung up and stared at the phone. Cynthia had given out her number. She couldn't believe it. Why would she? She knew how Susie felt

197

about Alan. They'd joked at the party about him giving her the creeps. He had as a teenager and it seemed, fifty years on, those feelings hadn't gone away.

The phone rang again. Same number. She stared at the phone in the middle of her desk and made no attempt to pick it up.

'You okay?' Luke asked from his desk. 'You've gone white. Was it bad news?' He stood up and walked round to Susie's desk. It was lunchtime and the office was quiet. She was on late lunch and had planned on going for a walk, but knowing who was on the other end of the line had sapped her strength and suddenly she wasn't sure she wanted to leave the safety of the office and a locked room.

'Someone from the school reunion,' she said, weakly. 'I didn't know he had my number. My old friend, Cynthia, gave it to him. He said something about asking me out for a meal . . . because we've both got lots in common, like dead relatives.'

'He's a widower?'

'No, his mother's dead. His wife's in prison, but it sounds like his divorce has gone through.'

'You're both unattached.' Luke sat on the corner of her desk and crossed his legs. 'That's perfect. A fundamental requirement for most sustainable relationships.' He was teasing her.

'It's not necessarily a precursor to a happy-ever-after,' Susie said.

'So, you are hoping for a happy-ever-after with someone.'

'Absolutely not. I'm not looking for a relationship. Full stop.'

'Hmm . . .' Luke crossed his arms. 'Methinks the lady does protest too much.'

'Idiot,' Susie laughed, swatting his arm. 'Why would I even consider going out to eat with someone whose opening line is that he wants to treat me to a meal because I'm single? Sounds like he is expecting far too much from an evening.'

'Perhaps.' Luke tilted his head to one side. 'Devil's advocate here. You need to eat, and if he's offering to pay, is that such a bad thing? He must have some redeeming features.'

'Must he?' Susie pursed her lips and tried to remember. 'I didn't know him well at school. We were never in the same classes. I think he went down the science route. The only time we had any sort of a conversation was in our last term when we were partnered together in dance lessons, and then someone put out rumours about us being an item.'

'So, you both dance? Maybe he could take you clubbing.'

'Are you listening to me? I'm not going. Anyway, he was rubbish at dance. And these days, he wears a baseball hat indoors all the time to disguise a comb-over. Did I tell you that his ex-wife tried to kill him? That's why he divorced her and why she's in prison.'

'You're joking.' Luke turned round and was focused on her now. 'No, I can see you're not. What on earth did she do?'

'I don't know, I haven't asked.'

'Aren't you a little bit curious? Go for this meal and find out. That way you can tell him you're not interested and, in fact, you've found love again and are happy. So, please would he leave you alone.'

'That would be a lie.' Susie coloured. Well, not entirely. She was happy, but if it had been Bob inviting her out for a meal, she would have jumped at the chance. Except that was friendship. Love was absurd. Neither of them were looking for love.

Luke frowned. 'Or I could come out at an agreed time and pick you up? You can tell him I'm a relative, toy boy, friend, lodger, whatever. That way, if you're having such a fabulous time you don't want to leave, you can send me a message, an escape code, to stand me down. Then I get to check him out and you can find out what his wife did.'

Susie's eyes smarted. 'You'd do that for me?'

Luke twisted his mouth. 'I'd do it for any of you. You're all like extended family to me.'

Susie's phone vibrated to signal a text message. 'Alan,' she mouthed. 'He says he'd like to take me out for a meal tomorrow night. He's suggesting the bar and grill in town . . .'

'Bloody cheapskate. Write back and tell him you don't have time to get a Hep C injection and suggest TOTU.'

'And he says, "leave the car at home, we could go on somewhere afterwards". He's finished the message with a winking emoji and xxx. No bloody way. I can't do it.'

Luke took the phone from her hand and read the message. 'You are right, girl. He comes across as quite high up the creep radar. Why on earth did you give him your number?'

'I didn't. I wouldn't. Cynthia did.'

'And she's a friend?'

'I used to think she was, but now I'm not so sure she ever was that good a friend.' As Susie said the words, she realized there was probably more than just an element of truth in them. At school, they'd been inseparable, but Cynthia had borrowed her clothes, jewellery, pens and anything else she needed, and some items she never got back. When the trouble blew up with Alan in the last term, Cynthia had blamed Lucy Miller for the rumours, but Lucy had been ill at the time and wasn't back at school until after Susie had left. There was no social media in those days. No mobile phones. She wouldn't have any idea about what was going on unless someone had told her . . .

'What did you do to upset her?' Luke asked.

'Search me.'

'Tell Alan you don't want to go out with him, for any reason, and that you'd like him to leave you alone. Then block Cynthia. You don't need that sort of negativity in your life.'

'You're right.' She typed a short brief message into the phone and then blocked him and Cynthia.

'Damn. That does mean you can't ask him about his wife,' Luke said. 'I wonder if the case is mentioned on the internet. Have you looked?'

He got up and went back to his desk. Susie smiled. No, she hadn't, but she had no doubt Luke was just about to.

CHAPTER TWENTY-EIGHT

Walking down the high street, Susie smiled as she spotted Norman just outside his office. Despite the autumn heat, he was still in a suit, still every inch a solicitor. She raised a hand when he looked her way. He smiled and waited until she was beside him. 'I was just coming to see you,' he said. 'Are you on your way back to the Register Office.'

She nodded and they fell into step together, making small talk about the weather and the potential hosepipe ban. At the zebra crossing she spotted a man with a baseball hat and couldn't help thinking it was Alan from the school reunion. He looked at her for a moment, and she felt cold and slightly uncomfortable. Norman said something about his dahlias and she turned to reply. When she turned back, the man with the hat had gone, but she had the feeling he was still around. 'How's it going with your lodger?' Norman asked. 'Is she still with you?'

'Good, thanks.' And it was going well. 'Rumour has it you're playing music again with your old band.'

He looked at her and nodded. 'Bob Diamond,' he said knowingly. 'I guess he told you. There's still a long way to go before we're anywhere near ready to play Redford Music Festival. But, and please don't tell Bob, I am starting to think it's not such a crazy an idea as I first thought when Freddie first mentioned it. Now that we've made contact with The General again, it looks like he's on board too.'

Susie waited until he'd checked in with the computerized system before she took him into one of the small appointment rooms.

'I've received the authority from the General Register Office — Max and Jodie's births now need to be re-registered,' he said.

Susie nodded.

'Terry's details are to be taken off their certificates.'

'That's good news, but I'm afraid I can't help. The births need to be corrected in the office the births were originally registered in. GRO will have written to the appropriate office,' she added. 'Does the letter tell you which office? The GRO normally recommend you give it a week or so before you ring them, then you can order a certificate from them online.

'But that's not why you're here, is it? You've booked a death appointment — aren't you here to register a death?'

'For one of my clients.' He took some papers out of his bag. 'No family, but . . . while we're on the subject, there is something else you should know. I contacted the company Terry worked for when he first started work. It turns out that he had a pension with them.'

'I didn't know him then,' Susie said, feeling not for the first time that maybe she didn't know him as well as she'd thought.

Norman wasn't watching her as he said, 'He filled in an expression of wish or nomination form for his pension trustees, saying that in the event of . . .'

'His death,' Susie prompted.

'Yes.' Norman swallowed. 'His pension should be split between his wife and any children in equal measures. He never changed the form. It's not unusual — many people don't. You can't leave pensions in your will, so some time ago I contacted the company to let them know of his death.'

There was a slight hesitation before he said the last word. 'I asked them to hold fire until we knew the outcome of the DNA test results and explained his concerns.'

'If he wrote it when he was still married, surely that would be his ex-wife.'

'He said "wife". He didn't specify anyone by name. Divorce normally trumps marriage and negates the relationship, in the same way that adoption trumps birth, in that an adopted child cannot claim any right to his/her birth parents' estate.'

Susie knew that, but Norman was in full swing.

'If he'd have stated names, we possibly wouldn't be having this discussion. However, this is a slightly unusual case. The trustees and I agree and believe that, considering what's happened, the only proper beneficiary is you. The tests prove conclusively Terry had no children of his own, and as his current wife, you are the sole beneficiary.'

Susie wasn't sure how to react.

'It has grown into a sizeable pot over the years. They will be distributing the money in the next week or so. It doesn't go anywhere near probate, so there is no reason for it to come to me. I have given them your address, bank details and provided them with all the proof of identity, etc. they required.'

'Thank you,' Susie said quietly. Because she didn't know what else to say.

'I know that you are shaken by all this,' Norman said. 'I understand you may feel differently towards Terry just now, but I still very much believe that you were the love of his life. He told me on more than one occasion how he felt, but when it was first suggested that he might have a form of dementia, he made sure everything was in place. He wrote the letters and insisted his will was signed and lodged with me. He gave me details of his share portfolio and pension pots. He was a good man. You might feel he lied to you, but he did what he thought was right to protect you, and whenever we talked of death, he always said that he wanted you to have a good life after he was gone, and hoped you'd take every chance that came your way. I looked at death differently after my chats with him, and he made me think about putting my own affairs in order.' He paused, and Susie wasn't sure if she was supposed to react. Should she say something about how he had a good few years yet, before he needed to worry about that sort of thing?

'I hope my estate is as easy to sort as his was. Although I have put certain conditions in place that my own executors might find difficult to comply with.'

Susie burned to ask him what, but Norman's face was blank. 'Now, I've taken up enough of your time,' he said. 'And we have a death to register, but you know where I am if ever you want to talk . . .'

CHAPTER TWENTY-NINE

'How was your weekend?' Charlotte asked as they sat down with mugs of tea and breakfast rolls that Maddie had brought in from the bakers, for their usual Monday morning Register Office catch up.

'Great,' Luke said. 'The girls are now enrolled in gymnastics on a Saturday morning, which gives me an hour and a half to sit in the corner of the Sports Centre café and read the paper. You have no idea how much I enjoy that time.'

Charlotte and Maddie had covered last Saturday's weddings and Susie smiled as she listened to Charlotte describing the problems they'd experienced with one of the hotels when the room she was told the wedding was being held in wasn't actually one of the hotel's licensed ones. It had all got sorted, but Charlotte's story, probably heavily embellished, involved an awful lot of eye-rolling.

'And you, Susie?' Luke asked. 'How did you spend your weekend?'

'In Wales,' Susie said. 'I went on a zip-wire experience. The fastest one in the whole world. While you were here in Redford, I was hurtling down a Welsh quarry at almost 120 mph.'

There was silence. One of those stunned silences that was so silent, it was almost loud. Susie wasn't entirely surprised. There had been a moment when she'd considered it was the single most stupid thing she'd ever signed up to do in her life, somewhere around the time she'd been stood in the shed, at the top of mountain, waiting to be attached to a thick metal cable, and staring down at the jagged slate hills below her. 'It's not as dangerous as it sounds,' she said defensively. 'You get strapped in and have to wear a helmet. They make sure you're secure before they let you go.'

'Let me get this straight,' Luke said after another lengthy pause. 'You allowed yourself to be dangled from a wire and pushed off to travel at speeds greater than 100 mph, headfirst into a quarry. I don't think I've ever gone that fast in a car.'

'Crazy, eh?' Susie said, feeling her smile practically touching each ear. The way it did every time she thought back to the weekend. 'It was thrilling. I loved every second of it.' She and Tara had got off at the end, hugged each other and just laughed until tears ran down their faces.

'Why?' Luke asked, shaking his head.

'I needed to push boundaries, climb out of my comfort zone, prove to myself that there's still life in this old woman yet.'

'Yes, but isn't that why you've been doing lots of new things this year?' Maddie asked.

'Like the pole dancing and felting March hares,' Charlotte added.

'This was more for me. I needed to know I'm not just some middle-aged widow destined to live in the past. I am ready to try new things. It's what Terry would have wanted. Life is good and it's out there. There is no room for regrets. Futures should be built on happy memories, but that should be the starting block, not the finishing line.'

'Jeez, she's gone all philosophical.' Luke laughed. 'Before we know what's happening, she's going to start wearing strange clothes because old ladies only wear purple or something.'

'Nothing like that.' Susie grinned. 'Although purple is my favourite colour, and according to a colour analyst I saw recently, it suits me. It's just that this year has taught me, if nothing else, I need to leave so-called friends, bullies and failed relationships behind. There was a reason I lost contact with my school classmates. I used to think it was a failing on my part that I didn't make more of an effort to keep in contact, but relationships generally fail for a reason.'

'Forgive and forget. You, of all people, should find that easy. You're so lovely about everybody,' Luke said.

He didn't look like he was joking.

'You say that, but I don't think I can. I might have thought I'd forgiven them, but when it boiled down to it, I never forgot what they'd done, or that it was down to me to forgive them. They never apologized for what they did to me. And any show of friendship on my part just seemed to grant them permission to hurt me again. I realized that when Cynthia used me to get a holiday and then tried to blame me for the fact it cost her money and she didn't have a brilliant time, that I had nothing to be envious of her about. I might not have had hundreds of exotic holidays, like her, but she's not happy and I am and that's more precious than a French vineyard or an Italian opera. It's time to let go. My life has moved on. I have great friends, a great housemate and a great job, and I'm happy.'

Charlotte started to clap, then Maddie, then Luke. 'Well said,' he added, patting her on the back.

Susie performed a mock bow and blew them all kisses. 'Now, were you saying you wanted me to cover deaths or births this morning?'

* * *

'I don't suppose your middle name's Jean,' Maddie asked later in the day, when she popped into Susie's room with the latest update from the GRO.

'I don't have a middle name,' Susie laughed. 'And do I look like a Jean?'

Maddie shook her head. 'No. Ignore me, it's nothing.'

Susie looked at her. 'Why did you ask?'

'Daft I know,' Maddie said. 'But Josh's dad has taken to going to Wales about once every couple of months to see a woman called Jean. He won't discuss anything about her, other than to say that he had a nice time. what with you being in Wales at the weekend, and him being away this weekend too . . . Well, I just wondered if the two of you had gone together. And maybe the reason he was being so secretive about this woman was . . .' Maddie looked embarrassed, '. . . was because Jean was really you.'

Susie smiled. 'I went on a zip-wire experience. I took Tara. We had a lovely time and really enjoyed it. I can honestly say one person we didn't see for the whole duration of the trip was Bob.' She tucked the update into her folder to read later and smiled.

Not a lie — she hadn't seen him. She had wondered if he'd suggest taking them when she told him they were going. She'd even wondered about asking him if he would, but a quick glance at the map showed it would have been daft. They were going to north Wales and he was going to the south.

'I hope you don't mind me asking?' Maddie said. 'Only, the two of you get on so well. And if you were Welsh . . . No, sorry, you're not. It doesn't matter.'

Susie looked at her boss for a while, willing her to finish the sentence. "If you were Welsh Jean", then what? She briefly considered explaining that she was, for message and call purposes, but that he hadn't taken her anywhere near Wales. That would only raise more questions she wasn't sure Bob was ready to answer. 'Have you asked him about his trips?' she said, trying to inject some lightness into her voice.

'There's no point. It's weird. Ask him about a car he's seen at auction, he'll spend ten minutes describing every detail, but ask him about Jean and he goes completely silent. Poppy and Josh think he's up to something.'

Susie glanced round the room, checked to make sure it was tidy and ready for her next appointment, and walked to the door.

Maddie followed. 'Do you think it's too early for him to have a new relationship?' Maddie bit her cheek. 'I mean, we'd all be happy for him, but he seems to think he'd be letting Poppy and Josh down in some way. That he would be being disloyal to their mother's memory.'

'It's difficult,' Susie said. 'I know from bereavement counselling and the people we see here, that everybody reacts to death in a different way. I suppose I'm different in that I had a long time to get used to the idea that at some point I would be alone. I'm not sure it made getting over Terry's death any easier. I still hate not being able to tell him about my day. It's always lovely to talk through awkward things or new ideas with someone. Even when he was in the home, he was still around, and I never felt lonely. I don't know for certain what I want from the future, but I am trying to find out. The zip wire was something I'd always thought might be fun, and it was brilliant — not as erratic as a roller-coaster ride, but probably the closest thing to flying free. I'm still buzzing.'

'I can tell.' Maddie smiled. 'You look different somehow this morning. Josh would probably tell you the same about biking. He says that makes him feel alive and it's his way of relaxing. He goes out for a ride on his bike some days, just to clear his head.'

'Maybe that's what I need. Just lately I feel my head might explode with everything that's going on. I know Bob loves bikes too.'

'He used to. Sadly, he doesn't ride anymore,' Maddie added. 'A promise he made to Elaine in the early days of their marriage. Although between you and me, I think he rides sometimes. Josh said his bike had done a lot more miles than he remembered when we got home from the States.'

'Would it bother you if he did?'

'What do you mean?'

'You make promises when you get married,' Susie said. 'Till death us do part and all that. Don't you think all promises should be like that? Elaine's been dead a while now and if he enjoys riding, then shouldn't he be allowed to do it? He didn't break the promise to her when she was alive.'

'I see what you mean.' Maddie looked thoughtful. 'And we do see a lot of widowers getting remarried — "forsaking all others as long as you both shall live" — and all that.'

'Exactly. Nobody bats an eye then.'

'Are you thinking of getting married again?' Maddie tilted her head. 'Is that what you're trying to tell me here?'

'We're not talking about me.' Susie snorted. It must have come across as an indignant snort, because Maddie's head jerked up, and she put her hands up in mock surrender.

'No offence intended,' she said.

'Sorry,' Susie added. 'I've got no plans, but I was interested in whether you thought you should have to carry on keeping promises, or whether they should be laid to rest along with the body of your dearly departed.'

'The latter, I suppose.' Maddie nodded. 'Yes, I suppose you're right. If Bob wants to ride a bike again, and it would make him happy, we should let him. Maybe I'll suggest to Josh that he has a word with his dad and offers him use of his bike on a regular basis.'

'Is it really that brilliant being on a bike?' Susie asked.

Maddie nodded. 'I love it. I know some people hate the idea of being a pillion passenger, but it is my quiet time. I feel completely free and relaxed. Okay, I'd rather not do rain or cold weather, but on those days we take the car.' She turned as they reached her office. 'Look, why don't I ask Josh to give you a lift home one night. It's not far, but it might give you a feel for what it's like. And if you don't like it, or want to get off, that's not a problem. We have an escape signal in place. If I want him to stop for any reason, then I squeeze his left shoulder. So far, I never have, but you could if you didn't like the ride.'

Susie looked down at her outfit. She was dressed in a tight skirt and court shoes, and she'd brought the car this morning. 'If you're sure he wouldn't mind,' she said. 'I'd love that.'

'Maybe you'll love it so much you'll think about getting your own bike,' Maddie said. 'I must admit, I'm tempted to take my CBT and get a small bike. It's so much more convenient for short distances, and round town, you can nip between traffic queues. But it's not practical with Miss Phyllis. And now, I won't be doing it for . . .' She blushed. 'A few months. Well, maybe a year or so.' She coloured as she said the last bit. Susie smiled.

'Mrs Diamond are you telling me what I think you're telling me?'

'No. Well, yes, but we haven't told anybody else. I'm not even close to twelve weeks yet and we haven't had our first scan.'

CHAPTER THIRTY

'Max,' Susie said. 'You should've rung.' She took a step back and Max was in.

He eyed the pole in the centre of the room suspiciously. 'And why would I have done that? So that you could give your fancy lawyer enough time to get an injunction against me. I just want to talk.'

'No,' she said simply, 'because I'm busy today. But seeing as you're here, sit down. I can give you five minutes.'

'I need money.'

Talk about come straight to the point.

'What interest is that to me?'

'You shouldn't have taken Dad's pension fund. That money was supposed to be for us.'

'I haven't taken anything that didn't belong to me.' Susie had been thinking for some time that maybe she could give both him and Jodie some of the money. That maybe she could give Tara some too. It was nice, she could do a lot with it, but she really didn't need all of it. But faced with Max sitting in her house and demanding it, the hairs on the back of her neck stood up. She became more militant and determined not to.

'You've gone against my father's wishes.'

'Your father.' She laughed. 'You mean Terry. He's not your father, is he, Max? That's already been proved. If you want to talk to your father about giving you a loan, then your best bet would be to speak to your mother and find out who he is. Although, if you seriously want his help, you might want to try being polite to his wife. I assume there is one, which is why he never married your mother in the first place.'

'That's not fair. My mother's a good woman. She'd still be married if you hadn't taken Dad away from us.'

'I didn't take Terry away from anyone. He and your mum had split up long before I came on the scene, as you've been told time and time again, so I don't know what warped version of events she's been spinning you all this time, but clearly, it's not true. And even if Terry had been your father, I'd still have to think twice about giving you a single penny after everything you put us through.'

'I don't know what you mean.' Max's eyes looked cold, and he pressed his lips together in a narrow line. He didn't resemble Terry in any way, shape or form. How had they not have questioned his parentage before?

'You've made my life hell all the time I was married to Terry. Refusing to acknowledge me as anything more than an inconvenience.'

'Which, as it transpires,' Max's mouth twisted into a sneer, 'was all you actually were.'

Susie really did dislike this guy. 'Get out, Max. And don't come back. I'll let Norman know you have been round and ask him to ensure the injunction is lodged. Next time, you will be arrested.' She turned on her heels and walked out of the room.

She'd got as far as the hall when her arm was jerked back, and she was spun back to face him.

'You can't do that.' His eyes blazed.

Susie was frozen with shock. Her stomach clenched. *Don't let him get to you.* She shook her arm free and glared back at him. She was more than angry now, she was furious. It must've shown in her face.

His chin wobbled, and he swallowed. 'You can't do that.'

'Just watch me. I want you out of here now and don't ever come back.'

'Make me go now and I'll never let you anywhere near my children.'

'What? I can count on the fingers of one hand the number of times I've met your children. If you mean that you're going to unfriend me on Facebook, you're too late. I shut down Terry's profile when he died, and personally I have never and would never accept a friend request from you on any social media platform.'

'You're being unfair on them — they'd like to get to know their grandmother.'

'I think we're both clear that I don't have grandchildren. I'm not related to you or them by blood, marriage, civil partnership, surrogacy or adoption. It's no good trying to force a relationship now. It's not like we have numerous happy shared memories we can reminisce over. It's far too late to start building bridges, and to be honest, it's the last thing I need right now.' She'd met her share of crazy people this year — she'd put Max, Alan and Cynthia at the top of the list. She didn't need any more.

Max took a step towards the door. As he passed the lounge, he looked at the pole again. 'Got many clients, Susie?' he asked. Susie bit the inside of her cheek to prevent herself from making any unpleasant comments. No. Sod it. Now wasn't the time for restraint. 'Fuck off, Max,' she said, and felt immediately better for it.

A head peered round the staircase. Tara's grin stretched across her face. 'Did I just hear what I think I heard?' she asked.

Max went, slamming the door behind him.

'Well done, girl. That told him.' Tara came across the room and slipped an arm round Susie. 'You did great. I didn't think you'd stand up to him.'

'Neither did I.' Susie walked to the window and watched as Max clambered into his car and set off with a tyre-spin and a puff of smoke from his exhaust. 'Stupid thing was, I was thinking earlier about sharing some of the money with Max and Jodie.'

'I thought Norman made it plain that Terry was clear in his wishes?'

'He did, but I just . . . It doesn't matter anyway because Max went and blew any generosity I felt towards him. How can you say you never liked somebody, then expect them to hand over wads of cash? What have I ever done to him that deserved that sort of emotion?'

'Nothing.'

Susie was exhausted. The encounter with Max had taken it out of her.

'Trouble is,' Tara said, 'you're too lovely. You think well of everybody, even Max. Some people just aren't that good.'

'It's a lot of money,' Susie said. 'I could give him some . . .'

'And next week, he'd be back for more. You know he would.'

She was right. Susie sighed. 'Norman told me I should go wild with it.'

Tara laughed. 'I can't wait.'

CHAPTER THIRTY-ONE

Josh lifted Susie's vizor. 'How does the helmet feel?' he asked.

Susie nodded as he watched her. Even with the earplugs he insisted she wore, she could hear him. The helmet felt comfortable and more balanced than the one they'd given her for the zip-wire experience.

'It's Maddie's helmet and leathers. I figured you'd be about the same size.'

In Wales, at the top of the run, once the officials had fitted a camera onto her helmet, she had struggled to lift her head. That hadn't been a full-face helmet either. This one felt far more comfortable. The leathers felt restrictive. They were warm but cumbersome. She felt a bit like the Michelin man, and they squeaked whenever she did manage to move.

'Once the engine is running and we're on the road, we won't be able to hear each other.'

'Maddie told me you have a stop sign,' she said. 'If I don't feel happy, or think something's wrong, she said I should squeeze your shoulder.'

Josh nodded. 'She never has so far. Now, don't try to get on or off the bike until I say. You can step on the footrest and swing your leg over. I'll tilt it so it's a bit lower on your side. Once on, centre yourself and face forward. You should

216

be able to see over my shoulder and hopefully enjoy the ride. It is a legal requirement that your feet always stay on the footrests. You can hold onto the grab rail at the back or on to my waist, whichever you prefer. When we go round corners, lean with me. Okay so far?'

Susie nodded.

'When we get to the end of your road, squeeze my shoulder if you want me to stop. If you don't, I'll take you down the dual carriageway. It means we can go a bit faster.' Josh smiled encouragingly. 'Then we can stop for a coffee by the river and you can tell me whether you'd like to go anywhere else.' Maddie gave him a thumbs up. She dared not nod.

'If you're okay then and ready to go, pull your vizor down and we'll be off.' He put on his helmet and waved at the window. Susie turned. Maddie was looking out, so she waved too, pulled down her vizor which was easier said than done wearing an enormous pair of gloves, as Josh's motorbike roared into life.

They stopped by the river, and Josh bought them both a hot drink. 'What do you think?' he asked, handing her one of the cups.

'Brilliant.'

'I haven't put you off.'

'Not at all.' Anything but.

'You're a good pillion passenger. Are you sure you haven't done this before?'

She shook her head.

'It's easier when the person behind you doesn't move all over the place. That makes it harder to balance the bike.'

They watched some starlings settle into the trees on the opposite side of the river while they drank in silence.

Susie's turned into a bit of a biker. She's acquired a full set of leathers and a bike, so if you see this old woman on a road near you, give her a wide berth.

Maybe she could get a fluorescent jacket. One of those Polite Notice ones that horse riders tended to use. *Polite Notice: Keep wide and clear. Novice rider — could fall off at any time.*

'Well?' Josh asked, an hour later as he rode up her drive and stopped neatly in front of her garage. 'An adrenaline rush?'

'It was incredible.' Susie grinned. 'I felt so free.'

'I haven't put you off?'

'No way. It was even better than the zip-wire experience. I can sort of understand why you love it so much. It's really got my blood flowing.'

'We didn't go quite as fast as you did on the zip wire,' Josh laughed. 'Although, I might have hit eighty at one point. Just don't tell Maddie.'

* * *

Susie gushed enthusiastically about riding down the Templeton dual carriageway. 'What do you think? Can you see me as a biker?' she asked Tara.

'I have a bike,' Tara said when Susie finally ran out of steam.

'You do?'

'Promise you won't be angry.'

'A push bike?' Susie looked confused.

Tara stared at something on the floor and shook her head. Her hair moved vigorously.

'A motorbike?' Susie frowned. 'What? Where is it?'

'It's in storage.'

'Why couldn't you put it in the garage here. It's a double one.'

'It's a long story.' Tara was uncomfortable, Susie could tell that. The girl was positively twisting her hands together.

Susie pointed at the sofa. 'Sit. It's not your bike, though, is it? It's Jason's.'

For a split second she wondered if Tara was going to refuse, but it must have been clear from her expression that this wasn't a matter for debate.

'You told me you didn't know what he was talking about when he came round here demanding the bike back.' Susie felt her blood pressure rising. Her eyes were probably flashing. Steam rising from the top of her head. She was cross. Cross with a capital C. She flopped down on the settee opposite Tara. 'You lied to me.'

A slight twitch of her head which Susie perceived to be a nod.

'Is that why he gave you such a hard time? You had his bike. And all this time you told me he was just being rude, because that was the sort of man he was. If you stole his bike, I get why he might not have been happy.'

'I did not steal it!' Tara shouted. 'It's not his bike — technically it is mine. Well, it's both of ours. We bought it together, only he put it in my name. We bought the bed, TV and fridge together too, but I left them behind when I moved out. All I took was the bike. And he did want me back. When it all went tits up with Alice, he did try and get me to go back to him. He even came round with a bunch of flowers. Said he'd taken the house off the market and I could move back in.'

Susie remembered a tired-looking bunch of carnations that appeared in a vase in the middle of her worktop a few months ago. Tara had been cagey about where they'd come from. They looked like they'd come straight from a crematorium or a shrine by the side of a road. 'Why?' she asked.

'Because he loved me. Or more like he wanted someone to clean and cook for him.'

'No. I mean why did he put it in your name?'

Tara sighed. 'He's got points on his license, and he's already insured for his car, so the price he was quoted for more insurance was insanely expensive.'

'But you don't ride. Have you even got a license? How can that help?'

'If the bike and insurance are in my name, he can still ride it third-party under his car insurance. And yes, I have a provisional license. I didn't mean to lie to you.' She looked genuinely crestfallen. 'You're just so lovely and going through such a difficult time with Max and Jodie that I didn't want you to worry.'

'I'd have rather known the truth from the word go.' Susie looked down at her carpet. It was spotless. Tara had hoovered this morning. 'Why didn't you go back to him?' she asked.

Tara looked unhappy. 'I guess I'll have to, if you don't want me here any longer.'

'I didn't say that.' Susie's mouth opened before her brain was fully engaged. It was true, she didn't want Tara to leave. It was nice, more than nice, to have the company. She imagined it was like having a daughter, or at the very least, a friend. They laughed and talked a lot.

There had been difficult times this year, but she'd shared them with Tara and for the first time in a number of years, she felt she wasn't on her own. Tara had been understanding when she let rip about Max. And when she let off steam about Cynthia and Alan. Susie hadn't been so open about her feelings for Bob, but Tara knew she liked him.

She didn't think they had secrets from one another. It hurt to find out they did. Possibly more than it had hurt to find out Terry had kept his paternity tests a secret. He'd kept that a secret to protect her, to save her from concern. God knows how many times she'd read his letter. That was the only conclusion she could come to. If he'd told her that he didn't think Max and Jodie were his children, she'd have probably talked him out of going for the tests. She'd have said that it didn't matter, that she'd taken them on as part of the deal with him. But with Tara it was different. Tara had no reason to lie.

'Is there anything else you haven't told me?'

Tara shook her head.

'Can you ride it?'

Another shake. 'I never learned. I'm no good at tests. I didn't do well at school. Jason said there was no point me even thinking about learning to ride. It would just be a waste of money.'

Deep breaths. Susie had a bank deposit burning a hole in her pocket. 'How much does he want?'

Tara shook her head. 'I don't know?'

Susie had to control her temper. There was no point in either of them getting bolshy. 'How much did you pay for it?'

'Three thousand pounds.'

'We'll offer him one thousand on two conditions. One, he can keep the television and the fridge, but he must agree to leave you alone.'

'I can't afford . . .'

'I'll speak to Norman before we make the offer. He might want him to sign something, just to make sure there won't be any more problems. I could do without being blocked in or accosted at the door by Max or Jason.'

'What's the other condition?'

'You learn to ride your bike too. We'll learn together. You'd be doing me a favour. I'd like to be able to ride a motorbike and could do with all the moral support I can get.'

Tara opened her mouth, her eyes wide.

'And before you argue. Yes, I can afford it.'

'Why? I mean, why would you do this for me?'

'Why not? Strange as it may seem, I have actually grown fond of you. I happen to like your company. This year has been difficult for both of us, and you've got me through some pretty tough times.'

The girl looked close to tears. 'Really?'

'No. You're right. It's just that this is a nice area and I want a quiet life.'

Tara looked momentarily concerned, but then seemingly realizing she was being teased, her face broke into the widest smile. 'No, you don't. You want dates with a biker, who just happens to own a garage and has his own teeth.'

'Stop it,' Susie said, amused by the thought. 'Is that agreed, then? You and I are going to do a motorcycle training course?'

'I can't.' The smile dropped and Tara's head fell. 'You're too kind, but Jason's right,' she muttered. 'There's no point. I'd never pass the theory part, let alone the rest of it.'

'I've told you my conditions.' Susie sat back and crossed her arms. 'We do it together — and maybe you can prove Jason wrong — or no offer.'

CHAPTER THIRTY-TWO

Bob had picked up the phone and considered giving Susie a call several times since last week's band practice, when Norman had been interrupted halfway through his "Born to be Wild" guitar riff by a phone call. Bob had been convinced it was Susie he'd been talking to, when he'd overheard Norman marching up and down saying something about Max and injunctions.

He couldn't ask.

Norman wouldn't tell him anyway, so he'd been worried ever since. He just couldn't think of how to phrase the question.

When Susie had picked up the phone and giggled, he'd felt a lot lighter.

'Who am I supposed to be this evening?' she asked. 'I thought Welsh Jean had been dumped now you've done all the courses.'

He hadn't expected to be invited over, but when she'd suggested he could drop in, if he was passing with Miss Phyllis, he'd practically sprinted round.

She dropped a kiss on his cheek and invited him in.

'Tara's in tonight.' She dropped her voice. 'And it's goulash for tea.'

It would probably have been a good time to admit he'd had a big lunch, but when she walked ahead of him into the kitchen and laid a place for him at the table, he realized there was no other place he'd rather be. He carried the cookpot to the table, while Susie got plates out of the warming drawer.

Tara put a glass of red wine in front of him.

'How is Bob likely to be affected by drinking alcohol?' Susie asked.

Strange question.

He'd been just about to say that he wasn't driving, but only planned on having the one glass anyway, when Tara butted in.

'What are my choices?' she asked, putting the bottle on the table and sitting down.

Susie put a plate of goulash and rice in front of him. It smelled heavenly. He looked up and smiled, but Susie was looking at Tara.

'A. His sense of danger increases.'

It's pretty high at the moment anyway.

'B. His judgement becomes impaired.'

Keep smiling.

'C. The speed of his reactions will increase.'

Pulse definitely racing at the moment.

'Or D . . .'

'B.' Tara picked up her fork. 'We're learning our Highway Code,' she added and took a mouthful of her goulash.

'Tara has got her theory test tomorrow,' Susie said, sitting down.

Tara threw Susie a look, that Bob took to mean *I wish you hadn't told him that*, but she was still chewing and couldn't express any thoughts vocally.

'Good for you,' Bob said, taking a similarly large mouthful of the dish.

'It's okay,' Tara said, we can talk about other things. We've been answering questions all day. I've done three practice tests already — how many have you done?' She looked at Susie.

Susie shrugged. 'About the same, I suppose. Soured cream?' She moved a pot in front of Bob. 'Imagine I'm a lorry,' she added.

'Sorry, can't,' Bob said.

She ignored him. 'I'm walking down the hall and going to turn left into the lounge, what should you watch out for?'

Tara put down her fork, 'Oh, please.' There was a moment of silence. 'That you're not going to move to the right to give yourself enough room to get round the corner — okay?'

Susie nodded.

Anyone looking less like a lorry, Bob couldn't imagine. Susie was dressed in jeans and fleece top but still looked good tonight. Bob hadn't seen her recently, but they'd talked a couple of times on the phone. She'd rung to find out how he was, and he'd rung her to say thank you for her help. He'd thought about ringing on several other occasions. Sometimes just to hear her voice.

'How are things going with Reggie?' She laughed. 'Have you persuaded him to play with Brothers in Boxers again?'

'Persuaded him?' Bob shook his head. 'He's firmly back in charge. He's been to most of our practice sessions and now he's talking about rereleasing "I Wish I Was Heaven Bound with You". Someone called George seems happy to run him around.'

'George? Treetops' manager's husband?'

'Possibly. A nice guy, great sense of humour and seems happy to help out with a tambourine. It's funny, Reggie really comes alive when he gets behind a keyboard or a baton. Probably sounds daft, but in some ways, I think we all do. I'm enjoying the sessions and Norman seems to as well. There's something cathartic about being able to sing and play music. I'm not sure that Freddie has told Reggie that we're playing the Redford Music Festival next year.'

'You are? I love that music festival,' Tara said. 'It's a great weekend.'

'You came home every night,' Susie said.

'I'm getting too old for communal camping,' Tara said dismissively.

'You're nearly thirty.' Susie laughed. 'Wait 'til you get to my age.'

'I went this year.' Bob grinned. 'So that trumps your age card.'

Susie stared. Her eyes seemed to be flickering over his, presumably trying to work out whether he was joking.

'Who did you see?' Tara asked.

'We went to catch Lily Brooks in the Crystal Country area and ended up staying much longer than we intended to watch a couple of the heavier rock bands on the main stage later on.'

'Did you plan rest breaks?' Susie giggled. 'If so, how often and how long?'

Bob laughed. 'I followed government recommendations to the letter,' he said. 'At least fifteen minutes every two hours.'

'Don't be ridiculous. You were at a music festival,' Tara said, 'not driving a long distance.' She got up and started to clear away the empty plates.

'That was lovely,' Bob said. 'Just what I needed.' He got up to help. Susie put out a hand.

'Sit down,' she said. 'There's pudding too. I've been experimenting with rhubarb custard roulade.' Susie placed a huge plate of expertly rolled meringue on the table.

It was good. No, it was better than that. The crispy shell and the soft mallowy insides were perfect.

Susie was watching his expression as he put down his spoon. 'More?' she asked. 'I never get quantities right.' He shook his head, much as he'd like more. He had already had a large lunch that he hadn't owned up to, and he was supposed to be watching his calories. But bloody hell, if he was going to blow his calorie budget, this was the way to do it.

'I'll take it in to work tomorrow afternoon. I know they'll love it, but it is always best the day it's made,' Susie said.

'Afternoon?' Bob wondered if he could just show up at the Register Office, not for an appointment, just for another large slice of dessert.

'We've . . .' Tara started.

'Tara's test is in Templeton. I'm taking her tomorrow morning,' Susie said. 'Talking of which, young lady, should we try the Hazard Perception videos again?'

'Do we have to?' Tara made a face. 'Do you know we haven't watched any TV for the last month? Every night she sits and makes me go through questions and watch videos.'

'Good, sounds like you should fly through. I better get going. Next time — my turn to cook.' Bob kissed Susie's cheek softly. He wished it was one of those moments you hear about when she'd turn her head and their lips would meet, but she didn't move. Perhaps for the best — Tara was in the room.

'Samosas,' she said, quietly. 'You promised me samosas.'

CHAPTER THIRTY-THREE

Standing in the rain, outside the motorcycle training centre, Susie hugged Tara. Susie was at that embarrassing hysterical stage and would soon need a slap to stop her sobbing.

'You okay?' Tara asked, taking a step back.

Susie hiccupped and tried to smile.

When she'd booked the course they'd said it could be done in five days, from extreme beginner to qualified rider.

Yeah, right — she'd assumed that was a sales pitch, nothing more. Let's face it, she was an "extreme beginner". She'd ridden a push bike as a child, but not since, and her only experience of motorbikes had been as a pillion passenger on Josh's bike down the dual carriageway to Templeton and back.

Tara seemed much more confident from the start, looked like she knew what she was doing and asked intelligent questions.

At the morning break of the combined basic training day, Susie half-expected the instructor to laugh and ask whatever was she thinking? Tell her enough was enough. By the end of that day, she'd ridden a 125cc bike and was buzzing. Oliver, their instructor, said he was more than happy for them both to progress to the next part.

Day two, and suddenly the bikes were bigger. A lot bigger. Oliver made sure they were comfortable, that Susie could touch her toes firmly on the floor and was happy she could balance the bike.

She still had imposter syndrome, totally certain by day three that someone would turn around and tell her she wasn't ready to consider doing Module 1, let alone Module 2, and suggest she book in for at least another week, or give up completely and go back to knitting dishcloths or something more appropriate for her age.

She'd taken two weeks off work. She hadn't taken much annual leave all year and the council had a "Use it or lose it" mandate, so Luke had been quite happy when she'd asked for the time off.

'Just to do a few things about the house,' she'd told him.

'Yeah, right,' he laughed. 'You expect me to believe that? When you come back, I expect to hear you've done the Tough Mudder or been on a naked bike ride.'

'Great idea,' Susie exclaimed. 'Now you come to mention it, I can't think why they haven't made it onto my list. They sound like they might be fun. I'll look out the details. Perhaps next year we could do one or the other as a team-bonding experience. What do you think, Charlotte?'

Charlotte had an expressive face. She didn't have to say that she clearly didn't think either a good idea — her face did it for her.

Luke changed the subject to talk about planning the rota for Christmas.

She'd got away with it. The fact that she planned on spending at least one week with Tara in a full set of leathers and riding motorbikes was something she hadn't shared with anyone. Partly because she couldn't believe she'd get through it.

'Module 2.' Tara hugged Susie back, tears falling down her cheeks. 'We've passed,' she sobbed. 'I can't believe it.'

'Congratulations, both of you.' Oliver beamed at them from the doorway to the office. 'You're now both qualified to go out and ride any bike you like. And if you want any help looking for a bike, you know we'd— I'd be happy to help. Why don't I give you my number?' He gave Tara a long look. There was clearly something he wanted to add. 'I'll write it down.'

'We've only gone and bloody done it,' Susie said as he disappeared inside.

'Please don't cry anymore.'

'I can't help it. I'm so happy.'

'I knew you could,' Tara said. 'But I never thought . . .'

'Me?' Susie chuckled. 'I thought you'd sail through and I'd be the one still training for weeks to come.'

'I was shit at exams at school. School more or less gave up on me,' Tara said. 'But you were so patient, with all the Highway Code and theory test. I didn't think I'd be able to get through that. Jason always said there was no point in me trying.'

Jason was a wanker. Susie bit her lip. Hopefully, Tara was starting to come to the same conclusion.

'Oliver was lovely, too, wasn't he? Really kind.' Tara looked towards the centre door.

Love's young dream.

'Come on, we're getting soaked.' Susie set off towards the centre but didn't get more than a step closer before Tara grabbed her arm.

'Susie,' she said, her voice wavering. 'You know I can never thank you enough for everything you've done over the last year. Not just the money. I was broken when you found me. I couldn't believe it when you gave me the key to your home, and then when you let me move in. I've never met anyone like you in my life. You've taught me to trust and believe in myself.'

Quite a speech, and Susie was welling up again. 'Me too,' she said, hugging Tara again. 'I can't imagine how I'd have coped this year without you. We both had some demons to exorcize. We've been good for each other. And we have Terry to thank for the money. I like to think he'd have approved of us using some of it for this.'

She'd never had the closeness with anyone, certainly not Max or Jodie, that she had with Tara. That alone had been worth its weight in gold. She was sure Terry would've liked Tara.

'Seriously, you believed in me and that always made me feel special. I never had that when I was growing up.'

Susie squeezed her hand. 'Don't blow this by making me feel old. Promise never to call me "Mum" or, probably more appropriately, "Gran".'

'Wouldn't dream of it. How about Auntie Susie?'

'Absolutely bloody not.'

Tara giggled. She looked so happy. Her eyes sparkled and she had a spring in her step. 'Are you going to own up to Bob and tell him you've passed your motorbike test?'

Susie smiled. 'I will, but first I need to get my head round what we've done myself. I'd like to be a bit more confident about riding on my own before I start boasting about it. I still need to get out and do a few more rides.'

'Not me,' Tara said. 'I'm going to boast to everyone I know.'

Oliver was waiting by the door. 'We do confidence-building rides,' he said. 'We can take you out, or you can hire a bike from us for a day or two if you're happy to go out on your own.' He gave them each a business card and handed another piece of paper to Tara. 'This is my personal number. I'd love to hear how you get on.'

Susie looked at them both. 'Right,' she said firmly. 'I'm going to walk to the car now, while Tara gives you her number.'

'Su—' Tara looked panic-stricken.

'Oliver, give her a ring in a day or so's time. She'd love to hear from you and maybe you can arrange to meet her for a drink, and she will happily tell you how she's getting on.' Susie walked to the car and started taking off her leathers. She didn't look back. Sometimes people just needed to be pointed in the right direction.

CHAPTER THIRTY-FOUR

Susie stepped over the postcard from the Post Office on her way into the house. Someone had sent her something without the correct postage on. She bent to pick it up and examined it. The Post Office were now holding whatever it was hostage. If she wanted it, then she would have to call them and pay a small fortune before they would release it. She put it down on the kitchen worktop to deal with another day.

It was late — she'd been out after work celebrating Maddie's first anniversary.

Luke had arrived with a collection of different-sized boxes, all wrapped separately. Initially, she'd worried she'd missed a collection until his magnificent assortment of parcels turned out to be a pack of nine toilet rolls that he'd wrapped individually.

'Well, what can you buy the woman who has everything for her paper anniversary,' he asked. 'Anyway, it was Susie's idea.'

'It so wasn't!' Susie almost choked on her drink, and everyone hooted with laughter. It gave her a warm feeling. She was among friends.

Maddie seemed to be having a comfortable pregnancy so far. It was early days, but she didn't seem to have suffered from morning sickness or had any strange cravings, although she'd made short-change of any crisps on the table that evening — something that appeared to amuse Luke and Charlotte who kept insisting it was their turn to buy crisps and coming back with ever more peculiar flavours.

The pregnancy wasn't common knowledge yet. Maddie and Josh had had the first scan earlier in the week and they planned on telling their families at Christmas, but she'd told Luke and Charlotte a couple of days ago, partly because most of Luke's ideas of anniversary celebrations seemed to involve alcohol. Susie had smiled as they'd crowded round the small picture and Maddie explained why she wouldn't be drinking. 'I'm so lucky, so far,' she said. 'I just hope the birth will be as easy.'

'Of course it will,' Charlotte snorted. 'That's why they call it labour.'

They'd joked about the various children's names they'd registered over the years. Luke made them laugh with his recollection of a conversation he'd had with two new parents recently who wanted their new daughter's name to be spelled "M E L O N Y".

'Didn't you mention that it wasn't the usual way of spelling it?' Susie asked.

'Of course.' Luke took another sip of his drink. 'I even wrote down what I thought the spelling should be and the woman told me I'd got it wrong, because that would be pronounced "Mel-aney". Sometimes you just can't win. I made them sign a statement on the back of the register page to say they had specifically asked for the forename to be spelled like that.'

'Tell me you're not going to call your daughter "Nevaeh",' Charlotte said. 'I've had four of those in the last month.'

'Daughter?' Maddie asked. 'Did I say I'm going to have a girl?'

She'd told Susie that they'd both asked the doctors not to mention the sex, wanting to be surprised on the day the baby was born. If she did know, Maddie certainly wasn't giving anything away about either gender, or the names she and Josh had chosen.

'You know I'm running a book on date, weight, sex and name,' Luke told Maddie. 'Get in quick and you could make a killing.'

'Nice try. But when we were considering names we did look at what the names would be if we spelled ours backwards. Eiddam was bad enough, although the internet has all sorts of information about the sort of person an Eiddam would be, but do you know there really are men called Hsoj. It's pronounced with a silent h.'

'It's going to be a boy,' Luke said. 'I knew it.'

'I'm glad you do.' Maddie looked at him. 'Because I honestly don't have a clue.'

At various points in the evening they interrogated Maddie about what colour she was painting the nursery and what colour clothes she was buying. But she gave nothing away. Luke and Charlotte stayed in the bar when Maddie and Susie left. They'd ordered more drinks and were talking about hitting the town later.

They invited Susie, but an early night or dancing till dawn — difficult decision. 'You forget, I've got to the age when nine o'clock is the new midnight, and I need to save myself for tomorrow.'

'Tomorrow?' Maddie asked.

'Weekend off.' Susie laughed. 'People to see, songs to sing. You know the sort of thing.' Maddie wasn't the only one with a secret. She hadn't told anyone where she was going. If it was fabulous, she'd tell them at the staff meeting on Monday. If it wasn't, then nobody was going to be any the wiser.

In the comfort of her own home, she slipped off her shoes and poured herself a small glass of wine — tomorrow was going to be a late night. Unless Donny's encore went on for longer than half an hour, she should easily make the last train home, but it still wouldn't get her in before the early hours of Sunday morning. She checked the train app to make sure she had loaded the tickets into her wallet and her concert ticket was to hand. She smiled. It was going to be fabulous, she knew it.

* * *

Bob washed down the kitchen surfaces. There was no sign this evening of Poppy or Tony and he was grateful for the peace. It hadn't been a great week.

The organizers of the Ace-to-Ace ride had been kind. He explained that he had to delay next year's ride due to health issues. They agreed to put his booking back a year. They wouldn't be happy for him to undertake the ride with that hanging over him, either. There was a waiting list for the ride and they said they'd easily fill his place. He should just concentrate on getting fit and back up to speed again.

Bob contemplated getting a stiff drink. A year — that wasn't the end of the world. The cardiologist had been kind, too, when Bob had explained the real reason for pushing him on the subject and what he was planning to do.

He told Bob firmly that he wanted him to wait a little longer before he did something that strenuous. 'In all honesty,' the man had muttered into his beard, rather than looking at him, 'I couldn't recommend you do it next year. But, stents do settle completely given time. I'd like another six months, and if those test results show similar results, I don't think it is totally out of the question to start training for the following year. That's a lot of hours on a bike, though,' he'd added. 'Why not do a couple of shorter rides first? Bring yourself up to speed, and see if you're up to it. You might find that the concentration levels will be too much.' He didn't say "at your age" but something about the way he said it made it sound as if that was what he was thinking and possibly that Bob wouldn't just have a problem with his heart.

But he hadn't said, "No".

Another year, that was all. That would be okay — the college had asked him for more help and were offering additional hours. They'd even asked him whether he'd consider doing an adult teaching course, so he could maybe take the odd class or two on his own. They clearly didn't think his brain was shot to pieces.

Bob sighed. The dream was very much still on the table, but it was sensible to postpone it. He'd done a lot of riding this year. There was no reason why he couldn't do a couple of holidays next year. Maybe Scotland — even the Alps. He'd enjoyed his weekends in Wales. A holiday on a bike wouldn't be so bad. If he got to the end of it and never wanted to see a damn bike again, he could pull out.

His dream hadn't been stolen, just delayed. He didn't need to tell anyone. It wasn't something they even knew he was considering at home. He twiddled his spoon and laid it in the saucer.

But Susie did. She'd helped him fill in the application. She'd been his excuse for the Welsh courses — his Welsh Jean. What would she think?

She seemed so focused on what she wanted to achieve.

He wondered whether Poppy and Josh knew Welsh Jean wasn't a real person. He hadn't mentioned her since the hospital scare, but strangely, neither had they. If they ever asked, he'd planned on saying they were over. That the distance was too much. That they weren't looking for love. Except he wasn't sure what he was looking for these days.

What did he want? He'd never considered another relationship. But then, he'd never met anyone who made him feel like Susie did. Susie Keane had breezed into his life and made an impact. There was the way she made him feel whenever he saw her. The way his insides jumped, his face wanted to smile, and he wanted to touch her . . . hold her.

She'd said something about expecting probate soon, last time he'd seen her. She'd asked whether he thought she should throw a party. 'You do for divorces these days,' she'd said. 'After a funeral, you have a wake. So why not? It doesn't seem like an occasion that should go unnoticed — it's taken a long time coming.' They'd laughed and he'd said that he hoped he'd be on the guest list.

Bob looked down at his phone. He'd had an email that morning giving details of another track weekend in Wales early next year. He'd been tempted to ignore the doctor, book it and go anyway, but the cardiologist had said that they should know in the next few months whether the stent was causing a problem. 'We can operate again, if necessary,' he'd said. 'You're still young and healthy. You have a long life ahead of you. Don't cut it short by rushing the recovery.'

He wondered what Susie thought. Suddenly he needed to see her, talk it through with her.

CHAPTER THIRTY-FIVE

'You say she's got an optician's appointment?' Bob tried to sound casual the following morning, as he stood on Susie's doorstep. The last thing he wanted to do was sound like some sort of crazed stalker. At the best of times that wouldn't have been good, especially when Tara, standing in the doorway, was clearly wearing a very skimpy outfit under her dressing gown. 'Do you know which one?'

What did it matter which one? She was out.

'She mentioned something about a date with Donny,' Tara smiled. 'I'm guessing Lomakins, the one in town. He's the only Donald I can think of.'

'Is something wrong with her eyes?'

'I think sometimes she finds her arms are too short, and she has to squint when she tries to read something small.'

'I know the feeling.' Bob smiled.

'I assume it's just a check-up. I didn't ask.' Tara flapped a hand. Her dressing gown slipped off one shoulder to reveal a black shiny leotard. Surely it couldn't be PVC, could it?

'Was she expecting you?'

'No.' Bob looked at his watch — it was already 12.30 p.m. 'I should get going. Tell her I called.'

'She was out first thing, before my pole-dancers arrived. That's nearly three hours. I expect she'll be back soon.'

Three hours — opticians could probably do complete eye replacement operations in that time. She might've gone on somewhere else. 'Should you get dressed or something?' Bob asked without looking up.

Tara chuckled. 'You sound just like my dad. Why don't you make us both a drink and I'll go and get changed? You know where the kitchen is.'

Bob was about to refuse. Make his excuses and leave, but she disappeared upstairs, leaving him to close the door, and Miss Phyllis had already run down the hall.

Susie's kitchen was bright and light. She'd told him once that they'd had it replaced when Terry got his diagnosis. Just in case they ever needed wheelchairs in the house, all the doors had been widened and the kitchen wall replaced with bifold doors so somebody could be wheeled out onto the small courtyard area which was a bit of a suntrap. The bifold doors stood open this morning. Miss Phyllis made a beeline for the garden and settled under the shade of one of the fruit trees. Bob found tea-bags and milk and washed the two mugs that were on the side.

'She's not answering her phone,' Tara said, coming into the kitchen a few minutes later with, thankfully, less flesh on display. She picked up one of the filled mugs. 'That's not like her. She always has her phone with her.' Tara was busy, hunched over her mobile.

In years to come, Bob was sure everyone would be born with a phone hunch. He'd watched a documentary on evo-lution last night. Everything had to adapt to survive.

'I'll send her a text message.' Tara looked up and sud-denly seemed to notice his two bags on the worktop. Her eyes widened. 'Oh shit, when you said you were going to cook samosas for lunch, you meant from scratch?'

'Just an idea.' He shrugged. 'She mentioned samosas last time I was here . . .' His voice tailed off.

Turning up with a bag of ingredients had seemed like a spontaneous thing that she'd appreciate and a good idea yesterday, while he'd been listening to a naturalist's monologue about the evolutionary development of finches' beaks in the Galapagos Islands.

He smiled at Tara and made a move to gather up his bags. 'I should get going.'

'I love samosas. I'd like to learn how to make them,' she said.

'What?' Bob jerked his head up.

'If you're not doing anything else. Obviously, it's not quite the same, but I'm a quick learner and I could always show Susie how—'

Bob had been told often enough that his face was an open book, but his face must have shown his lack of enthusiasm for this idea, because she added, '—or maybe you could do it with her another time.'

'No,' he said. 'I've got everything we need with me.' And maybe Susie would turn up midway through cooking. She had to be home soon, probably hungry. He imagined her face as she smelled the spices and the way her eyes would twinkle.

There was a large granite island in the middle of her kitchen with a sink. The cooker was on the wall under the window. The design made complete sense, and Bob suspected Susie had had a hand in it. He chopped carrots and potatoes into small pieces and left them to cook in the saucepan with a bowl full of frozen peas, a dash of oil and a handful of mustard seeds. He added a small amount of water and covered them while he chopped onions and checked he had all the other ingredients he needed.

When the filling was cooling on the counter, he added the onions and spices.

Looking good.

'How do you know how much spice to put in?' Tara stirred the mixture.

'Taste,' Bob said. 'Here, have a spoon. What do you think?'

He watched as she took the teaspoon and gingerly tried the vegetables. Then she took a second spoonful. Always a good sign. He relaxed.

'It's good and it's got a kick,' she confirmed. 'Susie will love it.'

He made a stiff dough from flour and water and tried not to think about Susie as he kneaded it into a large oval lump. He pulled bits of dough off distractedly.

'Could Donny be a friend? Someone she met at the school reunion, perhaps?' he suggested. 'What do you think?'

'God, no. She didn't meet anyone at the school reunion she ever wants to see again. No. Donny's one of those names you'd sort of remember, isn't it?' She was onto her third or fourth spoonful of filling now. 'Well, I would, but then I had an Uncle Donald,' she added. 'The only person he allowed to call him Donny was his wife. He was Don to his friends and family and Donald to his mother.'

Bob smiled. 'I was always Robert to mine.' He worked the dough shapes in his hands to form small balls, then let Tara roll them into saucer-sized discs. As she finished each one, he covered one side with oil and flour, then layered them into a stack. Once there were ten in a pile, he rolled them out again until the stack became roughly small-plate sized and substantially thinner.

'This is fun,' Tara said.

'Now we come to the tricky bit: dry-frying and filling,' he said, pulling an old frying pan from his bag. Susie's kitchen was always beautifully clean and her utensils shiny. He hadn't wanted to burn her frying pan. His was beyond redemption, so he'd brought that along.

At home, he was major cook and bottle washer. Until this year, he'd never considered cooking to be anything other than a chore. Learning to cook properly at college had changed all that. Watching people enjoy his food gave him a warm feeling. Susie understood that. They'd talked about it before. He was a tidy worker, and Tara was too. He liked empty worktops. He only got out what he needed, and always put things away when he'd finished. On the other hand, leave Poppy alone in the kitchen for five minutes and the worktops, sink and probably floor would resemble a scene from a massacre. There would be crumbs over every surface from whatever she'd found in the cupboards to eat. Or tea and coffee stains from where she'd overfilled mugs.

Her cookery would probably make a good episode of *Sherlock*. *I think the suspect has dined well tonight, Watson. It seems like a last meal of cheese on toast, and it appears they have added mustard and pepper and finished with chocolate in some form.*

'I'm going out later,' Tara said. 'Can I take some of them with me?'

'Don't see why not. Looks like we're going to have enough for most of Redford. I never seem to get quantities right.' Bob covered the dry-fried disks with a damp tea towel.

'How do you know they're cooked?' Tara asked, as he flipped over another one in the frying pan.

'Those white bubbles.' Bob pointed at the cooker. 'We're not cooking them, we're just making them easier to handle, so turn it quickly, then lift it out straight away. Want to have a go?'

Tara separated the next disc from its pile and as soon as the frying pan was empty, dropped it in.

She cooked the rest of the pile while he mixed some more flour and water into a much runnier consistency. He cut a disc in half, folded it into a triangle and sealed one edge with his homemade glue. 'This is the tricky and time-con-suming bit: filling and sealing them,' he said, expertly spoon-ing some, but not too much, filling into the cone. He pressed the open edges together and finished it with more of his glue. 'There,' he said proudly. 'This is where I need help. We have thirty-seven more to go.'

Tara glanced up at the clock.

'Where are you going?' he asked as Tara concentrated on trying to imitate Bob's folds and then fill her cone.

He nodded with encouragement. She was a quick learner 'Any holes?' he asked, as she held it up for approval. 'You need to fill them with our glue, if there are. Otherwise, they will explode when we fry them. Where are you going later?' he repeated.

She looked embarrassed. For a second, he thought she wasn't going to answer.

'I've met someone. He's cooking supper. I could take some samosas.'

'Has Susie met him?'

Tara nodded. 'She likes him, but she doesn't know I'm meeting him tonight.'

'Where did you meet him? My lips are sealed, I promise,' he said.

'He was my motorbike instructor.'

Bob slapped his forehead. 'I am sorry, I forgot to ask how you got on. I presume you passed your theory test then?'

Tara grinned. 'And my Module 2. I can now go out and ride a bike without L-plates.'

'Congratulations on the test and finding a man who likes bikes and samosas. He sounds like a man after my own heart.'

'It's early days, but he's got a good sense of humour.'

That was important in a relationship. Bob thought about Susie's laugh and how that made him feel, and sighed.

'This feels like a real labour of love,' Tara said. 'Do you enjoy cooking?'

Wonderful change of subject.

'Susie says it's her happy place,' Tara continued. 'She cooks when she wants to think, or when she wants to forget. I know she's had a bad day if you can't move around here for cakes or cookies.'

'Does that happen very often?'

'Not since Norman sorted Max out and she blocked her so-called friend, Cynthia, on social media, but she always takes a lot of cakes into the office or Treetops whenever she's helping there.'

They carried on working their way through the pile of dough until the worktop had a pile of samosas ready for frying. The filling stretched, although the last two cones hadn't been filled as full as Bob would have liked.

Tara started deep-frying them.

'You can part-fry and freeze any you don't want to eat straight away,' he said. There must be thirty in the pile now and still another eight to cook. Bob began to tidy up and wipe down the work surfaces.

It was getting late. Still no sign of Susie, but it had been a good day. He'd enjoyed it. Tara had been great company.

Tara's phone buzzed. She grabbed it. She typed out a reply while Bob rescued the last batch and drained them.

'Susie,' she announced. 'She's in Brighton'.

Bob felt his phone vibrate and picked it out of his pocket. A text message from Welsh Jean.

Hi, it read. There was a picture of a pier and below it written, *Save some samosas for me. X*

'You told her, then?' Bob said, as he put his phone back in his pocket. He smiled. It had been a good day.

CHAPTER THIRTY-SIX

Bob looked genuinely surprised to see Susie when he opened the door. But so had Josh and Poppy.

Stood a little way back, Maddie winked at her.

Susie had been touched by a text message from an anonymous number last week. It had simply read: *I'm hoping you're Welsh Jean?*

They clearly weren't giving up. Maybe it was time to come clean. She hoped Bob wouldn't be too upset that she'd abandoned their pretence. Poppy and Josh obviously cared about him and what he was doing.

I believe I might be. Why would you want to know?

The reply came back immediately. *We wondered if you were in the area, whether you'd be free for Christmas Eve this year? We're having our Christmas lunch a day early and know Dad would love it if you could be there.*

Would he?

That would be lovely, she texted back. *Thanks for the invite.*

If you speak to him, please keep it a secret. He seems like he could do with cheering up just now. We can pick you up from anywhere and have plenty of room if you'd like to stay. The message was signed — Josh Diamond.

Susie had replied that she could get there under her own steam, but would have to leave by 3 p.m.

She grinned at Bob — it looked from his expression that it was a good surprise. He looked pleased to see her.

At yesterday's team meeting, they'd been talking about their plans for Christmas. Maddie invited her for lunch before her musical debut at Treetops.

'I've already had an invitation to your lunch,' Susie laughed. Maddie looked confused for a second, before the penny seemed to drop. 'So, you *are* Welsh Jean?' she said.

'Just a telephone number. I didn't lie to you. I really don't have a middle name and have never spent a weekend away with your father-in-law, in Wales, or anywhere else. Can I bring anything tomorrow?'

Maddie shook her head and then said she couldn't wait to see Josh and Poppy's faces. 'After our chat, I told them it couldn't possibly be you. Now they're convinced that you're some little old Welsh lady with a heart condition.' She laughed.

Everyone chuckled about Susie's role in the "one night only" performance at Treetops. Luke and Charlotte teased her about her budding relationship with Maurice and his catheter bag.

In the Diamond's kitchen, Susie was hugged by Josh. Tony handed her a sherry swerve and then one by one they disappeared into the dining room, leaving her alone with Bob.

Susie took a polite sip of the cocktail. It was very sweet. 'Anything I can do to help?' she asked Bob.

'What are you like with gravy?' He beamed. 'I've got some interesting lumps. What do you say, sieve it or blitz with a food processor?' He passed her a teaspoon full of gravy. It was good. The turkey was resting on the side. He looked happy and fully in control. The temperature on the oven suggested he was in the process of cremating the potatoes — just as she liked them.

'This really is a surprise,' he said, still smiling.

'A nice surprise?'

'Definitely. That lot have been so secretive for the last week, I started to fear what they were up to. But I can relax now I know that the surprise is you.'

'You were expecting someone else?'

'I never put anything past Poppy,' Bob sighed. 'But I'm glad you're here.'

She watched for signs he was joking, but he didn't appear to be. Her nerve endings tingled. Her heartbeat became stronger and faster, she was sure of it.

'You're not upset our Welsh Jean deception has been exposed?'

'What?'

Susie showed him the text messages. His eyes crinkled as he read the brief exchange. He looked up, and his eyes found hers and held her gaze.

There was so much she wanted to say, but more than anything, she longed for him to put down the bloody spoon, take her in his arms and kiss her. She lifted her glass to her lips and took another sip.

'How's your cocktail?'

'Too sweet for my taste,' she grimaced.

'You're being kind. It's disgusting. Pour it in the gravy. Mine's in there already. I'll get you a glass of wine.'

She didn't need to be told twice. Bob's eyes twinkled, and Susie thought he was whistling as he turned and filled two large glasses with red wine.

A pins-and-needles sensation on her right hip made her look down. Her phone was vibrating. Josh.

'Hello,' she said cautiously, wondering what was so secret that he couldn't walk from the dining room to the kitchen to ask her.

'Sorry, Susie,' he said, 'just hit the wrong number. Everything's fine. See you in a second.' She could hear women talking behind him. She couldn't catch what was being said, but it sounded like an "I told you we shouldn't let him do it" was in there somewhere.

'Everything all right?' Bob handed her a glass of wine.

'Fine.' She frowned. 'That was Josh.'

'I'm guessing I'm not the only one surprised you're here today.' He clinked his glass with hers, holding her gaze. 'Cheers.' He grinned. 'Ready for lunch?'

Susie nodded.

'Coming in, ready or not,' he said, opening the dining room door. The table was beautifully laid. Bob set the turkey down. Tony and Poppy followed with vegetables, Maddie and Josh brought the plates and Susie the gravy, now de-lumped, thanks to a sieve. It looked wonderful. Bob carved, and despite Susie's protests that she didn't want too much, it was all too lovely not to try everything. It had been a long time since she'd been presented with so much food.

She told them about her plans for spending the day with Tara tomorrow and that they'd planned to drive somewhere near the coast for a long walk. Maybe if the Diamonds were busy, they could take Miss Phyllis with them for a walk along the beach too. Miss Phyllis, pretending to be asleep, pricked up at the sound of her name.

Pudding was served before Poppy announced it was time for truth or dare.

'We haven't played that since you were knee high,' Bob said. 'We used to have to,' he explained to Susie, 'if we wanted to know anything or find something that she'd hidden. The rules are simple: you must be one hundred percent truthful and be believed. Otherwise, you have to take part in a dare of the family's choice. They decide on what that is when they've heard your answer.'

'Like a family court,' Poppy said, raising her eyes. 'But don't worry too much, the worst punishment used to be being grounded.'

'Okay,' Maddie said. 'Josh and I will go first. Truth, and before any of you argue, we have proof of what we are about to say.'

She put a small envelope on the table and pushed it towards Bob. 'You're going to be a grandfather in April.'

Bob looked at the small picture and smiled. 'That explains a lot.'

Maddie looked confused.

Poppy laughed and took the picture from Bob. 'He's right. Something's been happening: you've been putting on weight, your boobs are getting enormous and if you'd said anything else, my first question was going to be, where has all the Marmite and the bananas disappeared to?'

'You all knew?' Maddie laughed.

'Of course we did. It's been costing us a fortune,' Poppy said to Susie. 'Maddie turns up and before you know it, a whole bunch of bananas has vanished. On a good day she might leave one or two, but on a bad day, it looks like she's licked the Marmite jar clean, too.'

'I never lick the Marmite jar,' Maddie protested.

There were congratulations all round.

'My turn,' Poppy said excitedly. 'Truth and Valentine's Day, next year — save the date.'

'I thought you said I could tell them.' Tony pulled a face.

'I'll tell them,' Bob said, 'because this young man and I had a conversation recently. For some reason, he asked for my daughter's hand in marriage.'

'He said, "Yes".' Tony looked happy.

'I think actually I said, I'd rather you took all of her.' Bob grinned.

'And all it cost me was . . .' Tony stopped as Poppy smacked him playfully on his arm.

There were cheers from everyone.

'Why Valentine's Day?' Maddie looked confused. 'Was that the day you met? Oh no, don't tell me, that's the day you want to get married?'

Poppy's face dropped. 'Yes, we do. Why? We're going to come in and see you as soon as you're open again after New Year.'

Susie sighed. 'Please don't. We don't have any spaces left.'

'Are you sure?' Poppy looked on the verge of tears.

'Absolutely. Someone came in the other day and asked for a Valentine's Day wedding. We couldn't accommodate them. We're stretched to the limits. We're not even doing death or birth appointments that day, we just don't have capacity. Added to which there's an outside wedding booked, too, which has really left us short.'

Maddie nodded. 'I'm sorry,' she said. 'I wish you'd told me earlier.'

Poppy looked crestfallen.

Susie coughed. 'My turn,' she said. 'Truth. Is that how it's done?'

She looked at Bob, who nodded.

'It was me who took the booking for the external wedding. A man came in to see me a month ago and explained how important that day and venue were. Grey Towers fitted them in as a favour, so providing our superintendent registrar doesn't go into early labour, Luke and Charlotte will cover the office weddings, and Maddie and I will work the outside one, providing the couple get their notice in soon.'

Poppy looked close to tears.

'Because I'm sure neither of us would want to miss your wedding,' Susie added.

'You mean . . .'

'It's not what you know, it's who you know,' Tony said. 'My turn. Truth. We are getting married on Valentine's Day at Grey Towers,' he added. 'It's paid for and sorted. Susie helped with the arrangements. Lisa and Clara from Grey Towers want to take care of the cake as their wedding present. And Faith from the funeral directors will make sure there's a driver available for any limousine you want to use.'

'Hang on a minute,' Maddie said, stroking her stomach. 'Are Josh and I the only ones who didn't know about this?'

Josh coughed. 'Actually, I've agreed to be Tony's best man.'

'You're expecting me to conduct your wedding, and didn't think to ask me?' Susie guessed Maddie was trying to look indignant. She failed — she was clearly delighted.

Susie laughed. 'Yes, that's about the sum of it. We sort of assumed you'd want to, but if for any reason you can't — you know, early labour and all that — our old boss has agreed to stand in.'

There were more congratulations all around and everything stopped while Poppy had to dry her eyes. 'You really had me going there,' she said, slipping back into her seat beside Tony.

'Your turn, Dad,' Poppy said.

'Truth. But then there's nothing about me that you don't know already,' Bob said. 'I'm an open book.'

'You're lying,' shouted Poppy and Josh together. 'Now, we get to question you . . .'

'Who is Welsh Jean?'

'Susie, perhaps you can help with that one,' Josh said.

'Me?' Susie tried to look innocent. 'I don't know much about her, other than she's lovely, of course.'

Bob raised a glass. 'You won't find me disagreeing with that,' he said. 'Are you all telling me you don't believe in Welsh Jean? Why? You've never doubted Inflatable Eileen or Two-Paddles Frank. Why was Welsh Jean less believable?'

Poppy's eyes were still red. 'You disappear for weekends at a time, with only a rucksack, saying you're off to see a woman you never want to talk about. What were we supposed to think? And Josh checked the mileage on the car the last time you went. You'd done less than a hundred miles. We're not stupid. We knew that wouldn't get you to Wales and back.'

'You figured what? That I was staying in Redford with Susie?'

Maddie squeezed Susie's hand. 'I didn't tell the others I knew you were coming. I thought it would be more fun.'

'Hang on a minute,' Josh said. 'Don't tell me you've known all along that Welsh Jean wasn't real? In which case, where has Dad been going all this time?'

'Search me.' Maddie held up her hands. 'I only found out Welsh Jean's true identity in the team meeting yesterday.'

'Hang on a minute.' Bob looked at Josh. 'Are you telling me, you didn't invite Susie today?'

'We did invite her,' Maddie said. 'But yesterday I found out she'd already been invited by Josh.'

'I thought I'd invited Welsh Jean. Who, by the way, had said, "Yes",' Josh said.

Bob frowned. 'Welsh Jean? How did you know how to contact her?'

Poppy shrugged. 'We looked at the call history on your phone and found her number. You've looked unhappy and out of sorts lately. We thought you two must have had a row and we could act as cupid—'

'Intermediaries,' Josh butted in. 'We wanted you to be happy.'

'Thanks.' Bob ran his finger round the top of his glass, until it made a screeching noise.'

'Another sailor dead.' Josh shook his head.

'It's been a tough couple of months,' Bob said. 'Not because of Welsh Jean, although as you have probably guessed, she doesn't exist.'

'If she's not Susie . . .' Poppy looked confused. 'Where did you go?'

'I went to Wales.'

'Not in the car you didn't . . .' Josh said.

'Not in the car, you're right. I left that at Freddie Brompton's. The motorbike warehouse in town agreed to loan me a bike for the weekend whenever I needed one. I wanted to see if I was still up to long distances. Welsh Jean was just an invention so I could go away for the odd weekend without you all questioning me too deeply. I thought we were quite convincing.' Bob looked at Susie.

She nodded. 'I did too.'

'Why?' asked Poppy.

'There was something I needed to do.'

'Specifics,' Poppy growled.

'Specifically, three off-roading courses in Wales, and I wanted you to take me off all those bloody dating sites.'

'You never went away together?' Poppy sat straighter up in her chair, her arms crossed over her chest and her eyes narrowed.

'No.'

'Just hold on a second. Let's rewind there. Did you say off-roading?' Josh carved another slice of turkey and offered it to Maddie. 'More meat, anyone?'

'That's let the bloody cat out of the bag,' Bob whispered, as they all passed their plates across to Josh for seconds.

There were a few moments of silence. Susie was amused to see the looks on all their faces while they tried to compute what was going on.

'And the reason I am probably not as happy as you'd like, is because my stent issue,' Bob added, 'has meant I've had to put my dream on hold for another year.'

'What dream?' Poppy speared another potato.

'I'm booked on next year's ride from the Ace Café in London to the Ace Café in Beijing. At least, I was until recently. I've put it off for a year.'

'Thirteen weeks on a motorbike,' Josh said. 'That's a hell of a lot of riding. Are you sure?'

'You know I am,' Bob said. 'I've talked about it before. Which is why I've been riding again this year as often as I could. And the reason I needed Susie's help was that some of the best off-roading courses are in Wales. I have been spending time, not with Susie, but two or three days at a time riding some really challenging tracks.'

'You say you've put your dream on hold for a year,' Maddie said.

'The doctor won't give me a clean bill of health until I've had a year without issue with the stent. Then they say there's no reason why I can't do it. The trip organizers have agreed to carry my booking back twelve months and see where we are this time next year. I had to be completely honest with them. Even if I'm given a clean bill of health, I get the impression they'd feel happier if I was accompanied by someone who could keep an eye out for me. But it's not all bad news. Next year I plan on doing a few more long-distance rides, maybe holidays abroad. See how I get on.'

'I hope you're not expecting someone else to do something as foolhardy as the Ace-to-Ace, just to keep an eye on you. Oh, hang on a minute, please, tell me you're not expecting me to be your pillion passenger?' Josh asked.

'I don't know what I'm expecting.' Bob looked down at the table and put his head in his hands. 'Only that it's my dream and I'm not ready to give up on it.'

If they hadn't been in company, Susie might have reached across and given him a hug. Her hands itched to comfort him.

'Maybe next year, when I've done a few longer trips, I'll decide I'm too old to do it. After all, I will be a grandparent by then.'

There was silence around the table. Susie coughed. 'I will be a more experienced rider by then, too, and I do have a first-aider's badge.'

Bob's face was a picture, his expression a mixture that Susie couldn't fathom. 'Okay, Truth or Dare round two, and this time you start,' he said, looking directly at her.

'Truth.' She swallowed. 'I suppose my truth is that this year I decided I needed a challenge in my life.'

'You've had a fantastic year,' Maddie said. 'You've done so many things.'

'Mostly, because this man . . .' Susie was looking at Bob, 'showed me I could, and should, dream big. That nothing was impossible. Well, apart from getting legs the same size on my felted March hare. I've cooked, painted, crafted, pole danced, gone to museums, and to art galleries. I've dressed in a red dress and danced to *Wuthering Heights* on a harbour.' She grinned. 'I've even been to a Donny Osmond concert.' She giggled. 'That was surreal. I was surprised how many songs I remembered and felt the need to sing. If you get the chance to see him . . .' She looked at the assembled group. Nah, that wasn't going to happen.

Bob looked at her. 'Do you mean there's nothing wrong with your eyes?'

'Tara told me that the two of you figured I was at the opticians, until I sent the picture of the pier. Even then, she didn't twig. Thanks for the samosas, by the way, but you have created a monster. Yesterday, she was showing Oliver how to make them.' The look he gave her made her stomach flip.

'Anyway,' she said. 'You name it, I've done it this year.'

'Apart from the naked bike ride and the Tough Mudder assault course,' Maddie laughed.

'There are one or two things still on my list for next year. But, one day, Josh showed me the thrill of being on a bike and I enrolled on a motorbike course with Tara. We did our theory test together and then five days of pretty intensive training. For a while there, I thought it wasn't going to happen, but I'd like to tell you, I now have a full license to ride any size motorbike.'

The others clapped. Susie made a mock bow.

Bob was openly staring.

'Close your mouth, Dad.' Josh grinned at his father. 'That's really not an attractive look.'

'Now, it's a long way off, and I realize I need a lot of training to get bike fit, but perhaps if you're happy and Josh doesn't want to go . . .'

'Josh definitely doesn't want to go,' Josh interrupted. 'The idea of long hours sitting still on a bike behind my dad is not my idea of fun.'

'Don't listen to him,' Maddie said. 'I love being a passenger.'

'And don't forget, I'll have a new family to think about.' Josh turned to Maddie. 'I wouldn't want to spend thirteen weeks away from you and bump.'

'I was going to say,' Susie said, 'that maybe you'd think about me coming too.'

'As my pillion passenger?' Bob said.

'Whoa.' Susie smiled. 'I might want to drive the thing occasionally. I hadn't ruled out that option entirely. But you might need to rethink the bike idea, maybe something lighter. One with a better power/weight ratio.'

'Oh, I might, might I?' Bob's eyes were crinkled. He was laughing at her.

'So much makes sense now.' Josh smiled. 'She's right, Dad, the Triumph Tiger might be a lovely bike, but it would be far too heavy for Susie to handle with a pillion passenger too.'

'I don't know what to say,' Bob said.

'Okay,' Maddie said, 'I don't want to spoil the party, but have you seen the time? We need to get to Treetops, especially now that Susie's here. We don't want the leading lady and lead guitarist to be late.'

Everyone began to clear the table.

'What, you're all coming?' Susie stopped in her tracks.

'Certainly are,' Josh said. 'We've got tickets.'

CHAPTER THIRTY-SEVEN

'Ladies and gentlemen, welcome to Treetops . . .' Fiona had to shout over the Christmas-carol recording. She looked frazzled. A look not helped by the throat-slashing gestures she appeared to be throwing to the back of the room, where a group of women sat round a table and a CD player. Finally, one of them noticed her and waved back.

Susie clearly wasn't the only one who hadn't known tickets were on sale for the performance. Fiona and George looked completely exhausted when they'd all arrived. People kept turning up, announcing they'd bought tickets, and it had quickly become clear that chairs were going to be a bit of an issue.

'The Tandoori in town said they can't help.' George walked towards them with his phone in his hand. 'I can't think who else to call. All the restaurants are expecting to be fully booked this evening. Most of the local businesses are shut already.'

'I'll bloody kill him,' Fiona said under her breath when another family turned up.

'How many do you need?' Maddie asked.

'Who knows?' George shrugged. 'I can't find Reggie anywhere.'

'Okay,' Maddie said calmly. 'The Register Office is now shut until the New Year. We have seventy-five chairs in the main ceremony room, and thirty in the smaller room. We're five minutes away. If you can put a call out, explain the situation, and ask anyone with a car to help, then I'll open the building — we have out-of-hours access.'

Josh and Tony headed back to the garage to pick up a Transit, and Fiona made the announcement. She'd barely finished when many others rushed out. Within an hour, the room had been reorganized, the conservatory turned into the chorus and band area, while everyone with a ticket was seated in the lounge. There was a high level of chatter going round the room that drowned out the recorded music until Fiona took her place and spoke into the mic.

'Ladies and gentlemen,' she said again. 'Welcome to Treetops and thank you for your patience.'

Susie glanced nervously out at the crowded room. No sign of Cynthia or Alan, thank goodness.

The waving woman at the back suddenly pointed at the CD player. Fiona gave her a thumbs-up sign, and there was silence.

'For our Christmas musical, *The Best Little Whorehouse in Texas*,' she went on. 'Some of you may not know, but we're lucky enough to have in our midst the one and only General.'

'The General,' Reggie muttered, suddenly appearing at Susie's side.

'You may remember he topped the charts a while back—' Fiona was being diplomatic — it must've been at least forty years ago — 'with "I Wish I Was Heaven Bound with You". Well, Reggie, to his friends here—' the jury was still out as to whether Fiona and George thought of themselves as friends of Reggie, especially just then — 'has not only adapted and directed our musical this afternoon, but he's our narrator too.'

Reggie walked out into the centre of the room, waving and blowing kisses to the audience.

Everyone applauded.

Fiona waited for them to stop. 'I don't know how he's done it, but this afternoon a local band will perform all the musical numbers. A group that Reggie—'

Reggie coughed.

'Sorry. Sorry, The General, pulled together many years ago. This afternoon is the first of what we hope is going to be many concerts that they perform as part of their reunion tour. Before we start, please put your hands together for The General and Brothers in Boxers.' The audience stood and cheered. Fiona handed Reggie the mic and walked back through the conservatory to the kitchen, which doubled up as the dressing room for today's performance.

From her position in the kitchen doorway, Susie watched Bob and Norman walk briskly forward, while Freddie stopped en route to pat various audience members on the back.

The cheering continued until they'd all reached their spot on one side of the conservatory. Reggie followed, then spun round, holding up his hands to indicate the audience should sit down. The applause stopped and everyone sat.

On the other side of the conservatory was the chorus, primarily dressed as elves or Father Christmases. Brothers in Boxers started tuning up.

'I see Edna's agreed to take part, even if it's not *Oklahoma!*' Susie nodded over to where Edna had arranged herself in the middle of the front row. She wore an elf outfit, partly covered by a long, frilly, shiny skirt. 'Interesting looking costume. Have you lost more bed quilts or is that a shower curtain?'

'I flaming well hope not.' Fiona looked to where she pointed as Violet and Beryl, equally attired, sat down either side of Edna. Her eyes bulged. 'Jeez, I hope no one gets anywhere near that trio with a naked flame.' Her brow furrowed, and her jaw clenched. She seemed to be doing that a lot today.

'Reggie told me they'd negotiated and come to an agreement. I guess dressing up like a Can-Can girl was part of it,' Susie giggled.

Reggie stood in front of the music stand. With a conductor's baton in one hand, he nodded to the band, and with great aplomb started moving his hands.

Susie held her breath as Bob strummed his guitar. He was concentrating entirely on Reggie. Then Norman joined in. Next, Freddie on the drums and Reggie gestured to the chorus, who, after staring at him for a while, seemed to realize what he wanted them to do. One or two started singing tentatively. By the end of the first verse, Susie thought they were all opening and closing their mouths. They'd certainly got louder.

A television screen on either side of the room showed the words to the song. Big enough for even the most myopic resident to read. Reggie hadn't left anything to chance.

The audience could also see the words. They started to sing too. The elves and Father Christmases got louder. Reggie sang, and from the kitchen, Fiona, George and Susie joined in too.

The audience stood and shouted for encores. Everyone sang the last verse and chorus several more times. Eventually, Reggie made a cutting motion with his baton and spoke into his microphone. 'Thank you,' he said. 'But now . . .' He put on a hat. 'Ladies and gentlemen, welcome to the Christmas Ranch.'

'He's made it more Christmassy and more English, apparently,' Fiona whispered, as Brothers in Boxers started the next song. 'Oh God, why did I agree to this?'

Susie squeezed her arm. 'It'll be fine. Reggie's a professional. He knows what he's doing. Nothing can go wrong now.'

'I hope you're right. We've not done a risk assessment. If someone from the council turns up, we'll probably get shut down. It's Christmas Eve, and most of our residents are dressed in flimsy elf suits, which means half of them will probably die from hypothermia before the performance is finished.'

The song ended and Reggie announced that it was the night before Christmas and all the department stores were shut. The Father Christmases, as their reward for working so hard, were going to be allowed to visit the Christmas Ranch and party all night with the elves before they took their reindeers out and delivered Christmas presents to well-deserving children.

Susie tried and failed to suppress a giggle.

'Even I find that thought traumatic, and I don't believe in Father Christmas,' Fiona whispered from behind her. 'Not only that, it's going to take for ever to get the place back to normal. There's no way we're going to have the conservatory ready in time for supper. Medication is going to be late tonight. And the residents have already been through the kitchen. They're scavengers, the lot of them. I retrieved half a Christmas cake from Bernard just before we started, and we're still trying to locate two bottles of sherry. Go girl, you're on.'

Fiona gave Susie a gentle shove through the door, as Brothers in Boxers, started playing "A Lil Ole Bitty Pissant Country Place". Not the most graceful entrance, but Susie flicked open her fan and started singing. She was relieved to hear the cheers at the end of the song. When she turned round, Bob was clapping and wearing the widest smile. A lovely, warm feeling engulfed her.

Reggie introduced Sheriff Ed Earl Dodd. Maurice pushed his walker into the conservatory. 'I'm the sheriff,' he said, 'but my name's Maurice, not Ed Earl Dodd.'

There was a ripple of laughter from the audience.

'You're right,' Reggie said. 'Ed Earl Dodd was the previous sheriff. My mistake.' He looked at the music stand. 'Maurice here has recently taken over as sheriff of our sweet county and is having a bit of a fling with Miss Mona.' He nodded at Susie, gestured to the band, raised his baton and the music started. Susie sang "Sneakin' Around". Maurice didn't. He opened the top of his walker and fiddled with something that looked surprisingly like a catheter bag. Susie tried not to stare. Why wasn't it attached to his leg?

She missed a line, but it didn't matter. The audience sang along, laughing and clapping. She could understand why singers enjoyed performing so much. As the number finished, Maurice didn't wait for the applause to end. He was off. He pushed his walker straight through the audience.

From out of the corner of her eye, Susie could see Fiona speaking to one of the care assistants. Maurice had made multiple attempts to break out of Treetops before but had always been happy to come back as soon as the staff, or the police, found him. The audience seemed to think his exit was part of the performance and carried on cheering wildly. Maurice raised a hand in acknowledgement as he reached the door.

'We probably don't need to worry about him too much,' Fiona said, as Susie walked back to the kitchen. 'That catheter bag looks quite full. I was going to help him empty it between scenes, but I've sent someone to find him and help. Besides, he can't get far. We've taken his shoes away from him. All the staff know we must keep an eye on his slippers.'

'He was wearing shoes just now,' Susie said.

'No way. He couldn't have been.' Fiona looked at her husband. 'Who gave him shoes?'

'His family are here, So I suspect from the box-sized present they brought in with them that maybe they did. Don't look at me like that. We're a residential home, not a prison. If someone wants to bring something in, they can. And if Maurice wants to open his presents early, that's up to him too.'

'At least he was only opening his own,' Fiona laughed. 'I've put a pile of presents in my office that need re-wrapping before tomorrow.'

'Press are here,' one of the nursing assistants said. 'Apparently, the *Redford Chronicle* have heard that Redford has a whorehouse in it'.

'Give me strength,' Fiona said.

Several times over the next hour, Susie grinned at Bob and he grinned back. Each time, the flutter in her chest made her feel ridiculously happy. She was a middle-aged woman, far too old for a teenage crush, wasn't she? Then he'd smile back. Did he have feelings for her too? Could there be a real connection there?

George's "Sidestep" was impressive. The audience cheered and demanded an encore. George was happy to oblige. They were well into the story. On cue, they hissed and booed when Reggie announced the mayor had ordered that the Christmas Ranch be closed.

There was a dodgy moment towards the end of the song that announced the arrival of the Father Christmases. Edna, Violet and Beryl started a seated dance, kicking their legs and flapping their fancy skirts about in the front row.

A hush fell over the audience when, after a vigorous flap on Beryl's part, it became clear she wasn't wearing bloomers.

Susie giggled.

Fiona raised her eyebrows.

Susie shed the shawl she was wearing and stepped forward, ready to sing "Hard Candy Christmas" but was stopped in her tracks by Edna marching over to Reggie. He handed over the mic. 'Seeing as we've been shut down . . .' she said.

Susie retreated to the kitchen door.

'What's happening?' Fiona groaned.

Susie assumed Edna was going to thank the staff and performers for this afternoon's production.

But no.

'These poor creatures are all out of work. And it's all your fault. Every one of you.' Edna walked into the lounge and flung her arms out theatrically, narrowly avoiding the first row.

There were odd noises coming from the elves, who were fiddling about trying to retrieve something from under their chairs.

'I hope you're all happy,' Edna shouted.

The audience was remarkably quiet.

Susie had two more songs to get through. That was going to be hard enough without giggling. Once she started along that route, there'd be little chance of being able to stop.

They both needed to have their wits about them for "Hard Candy Christmas", but instead of looking ready with baton poised, Reggie had sat down. What was going on?

'Ladies and Gentlemen, in *Oklahoma!* there was a picnic basket auction,' Edna said into the microphone. 'We weren't allowed to do *Oklahoma!*, but tonight, we are going to have our own auction.'

Beside Susie, Fiona groaned, her head in her hands. 'What on earth . . . ?'

'You have to bid for your chance to spend Christmas with an elf of your choice. Tonight, they are all for sale,' Edna shouted into the mic.

'No way, she can't be serious.' Fiona's face was completely drained of colour.

There were murmurs coming from the audience and some concerned looks.

'Do something?' Fiona hissed at George.

'Like what?' he asked without looking up.

Edna had centre stage. 'Every one of our elves comes with their own Christmas treat. Show them your crackers girls.'

The elves waved what looked like homemade crackers in the air.

'Don't they look impressive? Come on, this is a one-off opportunity. Let's face it, most of them are unlikely to be around next Christmas.'

'I'm glad Edna said that.' Fiona's eyes were shut and she'd started rocking.

'Here's hoping,' George said.

'What am I bid,' Edna asked, 'for our lovely Miss Emily?'

A hand shot up at the back of the room. Someone shouted, 'Twenty pounds.'

'Any advance on twenty pounds? No. Going. Going. Gone. Sold to the man at the back.'

Fiona's eyes snapped open.

'Don't worry. That's Emily's son,' George said.

Fiona looked relieved. All the elves went for similar amounts. It seemed most families didn't mind paying.

'And now for my cracker,' Edna said, finally. 'What am I bid for this?' She waved a tiny tube in the air.

A laugh went round the room, then silence, until a voice from the back of the hall said, 'Fifty pounds.'

'Who's that?' Susie asked George.

'Isn't that Nick Flynn? You know the Olympic Champion. The one whose horse Edna sponsored.'

'Right.' Susie shook her head. She didn't, but before she had time to say, the man next to him shouted, 'And two bits.'

'Who's he and what's going on?' Susie watched, enraptured.

'That's the editor of the *Redford Chronicle*,' Fiona said. 'Oh God, what are the headlines going to be next week?'

Edna frowned. 'Gary Mansfield.' Her hands were clamped to her hips. 'Or should I say, Jud Fry, is that really your best offer?'

'Did you ever see the original film with Rod Steiger?' Fiona asked, shaking her head. 'He played the baddie, got into a bidding war with the hero, ended up winning the auction and taking Miss Laurie to the ball.'

'One hundred pounds.' The bid was back with Nick Flynn.

'And what, it all ended up happily after all?' Susie whispered.

'No, he fell on his knife after he'd tried to burn them to death.'

'Jud, it's your turn. The bid's with you,' Edna challenged over the top of the microphone.

The newspaper editor nodded. 'And two bits,' he said.

'Any advance?' Edna asked.

'One hundred and fifty pounds,' Reggie piped up.

'Two hundred pounds,' Nick called out. 'But that's my final offer.'

The entire room held its breath. This was too bizarre for words.

'And two bits,' Gary Mansfield said, just as Edna started the "going, going, gone" bit.

Edna quickly scanned the room. 'Sold to Gary Mansfield for three hundred pounds,' she said.

There was a shocked gasp from the audience, who all turned to look at the journalist.

'Three hundred pounds. How did that happen?' Susie laughed. 'In the States, a dime was ten cents and a nickel five cents. Isn't two bits just a quarter of a dollar — twenty-five cents?'

'Yup,' George said.

'Edna, you must explain your calculations sometime.' Gary Mansfield laughed, stepped forward and kissed her on the cheek. The audience erupted.

Reggie stood up, and with a majestic flourish of his baton, the band struck up with the introduction to "Hard Candy Christmas".

Susie stepped forward and sang. She needn't have worried. Everyone sang along as if their lives depended on it, and as the song ended, the elves walked over to their families, leaving the choir empty.

'All our ladies found new homes but what of our leading lady?' Susie heard Reggie say. 'Obviously the sheriff wouldn't let Miss Mona drive away without coming to say goodbye.'

Except he just had. There was no sign of Maurice.

The words of "I Will Always Love You" came up on the screen. Susie stepped forward to sing it alone. The audience didn't seem to care that she didn't have a sheriff to sing to. She started to sing it to them. They were singing too. Before the end of the first verse, Bob walked towards her wearing a cowboy hat, his hand stretched towards her and sporting a huge smile. They sang the rest of the song to each other.

She forgot the audience. His dark-brown eyes sparkled. They were almost black. She couldn't tear her gaze away. At the end of the song, without breaking eye contact, they mirrored each other's smiles. And while Susie hoped nothing serious had happened to Maurice, she relished the tension between them that fizzed with expectancy.

They sang two extra choruses as an encore, turning and bowing to the audience as the music came to a stop. And still the audience didn't want to let them go. They were on their feet, demanding another encore.

'What do we do now? Do we just walk out through the main doors?' she whispered to Bob.

'No. Let's give them what they want,' he said, and nodded to Reggie.

Reggie put down his baton and sat down at the piano. 'One, two, three,' he said.

The music started. A familiar melody, but not one Susie expected.

Bob moved towards her, smiling. He took her into a ballroom hold. 'Could I have this dance?' he sang, and guided her through the various turns and transitions of a waltz. There was a confidence to his steps she definitely wasn't expecting and she glowed with happiness.

This time no words came up on the screen. People just clapped in time to the music.

There was a connection.

Susie's skin tingled where his hand rested just below her shoulder blade. He had a great sense of rhythm. The music stopped. She was breathless and completely overwhelmed.

The audience stood and applauded. Susie stood back and clapped Bob too.

He bowed to the audience then bowed at her.

'Our happy couple are off to a brand-new state,' Reggie said. 'Let's wish them well as they set off for their new life in Oklahoma. We'll be able to find out soon how they're doing, because our summer show will be coming from there.'

A noise behind Susie sounded a bit like a muffled scream, but she didn't have time to check before Reggie lifted his baton and the theme tune to *Oklahoma!* started playing.

The audience, still on their feet, started singing.

'That's our cue to leave.' Bob nodded towards the door. 'Shall we?'

He whisked her up into his arms and carried her out of the room to the cheers and whistles of everyone.

'Sorry if you thought that was a bit forward,' he said, setting her down gently as soon as they reached reception.

Susie unwound her hands from his neck. 'You're talking to the woman who just sang, "I Will Always Love You", to you.'

'I know, but to be fair, you'd have sung it to Maurice if he'd been there.'

Susie giggled. 'You're right.' *But I wouldn't have meant it.* 'I can't believe you remembered "Could I Have This Dance?" was one of my favourite songs.'

'Was it?' He was teasing her. His smile so wide, his eyes crinkled.

'It was that or "The Last Waltz" — Reggie's suggestion. But when I said it meant something to you, the boys were happy to play a little old country number.'

'And you dance. Rumour had it the last time you danced you sported a tie as a bandana and were throwing shapes to *Kung Fu Fighting.*'

Bob's eyes sparkled. 'I've had lessons since then. You're not the only one who's been on a voyage of discovery this year.'

'Maybe we could dance again together sometime,' Susie said.

'I'd like that.' He looked away. 'Very much.' There was an awkward moment. He hesitated a fraction too long. Something was on his mind.

'What is it?'

'What you said at lunchtime about doing the Ace run with me — I'm touched, but Elaine always moaned that it wasn't much fun on the back of a bike. She'd always rather take a plane or a car.' Another pause. 'If you change your mind, I won't be offended.'

Susie reached up and stroked his cheek. 'I'm not Elaine,' she breathed. 'Okay, so I've only been a passenger on Josh's bike, but I enjoyed that ride.'

Bob looked confused.

'Maddie loves riding pillion and I wanted to try it. She persuaded Josh to give me a ride home, only we went via the Templeton dual carriageway.'

Bob laughed. 'Like father, like son.'

Susie looked at the man in front of her and a feeling of complete happiness washed over her. Life was for living. Terry wasn't somebody she'd ever forget, but he wouldn't have wanted her to wallow in grief for the rest of her days, especially when she had so many happy memories to build a future on. The way ahead was paved with uncertainty, but she felt ready to take a chance on it. She hoped the look in Bob's eyes meant he felt the same.

'Who knows, I might get so good at this biking thing, it's you who will end up being the pillion passenger anyway.'

The expression on Bob's face didn't look like that was ever going to happen.

The audience's applause on the other side of the door died down. Suddenly, a woman's voice said, 'You're all invited to the after-show wrap party, you hear.'

Edna.

And someone, probably Edna, started singing "I'm Just a Girl who Can't Say No".

'After-show wrap party?' Susie mouthed. 'Is there one? Does Fiona know?'

'The General said something earlier about three-to-five songs max. Just to remind everyone who we are and to pacify a difficult old biddy.'

'Edna.' Susie opened the door. 'That's her singing.'

'I better get going, I'm expected to play,' Bob said. 'I won't be long.'

'And would I be right in thinking one of those songs is, "I Wish I Was Heaven Bound with You?"'

There was silence between them. They caught each other's eye. Susie's heart was beating so hard. Surely, he could hear it.

Without a word, they both leaned forward and her lips found his.

'Oof!'

Not quite the reaction she expected. It had been a fleeting kiss, but nice. She'd have liked it to last longer, except now, between them, was a man crouched over a walker.

'Maurice,' Susie said, trying to regain her composure. 'You're back.'

'These shoes are too tight and my catheter's full.' Maurice gestured to the bag on top of his walker. 'I can't get the plug out.'

'I'll get back to the band. See you later . . .' Bob turned when he reached the door. 'We have some unfinished business.'

EPILOGUE

'It's here, I just didn't fancy opening it,' Susie said, handing the letter to Tara, who had just poured out three enormous glasses of wine.

Bob laughed. 'It's quite thick,' he said. 'Looks like they had a busy year.'

Susie carefully slit the top of the envelope open with a paper knife and pulled out the usual charity card. Tucked inside was the double sheet of A4 headed "The Bailey Bulletin".

'I can't do this,' she said, but before she could decide what to do with it, Tara had snatched the letter out of her hands.

'*Dear All,*' Tara read:

The Baileys say it every year, but this year was no exception. Time has simply flown by in a whirlwind for them.

'Do they really say it every year?' Bob asked.

'Oh yes.' Susie put a plate of nibbles on the table. 'You need to check who it's signed by.'

'Looks like Cynthia, Alfie, Kelly, Giles and Widget.' Bob looked up.

'Sounds like they've bought another cat, then,' Susie said.

'Dog.' Tara flicked through the A4 sheet. 'Long name. Looks like it's foreign.'

'Well, Susie has had a busy year,' Bob said. 'One all.'

Alfie made the annual trip to the south of France on his own this year, and because of the room in the car, didn't return with a cellar full, but six vines. Assuming they become well-established, he aims to make his first wine in about four years' time.

'Susie made doughnuts to die for,' Tara added. 'Plus cinnamon buns and croissants.'

'The croissants only the once so far.'

'And her sourdough starter is still doing brilliantly,' Tara said. 'Definitely two-one to Susie.'

Cynthia organized a fifty-year school reunion. Everyone had a lovely time and requests keep coming in for the next one.

Susie's eyes widened. She really hoped not. 'School days weren't the happiest of her life, but Susie went to the reunion and faced up to her nemeses. She has no need to go to another.'

Cynthia was a VIP guest at an Italian opera festival and away for two months.

'Cynthia's lying,' Susie said. 'She should get points for that one. But she missed a bigger trick not mentioning that she went as a carer for a former pop star called The General.'

Tara clapped her hands. 'Love it. That will really piss her off if she ever finds out. Think of the mileage she could have got if she'd capitalized on that.'

'She hated every bloody minute of it, but not as much as The General, who spent a day pretending he was unconscious to get rid of her.'

Giles got his degree and is now taking a year out and travelling.

'Susie went on an assisted human flight, travelling at 120 mph over a slate quarry in Wales, with no parachute or safety net,' Bob said. 'You must get double points for that one.'

'What's next?'

Kelly has gone for a change of career and given up medicine in favour of a degree in criminology.

'They must be so proud,' Tara said. 'I don't see how you can top that one.'

'Susie dusted off her chords and took on the lead role in a musical extravaganza this year, to great acclaim. She is currently considering offers for next year and thinking about getting an agent,' Bob joked.

'No, I'm not. What would I do with an agent?'

'Hah, so are you thinking about it?'

Alfie is taking early retirement at the end of the year and he and Cynthia are looking to travel together more next year. She is looking forward to spending time in the Caribbean, and him in Canada. Join them next year to see who won the holiday battle.

'Everything hinges now on Susie's next year,' Tara said.

'No, it doesn't,' Bob said. 'She's streets ahead.'

'We have to do this properly,' Tara held up a hand. 'Susie, what are your plans?'

Bob took hold of Susie's hand before she replied.

'Next year,' he said, planting a kiss on her cheek, 'Bob and Susie are going to get to know each other better.'

'They plan on taking it easy and enjoying the ride.'

THE END

ACKNOWLEDGEMENTS

This book has been so much fun to research and write. I have a lot of people to thank for not batting an eyelid at my mad suggestions for a day out and patiently answering questions on a wide range of subjects.

Firstly, my sister who embraced the idea of trying our hands at something new on a regular basis. Concerts, workshops, zip wires, cookery and experience days, we've done a lot this year. Maybe felting is something we're unlikely to try again, but we do have two March hares on our windowsill, and we haven't finished yet — glass blowing is still on the list.

Thank you, Guy Turner and Sue McDonagh, for your patience and sensible advice with my bike questions — the jury's still out on which one Bob will choose. And huge thanks to Danny from Riding in Action, Swindon for explaining all aspects of motorcycle training for middle-aged women. I hope I got it right. I did all the practice theory tests online and yep: the Hazard Perception tests was tricky! Thank you to the Ace Café, London, for amazing breakfasts. But mostly thank you to everyone who sends an email or letter with Christmas wishes each year — we do love hearing your news.

Thank you as always to my brilliant publishers Joffe Books and the Choc Lit family authors for being so kind, my editor for pulling everything and being so lovely to work with. Thank you to the Tasting Panel for your lovely comments and passing the manuscript for publication.

And finally, 'Team Rose': Jane, Keith, Sarah Xenia, Hilary, Pauline, Dunford novelists — I love you all. Thank you for endless cups of tea, amazing meals and great suggestions. Living with a writer can't be easy! And Brian and Rocky for your constant companionship during the whole writing process.

THE CHOC LIT STORY

Established in 2009, Choc Lit is an independent, award-winning publisher dedicated to creating a delicious selection of quality women's fiction.

We have won 18 awards, including Publisher of the Year and the Romantic Novel of the Year, and have been shortlisted for countless others.

All our novels are selected by genuine readers. We are proud to publish talented first-time authors, as well as established writers whose books we love introducing to a new generation of readers.

In 2023, we became a Joffe Books company. Best known for publishing a wide range of commercial fiction, Joffe Books has its roots in women's fiction. Today it is one of the largest independent publishers in the UK.

We love to hear from you, so please email us about absolutely anything bookish at choc-lit@joffebooks.com

If you want to hear about all our bargain new releases, join our mailing list: www.choc-lit.com

Printed in the USA
CPSIA information can be obtained
at www.ICGtesting.com
LVHW041341191023
761544LV00004B/356